"You think I would kill my own husband?" she yelled, pushing mightily to get her ungainly body out of the cushions.

Seeing her struggle, Kimbrough naturally offered her his assistance. She put her right hand in his and said "Thank you" when she'd attained her footing. Then she hauled back with that same right hand and slapped him across the face.

"My husband lies dead upstairs," the duchess was crying, "his mistress next door. I have been accused of murder by an odd little man in a red vest. My maid has given notice, and I am fat. But you . . . you are the worst of the lot!" She sank back to the sofa, her face in her hands, sobbing. "And now I have struck a man to whom I've never even been introduced!"

The earl held out his handkerchief and tried to speak past the dust of contrition in his throat. "Carlinn Kimbrough, ma'am, at your, ah, service."

Also by Barbara Metzger
Published by Fawcett Books:

MY LADY INKEEPER
EARLY ENGAGEMENT
CUPBOARD KISSES
MINOR INDISCRETIONS
THE LUCK OF THE DEVIL
AN AFFAIR OF INTEREST
CHRISTMAS WISHES
A LOYAL COMPANION
LADY IN GREEN
AUTUMN LOVES: An Anthology
AN ANGEL FOR THE EARL

A SUSPICIOUS AFFAIR

Barbara Metzger

FAWCETT CREST • NEW YORK

A Fawcett Crest Book
Published by Ballantine Books
Copyright © 1994 by Barbara Metzger

Library of Congress Catalog Card Number: 94-94039

ISBN 0-449-22216-0

Manufactured in the United States of America

First Edition: July 1994

10 9 8 7 6 5 4 3 2 1

To Elaine Noel Edel, Madame Journet.
I wish I had known better, earlier.

Chapter One

"*F*acts is facts," quoth the Bow Street Runner. "They don't change for nobody, not even a duke." Mr. Jeremiah Dimm ("That's my name, not my brain") unbuttoned his red vest and leaned back in his stuffed chair, official ledger, pads, and pencil on the table next to him. He sighed once in contentment when his son poured another bucket of hot water into the basin in which the officer's aching feet were splayed. Then he sighed again and took his good luck piece out of the vest's pocket. The lad had to be taught right, if he was ever to be a successful thief-taker like his da.

"Now listen, Gabriel, facts is like this here rock." He dangled the stone from its string so Gabriel could see the streak of gold through it. "You can turn it this way and that, look at it from every side and every angle, and it's allus the same. You, me, everybody, we all see the same rock. That's a fact."

He held the stone in one beefy fist and let the string trail down. "Now, suspicions, they is like this string. Sneaky, snaky bastards a man can get to take on any shape. See, they can wrap they-

1

selves around your facts a hundred different ways." He illustrated his point by twining the cord one way, then another around the rock, finally ending the lesson with the string tied in a square knot around the stone, like a package. "You got to make sure the supposition fits the facts."

Young Mr. Dimm hung on his father's words, even though he'd seen the demonstration countless times out of mind. Anxious to follow in his father's illustrious if aching footsteps, Gabe nodded eagerly. "Like the Denning case."

His father agreed. "Like the Denning case. It would be easy as pie to pin the thing on the duchess. Witness saw her at the scene, she admits having words with Denning, and lud knows there was motive. But."

Gabe leaned forward. "But it doesn't fit?"

The older Dimm reached out for his occurrence book. "It fits too neat, if you was to ask me. And there be a dozen different theories that fit just as well. Problem is, there just ain't enough facts to make any quick resolution to the case. His nibs ain't going to be happy."

"His nibs" being Mr. Dimm's boss at Bow Street, the officer consulted his notes again, looking for insight. What he had was deuced little to look at.

Late that November afternoon, Duchess Denning had received a note, directing Her Grace to the carriageway between Denning House, Portman Square, and its neighbor, Armbruster House. There Lady Denning had come upon her husband's closed carriage, whose door she opened to find the duke *in flagrante delicto*, as it were, with Lady Armbruster. The duchess declared her intention of retiring to the country to have her child, with the duke or without, and damn his eyes, while Lady Armbruster fled out the other side of the carriage. Both women's testimony agreed to that point. Then the duchess made her cumbersome way back to the ducal property, let herself in the side library door while the servants were at their supper, and retired to her bedchamber to start packing. Which was where her maid found her when the Watch banged on the door, after the driver returned, as ordered, to restore His Grace's carriage to the coach house in the mews.

So facts were as thin on the ground as hen's teeth. Mr. Dimm had the note, which had been delivered by an urchin, the Denning butler reported. He had Lady Armbruster's pantalettes from the closed carriage. He had a recently fired pistol, the mate of which was still in Lord Denning's desk, and he had one very dead duke.

Both of the women involved were unavailable for interviews by the time Officer Dimm was assigned the case. Lady Denning's physician had prescribed a heavy sedative immediately after the local constable took her deposition, and Lady Armbruster had dosed herself into laudanum-laced sleep after telling the constable what little she knew, between hysterical bouts of "I'm ruined, I'm ruined."

She sure as Hades wouldn't be getting any invites to Almack's, if Mr. Dimm knew the ways of the ton, which he did, as much as any working man could, which was why his nibs had given Dimm the case.

If he could not question two of the people most directly involved in the crime, Mr. Dimm could at least spend profitable hours querying the employees, the neighbors, and the residents of both houses, and both Their Graces' associates and relations. Which he did, traipsing across the raw London landscape from servants' halls to gentlemen's clubs, from ladies' parlors to taverns, gathering blisters and gossip. He didn't find any witnesses to the crime or any more pertinent evidence, but he did get enough information to compile a list of suspects three pages long in his daybook, with every motive that ever existed for murder, and nary an alibi that could hold water. The only surprising thing he found from his investigations was that Lord Arvid Pendenning, Duke of Denning, had lived this long without someone killing the dastard ages ago.

If Jeremiah Dimm had the handling of the thing, all those suspects would be gathered up and hauled off to little cells in Bow Street and held there until one of them sweated out a confession or a valid accusation. But his nibs had vetoed that idea. Bow Street's funding would be slashed if the nobility found themselves treated like common criminals. Handle the toffs like lambkins, he'd ordered Jeremiah Dimm. Don't make the scandal any worse than it is, he'd commanded. Don't offend the innocent or the influential. But solve the bloody case, and do it quick!

So Jeremiah Dimm tracked down all his other likely prospects, besides the sleeping ladies, that is, taking notes well into the night. That was how, for once, he found his crowded little house on Hill Street in Kensington blessedly quiet of chatter and squabbles and cooking clatter. He lit a clay pipe and sighed again. A man could enjoy peaceful times by the fireside like this, if he didn't have so much else on his mind, and swollen ankles.

With smoke rising from the pipe, the Runner read through his notes. He had started with the servants at Denning House, interrupting their celebrations at the duke's demise. If ever there was a loose screw, His Grace was it. Extravagant in his own pleasures, Denning was a cheeseparing tyrant with his household. He was vicious and abusive to the men and not above taking liberties with the women. He was often in his cups, frequently violent, and capricious both in dismissals and paying earned wages. Of course, they had all claimed, conditions were much better since Her Grace had arrived three years ago. Half of the staff refused to believe such a kind, courteous female could commit ruthless murder; the other half thought she was justified, especially in her condition.

4

Dimm had no real suspicions of the servants. For one thing, there had not been a dismissal in a year, and the most disgruntled had left voluntarily for other positions, not the nubbing cheat. Life was bearable under the duchess, and good jobs were hard to find. Besides, they were all accounted for at the approximate hour of the crime, having early supper in the belowstairs dining room. The only ones missing were the chef and his two assistants, who were starting preparations for the family's dinner, and Her Grace's woman and the duke's man. Having helped her mistress from her bath and onto her couch for a rest, the maid, Eleanor Tyson, was in the ironing room, pressing the gown the duchess would wear to dinner. As Tyson noted, Her Grace's condition required a great deal of fabric to be ironed. Tyson usually ate later, while the family sat to dinner. Purvis, the valet, was laying out the duke's evening clothes while waiting his turn to smooth out any creases in the duke's neckcloths. But one of the footmen had placed his finger alongside his nose. Purvis, it seemed, was sweet on Tyson, and took any excuse to share her company. Good for them. Dimm shrugged and turned the page.

The servants, even those who staunchly maintained their mistress's innocence, admitted that the ducal marriage was less than ideal. Miss Marisol Laughton had accepted the dissolute duke in her come-out Season because her family was at *point non plus*, and he promised relief. Arvid, Lord Denning, had taken a bride almost twenty years his junior because she was a Diamond and he needed an heir. He hadn't come through with the commission for her brother or the annuity for her aunt; she hadn't conceived for nearly three years. Neither got what they expected, and the servants agreed Lady Denning got the worst of the deal. Her Grace's maid reluctantly revealed the use of the hare's foot to cover up bruises on Her Grace's fair skin, although those occasions were blessedly less numerous once Lady Denning was known to be awaiting a blessed event. Arguments between husband and wife grew more frequent, however, as the duchess's time grew near.

From the lofty butler to the lowest scullery maid, every member of the Portman Square staff knew Her Grace wished to leave for the family seat in Berkshire, to ready the nursery, to breathe healthy country air. And everyone in the house had heard the duke bellow that he wasn't about to give up any part of the Season for some puling female. Women gave birth in the streets of London's slums, he'd roared once from the sidewalk; his wife could damn well spawn in the luxury of Denning House. No one in all of Portman Square, and therefore in all of London, could think this was a love match. But would a lady, a lady moreover who was in an interesting condition, seven-and-a-half-months interesting to be exact, commit cold-blooded murder? Or even warm-blooded, finding him in the arms of another woman?

Your typical crime of passion? The jealous spouse? Inspector Dimm sucked on his pipe stem. He doubted it. The jury'd be like to suspend sentence in the case anyway, if Her Grace's undoubtedly expensive barristers earned their fees by claiming temporary insanity. The duchess's mind was obviously disordered by the pregnancy. Everyone knew breeding women came over queer sometimes. Jeremiah Dimm had seen his own calm and quiet Cherry grow attics-to-let when her time got near. He added a big question mark next to Duchess Denning's name and turned the page.

Now Lady Armbruster could have committed any number of emotional acts, judging from the constable's report and the servants' grapevine. She was nigh unintelligible with hysteria—and that was before she was informed that her lover was dead. What if she'd gone back to the carriage after the duchess left and discovered that Denning was indeed leaving her to follow his wife into Berkshire? Her reputation, what there was of it, was ruined, and all for nothing. Hell hath no fury like a you-know-what, Dimm muttered to himself, Gabriel having fallen asleep on the sofa.

Lady Nerissa Armbruster could only be a suspect if the murder weapon were already in the coach. Not even a gentry mort in the throes of unrequited love could be expected to creep into her lover's house, steal his pistol, and shoot him with it, not when her own husband's dueling Mantons were close at hand. Dimm made a note to check with the coachman in the morning. If they'd been driving out of London near Hampstead or through the City and its stews, the nob was like to have his barker with him. This meant that anyone could have come, argued with the duke, struggled with him for possession of the weapon, and run off after the shot was fired. But his rings, purse, and diamond stickpin were all found with the duke, so Dimm was ready to discount the casual robber.

Not so Lord Armbruster. The jealous husband arrives at Portman Square to see his raving wife running through the hedges with her slippers in her hand, shrieking of her fall from grace. On the other side of the hedges, His Grace is buttoning his trousers. Lord Armbruster grabs up the pistol and shoots his rival in the heart.

Dimm nodded. He liked the scenario. But what about the note to Lady Denning? And what about Lord Armbruster's claim that if he shot every man Lady Armbruster slept with, the House of Lords would be an echo chamber for octogenarians? Then again, Lord Armbruster hadn't offered a convincing explanation for his own whereabouts at the time, only that he was visiting with a friend. Dimm bribed his lordship's butler to find the location of Armbruster's love nest, rather than threatening the peer. The Runner made a notation in his expense book, hoping his nibs was happy. No one was at Armbruster's hideaway in Half Moon Street, not even a servant to bribe with the governor's money. Dimm made another entry on tomorrow's list, under *Lady A.* and *the widow* and *the pistol*.

If Lady Armbruster's husband hadn't flown into a jealous rage and defended his lady's honor with a bullet, perhaps someone had sought to avenge the duchess's disgrace, someone like Lady Denning's hotheaded scapegrace of a younger brother. At age twenty, Foster Laughton still hadn't mastered his adolescent humors nor found a channel for his energies. The army would have settled him nicely, Dimm reflected, but the boy hadn't been given the chance to make a man. Left destitute and landless by his father's ill-advised investments, the young marquis lived on a pittance and at his brother-in-law's sufferance. It was no secret belowstairs at Denning House that the duke had kept the youth dangling in London without the wherewithal to amuse himself like other sprigs of the nobility. So Foster got into trouble, associated with riffraff, and chafed at his sister's scrimping on her dress allowance to pay his bills. Denied his patrimony, cheated of his army career when he came of age, and forced to watch his sister's degradation, how much abuse could a young man's pride take? Not much, it seemed, as Dimm had found for himself that very evening.

"How dare you?" the youngster had blustered, threatening the older man with his riding crop. His handsome face an angry red, Foster had raged on: "I might have an empty title, but I still have my honor. I'll have you know I wanted to call the blackguard out any time these past three years for what he's done to my sister. I even did once, but he only laughed at me. Marisol forbade me to challenge him again."

"Dueling's illegal," the peace officer had felt obliged to point out.

Foster made a rude noise. "Yes, and I'd be forced to flee the country if I managed to kill the mawworm. Marisol reminded me of that, too, and how distraught she'd be without me. And then she reminded me that Denning's a crack shot who killed two men before she met him. She'd be even more distraught over that, so she had my word of honor." He looked away in disgust, beating the crop against his pant leg. "Word of a gentleman."

"So if you couldn't fight an honorable duel . . . ?" Dimm had prompted.

"I prayed some other poor bastard would do it for me. I did *not* shoot an unarmed man in a closed carriage, no matter how much I hated him."

Dimm tended to believe the young toff's high-minded attitude toward honor. But the volatile marquis could have argued with the duke, Dimm reasoned, threatened him with that whip until Denning pulled his own weapon. Another struggle over the hair-triggered pistol, the same dead duke. The young fool's own words even put him riding back to the mews from the park at just the right time. Alone.

"So you think your sister did him in?" Dimm had asked just to see the young man's reaction, after wisely taking a step out of range.

"Damn you to hell!" Foster snapped the whip in half in his hands and tossed both parts to the ground at the Runner's feet. "My sister is a lady, besides being one of the kindest, most generous females in all of London, and I don't care if you're the Lord High Magistrate himself, you shan't say otherwise in my presence. Why, she married that villain just to save me from debtors' prison."

"And he reneged on his promises."

"And that's enough to convict her? I promise you this, you put my sister on trial—you even charge her with such a crime—and I'll confess to killing the bastard. I followed him and Lady Armbruster home from the park, ran inside where I knew he

9

kept his pistols, waited for my sister to leave, then shot him. You cannot charge two people with the same crime. I'll be more convincing."

Dimm underlined his notation about finding if Denning had the pistol with him in the carriage. Then he tapped out his pipe, got up, and toweled off his feet. He padded over and threw a blanket over Gabriel, hoping his own boy never felt such a need to prove his manhood, hoping, too, that Gabe would have such a brave, loyal heart if he did.

As he placed another log on the fire, Mr. Dimm wondered if the new widow could really be such a saint. According to her aunt, who was next on his list, Marisol Pendenning, née Laughton, was ready to be canonized. His Cherry, bless her soul, would never have stood for him raising his hand to her, much less him smiling at another woman. Not that Jeremiah ever would have done either, of course. But what kind of woman tolerated such abuse? Poor downtrodden wretches he saw every day, broken-spirited wraiths whose husbands considered them chattel. But ladies of the ton? Leading hostesses of the *beau monde* who held intellectual soirees? He shook his head. Perhaps Duchess Denning swallowed her own pride for the sake of a dependent younger brother and an impoverished old auntie. On the other hand, perhaps one day, this day, she happened to choke on that swallowed pride.

Chapter Two

*A*nother log on the fire, another page in Officer Dimm's book, another suspect. Miss Theresa Laughton, spinster aunt to Foster and Marisol, was a lady of a certain age and a definite refinement. She even offered Dimm tea during their uncomfortable interview. Miss Laughton was also ready to confess to murder rather than see either of her chicks face charges. Of course, her hand was shaking so badly she could hardly hold her cup, and she frequently had to dab at her eyes with a tiny scrap of linen and lace.

"Not that I am crying for Denning, I hope you know," she'd confided to the Runner. "The man was a . . . a dirty dish. There, I've said it, even though one should not speak ill of the dead. Poor, poor Marisol."

"On account of Denning's being dead, or on account of her being one of the suspects in his murder?"

She rummaged through a work basket next to her and began stitching on a tiny knitted sweater. "What's that?"

"You said 'poor Marisol.' I wanted to know why."

"Because that awful man made her life such a hell, with his temper and his women and his nipfarthing ways. And now this awful scandal, just when the baby is coming, and the uncertainty of it all."

"What uncertainty might that be, ma'am?" Dimm wanted to know.

Aunt Tess waved a plump little hand around, trailing a skein of wool. "Oh, the settlements and things. Such a mess."

"Surely the widow is provided for?" He hadn't been to see Denning's man of business yet.

"What's that?"

"I said, Denning was known to be deep in the pocket. There cannot be any financial worries, can there?"

"Who's to say? The scoundrel had the terms of the marriage contract worded so that he agreed to 'provide' for us all, after paying Laughton's debts. Dear Foster was too young to understand, and Marisol was already making such a sacrifice for the rest of us, and I . . . well, I confess I have no head for business. The solicitor said there was so much money, not to worry. None of us ever saw a farthing of Denning's fortune. If dear Marisol ever complained that I was to have an annuity, Denning threatened to send me to a cottage in Wales. Provision enough, he said. And he withdrew Foster from university because the boy was a dunderhead anyway, he swore. I pray the Lord will provide for us now, for that sad excuse of a nobleman cannot be trusted to do so even from the grave."

"So you were entirely dependent on him?"

"What's that? Oh, the money. Yes, I cashed in my consols to give Marisol her Season. It was our only chance, you see." Miss Laughton set aside the knitting to wipe her eyes again. Then she squared her shoulders and raised her chin. "No matter if we are thrown on the parish, I am glad the duke is dead.

So you can put the manacles on me now, Mr. Dimm."

"Uh, Miss Laughton, do you know how to fire a pistol?"

"Of course I do. You aim the round part away from you and pull the little metal thing where your finger goes."

Dimm rubbed his chin. "And where did you say you were that hour or two before dinner?"

"Why, right here, in this little back parlor. Denning never comes near it, don't you know, but it has the prettiest view of the gardens."

Dimm opened the drapes, which were pulled for the night. He could see the roof of the stable complex, but not the alleyway. "Did you see anyone running through the gardens? Anyone suspicious loitering about or acting oddly?"

"Oh no, I was working on my knitting. The baby is coming soon, you know."

"Then did you hear anything? Quarrels, carriage doors slamming, gunshots?"

"What's that?"

So much for Lady Denning's family. Dimm relighted his pipe from a spill at the hearth, thinking of Gabe's brothers and sisters sleeping upstairs, all the nieces and nephews in nooks, cousins and in-laws nigh to bursting the rafters of this little house in Kensington. There was that huge Denning mansion, the ballroom bigger than Dimm's whole place, yard and all, for just four people. And one of them was dead. Dimm puffed and sighed, and went back to his notes.

The duke wasn't much for family either, it seemed. His mother was fixed in Berkshire, two married sisters lived in Wales and Scotland, and the only brother had rooms at the Albany.

Dimm had found Lord Boynton Pendenning there, trying out gray waistcoats, black arm bands, mourning boutonnieres.

"Such a decision, don't you know?" the pale, thin man had drawled, gesturing the Bow Street officer into his dressing room. "I mean, one wouldn't wish to appear the hypocrite, would one, with sackcloth and ashes? On the other hand, one must consider the proper degree of respect before paying a call on the grieving widow. Such a dilemma." He tied a black stock under the white cravat at his thin neck, then turned to ask his valet's opinion. "I tell you, I've been fretting over it ever since I heard the news."

Dimm blinked when the valet clapped his hands together in approval, but proceeded with his questions: "Where might that have been, milord—where you got the word of your brother's death?"

Pendenning waved a long-fingered, beringed hand. "Murder, you mean. The news is everywhere, don't you know. I suppose I was in some gaming hall or other; that's where I spend the afternoons. Before coming home to dress for the evening, of course."

"Mightn't you be a tad more specific, milord? Like, do you start dressing at four? Five? Six?"

"That depends entirely on the cards, my man. Let me think. Ah yes, the dice were cold at Pimstoke's, so I went on to the Pitpat." Dimm noted that Lord Boynton named less reputable gaming parlors, where the stakes were often higher than at the gentlemen's clubs, the company less select, and the games often rigged.

"The cards were against me at Danver's place," his lordship continued.

"But you got lucky in the carriageway at Portman Square?"

Pendenning turned from the mirror. "What, pray, can you be insinuating? That *I* shot old Arvid?"

"Begging your pardon, milord, for being blunt, but word is you're pockets to let."

His lordship nodded without disturbing his carefully arranged curls. "Dressing properly is not an

14

inexpensive hobby. Ask Prinny. Then again, gaming is not a steady income. I make no secret of either pastime."

"And greed do be a powerful motive in these here circumstances. Jealousy, too."

"What, jealous of Arvid's title? I never thought to step into m'father's shoes. Heavy old things, no sense of fashion, don't you know. I do admit the fortune is more tempting. But think, my good man. Why would I wait this long to do in old Arvid? Everyone knew we were at loggerheads since childhood. He never shared his toys, not even back then. It was no shock that he could never see his way clear to increasing my allowance now. Or make the occasional loan, not old Arvid."

"Then you two brothers were not close?"

"About as close as two gamecocks in a pit. He was a bastard, may my dear mother forgive me for the slur to her virtue. Still, I could have arranged for highwaymen, you know, or thugs to follow him home one night any time these past ten, fifteen years that I've been on the town and up River Tick. There are any number of ways to succeed to a title."

"Without getting your own hands dirty."

"*Naturellement non*, my dear sir. But again, I ask, why would I do the thing now?"

"Pressing debts he wouldn't honor?"

"But my so-charming sister-in-law has a pressing date with the *accoucheur*, as my loving brother delighted in reminding me. M'brother's heir is even now supplanting me from the womb."

"The babe could be a girl."

"With my luck? Not even I am laying money on that bet."

Next Dimm had trekked up and down St. James's to the men's clubs. His big toe started throbbing again just at the thought. He'd been going from White's to Brooks's to Boodle's, chatting up the various doormen and majordomos, trying to locate any of the recently deceased's friends. He'd have found the lost continent of Atlantis sooner.

Arvid Pendenning was one unpopular bloke. If he wasn't a shade too lucky at the tables, he was a mite too familiar with wives and daughters. He was arrogant, rude, or downright cruel to anyone below his rank, anyone less deadly with a pistol, or anyone unfortunate enough to play cards with him. Most club members seemed amazed the killer had managed to get a pistol ball into his heart, so small and shriveled that organ must have been.

Wagering in the betting books was heavily in the duchess's favor, if you could call it a favor to be the one considered most likely to hang for the crime. The bucks were already calling her the Coach Widow, drinking toasts to her aim. There was even, in one club, talk of taking up a collection to hire Her Grace the finest lawyer in the land in return for the favor she'd done them all. Boynton Pendenning ran a distant second in the race to the gibbet in the betting book, with young Foster Laughton trailing badly. It was the long shot, however, who caught the Runner's attention.

One gambler had put his money, a considerable sum, too, on Carlinn Kimberly, Earl Kimbrough. Dimm whistled. The Elusive Earl, they called Kimbrough, because he rarely came to Town, never took part in ton gatherings when he did, and refused to be feted as one of the past heroes of the Peninsular campaign. He'd sold out, what? Three, four years ago, Dimm recollected, when he came into the title. Then Kimbrough seemed to disappear from the gossip columns as well as the dispatches. Now, it seemed, the earl had traveled to London for the express purpose of confronting the Duke of Denning about a parcel of land that separated their Berkshire properties. By all reports this confrontation was acrimonious, *ad hominem*, and an education in the high art of name-calling without issuing a challenge.

"Absentee landlord" degenerated into "leech," "lecher," and "boil on the butt of humanity." "Bumpkin" became "manuremind" and "mold spore that should crawl back under its rock."

Kimbrough outright refused to duel, not when men were dying for better causes in Spain. He announced this right there at White's, looking down from his greater height into the duke's empurpled face. And Denning, according to the waiter on duty two nights ago, was fully mindful of the earl's reputation as being one of the cavalry's finest swordsmen. He was not about to throw down the gauntlet and let Kimbrough have choice of weapon. With footmen hovering, the proprietor wringing his hands, and wagers being entered in the book as fast as ink could flow, the two men nearly came to cuffs. Then Kimbrough stormed off, muttering curses that would have made his troopers proud.

He was still cursing when Officer Dimm had tracked him down at Pulteney's Hotel, just a few hours ago.

"Of course I heard about the bastard getting caught with his pants down. I'm sure everyone in London has heard by now. That's all the people here do anyway, isn't it—snicker and snort like pigs at the trough, then go repeat their filth to the next hog on line?"

The army lost a good officer when Kimbrough resigned, Dimm reflected, and society had gained an Original. Loud, forceful, a man of action, he was impatient with the claptrap of the polite world. As Dimm's dear Cherry would have said, may the angels bear her company, the earl was also a fine broth of a man. Big, broad, well muscled, and with a healthy tan, he had hands that were callused with honest labor. His eyes were a dark brown that looked through pretension, piercing eyes that, by force of will alone, would not miss their mark.

"Well, happen I'm here, milord, mind if I asks a few questions?"

"Of course not. You are only doing your job." Kimbrough stopped his pacing and took a seat, indicating his caller should do likewise. He lit a cheroot, after Dimm refused one. "But I'm afraid I cannot be of much help. I never even met the jade."

"The, ah, jade?"

"The duchess. The Coach Widow. Black widow, more like."

"Then you are convinced Her Grace was the perpetrator?" Dimm took out his pad and licked the point of his pencil. "My sore feet bless you for whatever evidence you have."

"Evidence? I have no evidence. I told you, I never had two words with the woman."

"You mean you didn't see her bring the gun out of Denning House, or hear the gunshot? I thought you must of called there to continue your arglebargle with Denning and seen something."

Kimbrough stubbed out his cheroot onto a saucer. "Why would I call on Denning when he flat out refused to sell me the land the night before? The man's as hardheaded as a jackass and as useless to have an intelligent discussion with."

Dimm closed his notebook. "Then why, begging your pardon, milord, if you weren't there and you don't know the woman, are you so sure she killed the duke?"

"Because I know her kind. Spoiled, feted by the ton, society's darling has to give up her own empty pleasures to bear the son of a bitch an heir. Then she goes off her looks and the duke strays. So she blows a hole through him, figuring that if she cries incompetence or some thing, she'll have all the money, all the power, and none of the inconvenience of a husband."

Dimm scratched his head. "A mite hard on her, don't you think? A' course, I ain't met Her Grace

18

yet myself. How does it happen that you don't know her, being neighbors and all?"

"I was in the Peninsula during her come-out Season and in mourning at the time of the marriage. I chose not to accept Denning's invitations the first time they spent Christmas at Denning Castle, so I suppose she dropped me from her list. I doubt she spent a month of her marriage in the country altogether. When I am in London on business, you can be assured I do not frequent the routs and revels where the likes of Duchess Denning will be found."

"Hmm. Well, can you tell me about that piece of land that Denning wouldn't sell?"

"What do you want to know? How Denning rechanneled a stream through the property line, changing the boundaries? How the new stream overflows its banks every hard rain and destroys my tenants' crops, or how their old wells go dry in the summer? Or perhaps you want to hear how I offered to buy the blasted land that should be mine by rights, and the limb of Satan refused. I came to London to try again, so work could be done over the winter before the spring rains. I have men with no income, and jobs that need doing, such as getting that deuced stream back to its proper flow, damn him. May he rot in Hell."

"He most likely will, from all I hear. Ah, one more question, milord, then I'll let you get back to your pacing. Uh, packing. The clerk downstairs didn't happen to notice your comings and goings this afternoon. Could you tell me where you might of been a few hours before dinner?"

"A few hours before—Devil take you, too, you long-nosed snoop!" Kimbrough rose and stomped to the door, flinging it back on its hinges with a loud slam. "Get out before I boot you out. I'm a bloody magistrate, you clunch, an ex-officer of the King's army, for heaven's sake, and a peer of the realm, for what that's worth. I wouldn't kill even that misbegotten maggot over a soggy acre or two!"

Jeremiah stood and shuffled toward the door. "I ain't the only one with a suspicious mind, so to speak. They have a bet on you at White's."

"You mean I'm part of this bumblebroth? Hell and tarnation!" The earl smashed his fist against the door, making a substantial dent in the heavy wood. "Blast! That's just what I despise most about this town. They've nothing else to do but ruin reputations and stir up scandals. Scandal's just what I wanted to avoid, with a young sister to fire off soon."

"Denning never made advances to that sister, did he?"

"I wouldn't have let that rotter within a mile of Bettina. And no, I never dallied with Lady Armbruster either. Damn your eyes, I didn't kill Denning, but I sure as hell might rearrange your nose for you if you're not out of my sight at the count of five!"

Jeremiah was gone by the earl's barked "Three." Alone in his little parlor except for the soft sounds of his son's breathing, it occurred to Dimm that his lordship never had explained where he was at the time of the murder. The devil was in it now. He'd have to go back and ask that question tomorrow, too. Dimm wrote *Kimbrough* at the bottom of his list. Maybe the earl would be gone by the time he got to it.

Jeremiah yawned. He should go up to bed, with tomorrow like to be another long day. But his bed was cold and lonely since Cherry had passed on, may she rest in peace, and his thoughts were all of her up there. Snugged in his chair downstairs he could keep mulling the Denning case. Gor'blimey, all those suspects, motives, and theories, and not a one of them feeling like a good fit. Something was missing, if he could just put his finger on it. He picked up his charm and dangled the rock on its string until the stone fell to the floor with a clatter that startled him awake. "Old fool," he muttered, "putting yourself to sleep like that German quack."

He sat up, wide awake. That was it: putting himself to sleep. The duke could have killed his own self! His nibs would love it!

Chapter Three

"Suicide? That's the most ridiculous idea yet," the grieving widow declared. "Arvid was too mean to do us all such a great favor."

Duchess Denning had agreed to meet with the representative of Bow Street at eleven that morning. She was reclining on a couch in a parlor done in the Oriental motif. Jeremiah felt an unaccustomed stab of envy—not for the vast reaches of the gilded chamber, nor the thick carpets, priceless vases and lacquer-work cabinets, but that the lady had her feet up on dragon-crested cushions, a blanket tossed over.

"Doctor's orders," she'd apologized for not rising to greet him at the door. "Swelling, don't you know."

He did indeed, and not just from his Cherry's five pregnancies, God keep her soul.

The duchess was going on: "Besides, what possible reason could Arvid have for taking his own life?"

Dimm looked around again at the opulence of the room, the pretty young wife big with child, and wondered himself. Her Grace was understandably haggard, her face drained of color by the black shawl over her shoulders, and her pale hair pulled back in a loose, untidy knot, but he could see the fine cheekbones beneath the added weight, the fine blue eyes. Yes, she must have been a Diamond of the first water, but there was something even more attractive about a woman in her condition. To his way of thinking, at any rate. That duke was more of a fool than he thought. Dimm cleared his throat and consulted his notes.

The coachman had earlier given his considered opinion that the duke habitually took a pistol along when he was involved in dalliance, which was to say most times he called for the closed carriage. Suchamany angry husbands and irate fathers had been scared off by the sight of that very same pistol, the driver swore. The butler confirmed the coachman's testimony. So the weapon was likely in the deceased's possession, not brought to the scene by someone else. "It's only a possibility, Your Grace. Another avenue what needs to be explored, that the deceased ended his own life because of the scandal over his discovered affair."

"You cannot have done your homework, Mr. Dimm, if you honestly believe my late husband gave a thought to public censure, before or after he acted."

Dimm nodded. That was what everyone said. "Still, there be reasons what are less obvious sometimes. Like His Grace's health might have been failing. Or mayhaps he suffered financial losses no one knew about yet."

The duchess merely raised an expressive eyebrow. Dimm had to admit his brilliant notion was not quite so convincing by the light of day. The duke's secretary refused to hand over his late employer's books and bank statements, not without a writ of investigation, but the figure he gave, just a rough estimate, the cully claimed, was more than

Jeremiah Dimm would see if he snabbled every crook on every reward poster from here to kingdom come. By about a hundred times. And the mortician who was laying out the body upstairs found nothing amiss with the duke's physical remains, except a great gaping hole in the chest, of course.

" 'E was tuppin' 'is ladybird, wasn't 'e? An' 'is own wife's breedin'. Can't say that sounds like a fellow about to stick 'is spoon in the wall."

Dimm couldn't say it either. He did have to make one last, feeble effort at solving the case with the minimum of inconvenience to any of the other highborn suspects. "Maybe he got remorse."

"And maybe pigs will fly," the duchess replied. "Besides, suicides cannot be buried in consecrated ground. What would you have me do, lay the Duke of Denning in a corner hay field? Arvid *is* going to Berkshire to be placed in his family's crypt alongside his father. My aunt is already having palpitations of the heart over spending another night with Arvid there upstairs, so we are leaving tomorrow to get on with the thing, unless you either come up with a suicide note or a warrant for my arrest."

"Now, there be no call to—"

Marisol held up a hand. "No, I have heard all the rumors flying around. I even know the odds being wagered on my guilt or innocence. The servants are very good about that kind of thing, you know. I did order the newspapers burned so my aunt and brother need not read the scurrilous attacks in the gossip columns nor see the outrageous cartoons. But I do know I am your likeliest prospect." She tossed back her head in a haughty gesture that only served to disorder her hair more. "And I do not care. Do you understand, Mr. Dimm? I do not care what anyone says. I am going home to have this child. That's all I ever wanted."

"Home being . . . ?"

"Oh, not my home. That's been sold off ages ago, if you are afraid I'll escape your clutches in the wilds of Lancashire. I'm going to Denning Castle, in Berkshire, where Pendenning children have been born for centuries."

"I understood you hardly ever visited there."

"That was Arvid's choice. He hated the country, disliked having to give up the pleasures of Town life, the high-stakes gambling and the high-flyers."

"And you, ma'am? You like the country? Begging your pardon for asking so many questions, Your Grace. It's me job, you ken."

Marisol nodded her understanding. "Berkshire is beautiful. All rolling hills and trees, flowers and farms. I loved it at first sight. I never lived in a city until my presentation and my marriage, you see."

"Yet you adapted something wondrous," Dimm noted, recalling what he'd heard about her triumphal Season, her standing among the hostesses of the *haut monde*.

"I was raised in the country, Mr. Dimm, not in a stable. My father might have been improvident; he was still every inch a gentleman. My mother's family could trace their ancestors to William the Conqueror."

So could Dimm's. His forebears were the chaps carrying all the gear and picking up after the horses. "I meant no offense, Your Grace. Just wondered why, if you liked the country so much, you made your home here in Town."

"You didn't know Arvid. I told you, he found the country dull. And he liked having me near him, he said, so he refused to let me live apart. He forbade the servants to help me, and they would have suffered terribly if I had disobeyed."

"Jealous type, was he?"

"Of me?" She looked down at her ungainly figure. "I am not quite the goddess to inspire passion, am I?" Marisol stopped to think a moment. "No, Arvid was more possessive than jealous. At first I believed he saw me as an ornament, part of his collection of *objets d'art*. Then I became an asset to the smooth running of his household. Recently . . . ?" She shrugged. "Recently he was just more perverse. He knew I wanted to be gone from London. That was enough to make him decide to stay."

"So you argued." That was a statement, not a question.

"So we argued," she acknowledged.

"And were you jealous of him?"

"Of his affairs, you mean? Of his birds of paradise and his opera dancers and Lady Armbruster? Why don't you simply come out and ask if I killed him, Mr. Dimm?"

"Because his nibs at Bow Street says that ain't the way to handle duchesses, Your Grace. But since you was the one what mentioned it, did you shoot the duke when you discovered him in the carriage with your next-door neighbor?"

"No, Mr. Dimm. I did not. I was no more jealous of Nessie Armbruster than I was of Harriet Wilson. My husband was a known womanizer when I married him, and a constant philanderer later. It never mattered before. It certainly never mattered after. In fact, I was more than happy when he took his attentions elsewhere."

"I see," said Jeremiah Dimm, wishing he'd never embarked on this line of questioning. For that matter, he wished he'd been given the Carstair case instead. What was a simple ax-murder or two compared to this mare's nest? No wonder all those newspaper chaps were camping in Portman Square. He wiped his suddenly damp forehead and took up a new line of inquiry. "Do you have any idea who sent that note, Your Grace? Might be that whoever wanted you to find your husband in the carriage meant to throw suspicion your way."

"No, I have no notion whatsoever. The butler said an urchin brought it, and no one had any reason to detain him at the time."

"And you don't recognize the hand?" Dimm held out the folded sheet.

Marisol took the letter reluctantly, as one might take a worm meant for fishing bait. She dutifully reread the message and studied the writing. "No, I'm sorry, it's unfamiliar to me. The script does look feminine, though a bit crude, as if disguised."

"You think it could of been one of your friends, passing on unpleasant news?"

"My so-called friends have never hesitated before about keeping me informed of Arvid's little peccadillos. They usually gave me the news to my face over tea, mixing a little spite with the sugar."

"But it must have been someone as knew you'd be home."

She shrugged. "That wouldn't be hard to surmise. A woman in my condition hardly goes for curricle rides in the park at the fashionable hour."

Dimm took back the note, folded it carefully, and placed it securely in the inner pocket of his waistcoat. "Notice anything unusual about the message?" he asked.

"You mean how the person misspelled *lying*? *Your husband is lieing, with a lady in the carriage alley*," she quoted from memory. "I remember wondering if he was lying there injured, telling a falsehood, or carrying on some liaison. Knowing Arvid, I guessed correctly, it turned out. Either my correspondent is a poor speller or undecided which crime was worse."

"As in some other woman altogether he might have promised the moon?"

Marisol shook her head. "I'm sure I do not know the latest *on dits* concerning Arvid's affairs. He could have had any number of mistresses. What he might have promised them besides money is beyond my imagination." She removed a ring from the chain around her neck. "I already had this, for all the joy it brought me. Even if my fingers were too swollen to wear it."

The duchess looked about to weep. Dimm hurried on: "So you went outside, even though it was a biting raw day and you had to go down that fierce-some tall stairwell in the hallway, then out and acrost the lawns. How come, Your Grace, if you didn't care?"

"I didn't go down for the confirmation. I went because I wanted something. I didn't think even Arvid could deny my request to leave for the country when he himself was found so much at fault."

"Were you surprised that the female was Lady Armbruster?"

"A bit, since I had thought we were by way of being friends, but her reputation was none too steady."

"Neither were her nerves, it seems, shrieking and carrying on like a banshee."

"Yes, I wondered why she was so distraught, once I had time to think. Surely she must have known I'd never have bandied her name around, but dallying with a married man in his own drive-way had to be a chancy thing at best."

"Do you think she came back to the carriage after you left, and shot Arvid? The duke, that is. No disrespect, ma'am."

"I wouldn't have thought she could hold the pistol steady enough, the way she was carrying on when she ran away. But why would she have shot her own lover? Even as high-strung as Nessie is, she must have known that couldn't stop the gossip. I'm afraid I cannot explain her actions. You'll just have to ask her yourself."

Dimm scratched his head with the pencil. "Now that'd be a fancy piece of investigation, even for Bow Street's finest. I suppose you didn't hear all the news making the servants' grapevine after all. Lady Armbruster got up last night and took herself another dose of laudanum, then another, and another. She'll be pleading her case at the pearly gates, not Old Bailey."

Marisol gasped and clutched at her chest. Dimm leaped to his feet, ready to race for the bell pull.

"No, no," she said, halting him in mid-wince, "I am all right. Just let me catch my breath a moment."

Dimm was all apologies for breaking the news to her that way. "Deuce take it, I should of known better. Are you sure I can't call for your woman or your aunt?"

"Aunt Tess is prostrate with the vapors already. I'd not have her disturbed with more ill-tidings. And Tyson is busy with the packing. Heavens, I cannot decide which is harder to comprehend: Nerissa Armbruster taking her own life . . . or killing herself over Arvid, of all things."

"If you don't mind, Your Grace, could you answer a few more questions?"

"Certainly, Mr. Dimm, if you think it will help. Be sure I'd like to find my husband's murderer as much as you."

The Runner consulted his book. "What do you think of Lord Armbruster?"

"As a dance partner or as a killer? No, please forgive my levity, sir. I am just a trifle addled right now. Perhaps a sip of Madeira, if you'd be so kind to pour." She indicated a decanter and glasses on the Chinese fan table. "And please join me."

When Dimm was reseated, thin-stemmed crystal goblet gingerly in hand, the young duchess gave her opinion of her next-door neighbor. He'd always seemed a courteous, soft-spoken gentleman when they'd met socially, she said. Of an age with Arvid, he had a much more refined air about him, making Nessie's preference for Arvid even harder to believe. Marisol had an even harder time picturing Lord Armbruster in a rage, shooting a fellow nobleman. "Doesn't he have an alibi? That's what you look for, isn't it?"

Dimm consulted his pages again. "Well, he does and he doesn't. He says he was visiting a friend, but he ain't giving up the friend's name. We located his pied-á-terre—that's a love nest, don't you know—but no one in the neighborhood seems to re-call who meets him there."

"Obviously a lady whose husband is less tolerant than Lord Armbruster. But there, if he was meeting his own light-of-love, what complaint could he have with Nessie? Not enough, surely, to murder her paramour. If he feared a cuckoo bird in his nest, he'd have done better to shoot his wife, if divorce was too distasteful."

Dimm drew circles with his pencil. "Stap me if I'll ever understand the gentry and their ways. Don't none of them keep to their vows?"

"I did, sir," Marisol answered with that touch of arrogance he was coming to recognize as the duchess on her uppers. She might be of an age with his daughter Sarah and friendly-like to a nobody like Jeremiah Dimm, but she was a lady through and through, right down to that steel in her backbone and that slightly long, straight nose in the air.

"Begging your pardon, Your Grace. You just seem powerful casual about Denning's lapses, and Armbruster's, too."

"And why not? It's the way of the world."

"That's what I mean, Your Grace. It's not the way of *my* world, not by half."

"Are you married, Mr. Dimm?"

"I was for twenty-two blessed years, until the good Lord saw fit to take my Cherry, and I never strayed onct."

"What, never?" she asked in disbelief.

"Never even thought on it, or my name isn't Jeremiah Dimm. I loved her too much to want any other woman."

"Then your Cherry was a very lucky woman, sir, to have you, and you were a lucky man to have the luxury of marrying where your heart desired. I suppose we are different, those of us considered more fortunate, for we have to wed for title and property, wealth and position. I would it were otherwise," she said with a new bitterness in her voice. "I do envy you your good fortune."

"I don't know how fortunate I am after all. Don't suppose I'd miss her so now, iffen I'd loved her the less."

"I am sorry. I did not mean to bring up sad memories. Who else is on your list of suspects? Besides my brother and myself, of course. I know Foster's name is being broadcast, but he is a right one, as the gentlemen say, although regrettably hot-to-hand. We needn't even discuss him."

The Prince Regent couldn't of done it better, Dimm decided to himself. Only thing was, the more pride she showed, the less likely he was to believe she put up with that blighter's behavior. He'd have to think on it later. "If not *your* brother, Your Grace, what about the duke's?"

"What, Boynton Pendenning? The man is a fribble. An expensive fribble, granted, who was constantly arguing with Arvid over money, but to murder his own brother? I cannot believe it."

"Neither could Adam and Eve, most likely, but it happens. Jealousy, greed, ambition. One brother has the world on a string; the other brother has a rope necklace."

"But if Boynton was so eager to step into his brother's titles and vaults, why wait to murder Arvid now, when I could be carrying the heir?"

"That's just what he said. A' course, babies has been known to die in infancy."

Dimm almost bit his own tongue off when the duchess clutched her stomach. "My baby! Do you think my baby could be in danger? Please, I pray you, tell me no."

Dimm prayed he could, too, but no use lying to the poor thing. "Well, a girl will be safe enough," he reassured her, "and a boy will be, too, if you can think of anyone else besides the heir presumptive what might of ventilated the duke. Sorry, Your Grace," he said yet again when she turned a bit green at his choice of words. Lud, his nibs'd have Dimm's liver and lights for this day's work. "Anyone at all."

"Why couldn't it just have been a passing thief seeing easy pickings in an empty coach until he saw Arvid still inside? Or someone he cheated at cards? He did, you know, even when we played piquet. He couldn't stand to lose. I just want it to be a stranger, someone I don't know and won't have to fear is hiding behind every bush. Not a neighbor or an in-law."

"Speaking of neighbors, how well do you know the Earl of Kimbrough?"

"The Elusive Earl? Not at all. Goodness, never say he is a suspect? When I said a stranger, I meant a nameless footpad, a faceless cardsharp, not someone whose name is a byword both here and in Berkshire."

"He had an argument at White's with the duke the night before the murder. A real loud brouhaha, they say."

"All of Arvid's arguments were loud. I daresay it was over that piece of property again?" At Dimm's grunted assent, Marisol explained: "I knew there was some bone of contention over the land, but Arvid never consulted me about business matters or anything of that nature. He simply forbade me to invite the earl to any of our parties the few times we were in Berkshire, so I never even got to meet the man. But the people in Berkshire think highly of him, and he was some kind of hero, wasn't he? And I understand he only comes to London to speak in Parliament on reform issues. That doesn't sound like a murderer to me."

"You never can tell. If there's one thing I've found in my years on the force, it's that every criminal is somebody's son or lover or mother or brother. There's a berserker in every one of us. One time or another."

Chapter Four

$\mathcal{A}$ berserker? Boynton Pendenning? Arvid's brother certainly did not look like some blood-crazed fiend, not in his cheek-high shirt collars, nipped-in waist, and padded-out shoulders. He looked like a middle-aged dandy, laughable or ludicrous—not dangerous. Then Marisol looked more closely, at the lines of dissipation around her brother-in-law's thin mouth, the pouchy gathers under his deep-set eyes, the unhealthy pallor to his indoor skin. Suddenly Boynton wasn't just an amusing rattle. He was also a hardened gamester, always a short jump ahead of his creditors, like his friend the Prince, a man who lived—or died—by his wits. He could have been desperate enough for fratricide, gambling on not being caught, gambling on coming into Arvid's legacy by hook or by crook.

Marisol's hand shook when Boynton brought it to his mouth in greeting. She'd had to permit him to call, of course, since she had been unable to receive him last night. They had to discuss arrangements for the funeral, the makeup of a cortege to trans-port Arvid back to Berkshire, the provisions that

might be needed for the reception following inter-
ment, and a score of other details Marisol felt
Boynton should decide, since he might well be the
next duke. She clutched her shawl more closely to
her at the thought, and wished she hadn't sent Inspector Dimm away with Arvid's secretary, Mr.
Stallard, to inspect the contents of the safe. Dimm,
she knew, was holding out a last hope of finding a
suicide note. Marisol thought his chances were
much better of finding a fistful of vouchers. Some
unfortunate cardplayer whose chits Arvid held
could have come to ask for an extension in payment. Arvid would never grant the poor soul more
time, of course. There could have been an argument; the pistol might have gone off accidentally.
And Boynton Pendenning could go back to being an
amiable here-and-thereian.

Meanwhile, she was alone with him except for
her aunt's little terrier. At least Max could be
counted on to yap at any loud noise. Or soft noise,
clatter of dishes, passing lorry. "How do you do,
Boynton?" she asked, motioning him to the chair
recently occupied by the man from Bow Street.

"Well enough under the circumstances, my dear,"
he answered. "Surviving m'great loss as bravely as
can be expected." She could see his lip twitching
and had to smile in return. At least Boynton wasn't
going to offer her any fustian about being grief-
stricken or shed crocodile tears for the brother he
loathed.

"Yes, I can see you are bearing up well," she
noted, while he preened for her inspection.

"You don't think the trailing black ribbons are
too much, do you?" he asked in mock anxiety.

Marisol pretended to consider the matter carefully. "Why no, they add a certain flippancy to your
otherwise somber elegance. Arvid would have
hated them."

"I thought so, too," he said in self-congratulation,
then he took out a jewel-handled quizzing glass

and surveyed her in turn through the horridly en-
larged eyeball he presented. "And you are looking
as lovely as ever, my dear, despite that abysmal
black thing around your shoulders, the slight puff-
iness I detect around your chins—ah, chin—and
the windblown look to your hair. Oh, did I neglect
to offer my condolences?"

"I believe you did, Boynton, but let's consider
them said, shall we? And give over, do, Boynton. I
don't need your Spanish coin. We both know I am
looking sadly pulled."

"And who's to blame you, under the circumstances? But you still have that Madonna-like quality to you, the glow those painterly types try so
hard to capture. I always knew m'brother had all
the luck in the family. Then to find himself a beautiful, tolerant, fertile bride." He gave an exagger-
ated sigh, polishing his looking glass with a
handkerchief edged in black lace. "Too bad Arvid
never appreciated what he had."

"I never did understand why you never married,
Boynton, especially if you hold such tender feelings
about women. A wealthy young bride could have
solved your financial difficulties and added comfort
to your life."

"Ah, but I could never have tolerated a female
more beautiful than myself, and looking at the phiz
of an ugly wife every morning would only turn me
off my kippers. There's no hope for it. I should just
scoop you up right now and carry you off to Gretna
Green."

"You and how many footmen?" she teased.

"Oh, at least three, I shouldn't wonder. Wouldn't
want to strain the seams of my coat, don't you
know. But just think, I could marry you out of
hand, get the fortune, the title, the heir, and a
charming life's companion, all in one throw of the
dice! Ah, those wretched laws of consanguinity."

Marisol nodded in sympathy, if not in agreement.
As if she'd ever give her life—and that of her child—

into the keeping of this jackanapes! She put her hands protectively over her swollen middle. "You might have it all soon enough anyway, mightn't you? The fortune and title, at any rate."

"If there is a god in heaven, ma'am, my niece will be as exquisite as her mother. That's what I pray every night."

"Before or after gaming, wenching, drinking to excess, and taking the name of the Lord in vain?"

"During, my dear, during. But seriously, Marisol, it's the devil of a coil, isn't it? The timing does leave all of us hanging."

Her Grace wished he'd chosen a more felicitous turn of phrase, but she had to sympathize with Boynton's quandary. "What do the solicitors say?"

"They won't say beans over there at Stenross, Stenross, and Dinkerly. Quiet as clams, those chaps. They say I'll have to wait for the reading of the will next week, like everyone else. Oh, they did mention all funeral costs and household expenses were to be covered until then, on your signature. Believe they were to meet with Arvid's secretary over the matter earlier this morning. I don't suppose proper mourning attire counts as a legitimate outlay, does it?" He picked a dog hair off his black superfine coat.

"I don't see why not," Marisol told him. "The Pendennings do have an image to maintain, to counter this awful, ah, embarrassment. Send your tailor's bill over; I'll sign it today before we leave. In fact, I think you might need two sets of mourning, since you'll be greeting all the neighbors at the church in my stead, and then again at the Castle."

He raised her hands and kissed the right, then the left, then the right again. "And I'll say a special prayer that my precious niece has her mother's generous heart. I'll just be toddling off, shall I, so I can have something ready by the funeral. I'll return later to settle any of those tiresome details you seem eager to thrust onto my shoulders, and I'll be sure to bring Weston's accounting."

"Why don't you come for luncheon? I have invited Mr. Dimm from Bow Street to take the meal with us when he is finished with Mr. Stallard. You might be able to help him decipher some of the names of Arvid's debtors."

Boynton raised his plucked brows. "A redbreast at the ducal table? My, my, how standards have flown in just a day. I'd be delighted to come, my dear, just to listen for Arvid gnashing his teeth upstairs. He does lie in the duke's chamber, doesn't he?"

"Yes, would you like to—"

Boynton held up a manicured hand. "No thank you, Your Grace, not before a meal." He took his leave then, but paused at the door and held up his quizzing glass again. "You really should do something with your hair before luncheon, especially if there will be strangers present. Image of the Pendennings, don't you know."

"Yes, I shall. But my head ached so this morning I couldn't let Tyson fuss with the curling irons. The hairpins seemed to be as heavy as horseshoes, but Arvid never did like me to leave my hair down. He thought it immature and undignified for a noblewoman of my position. He forbade me to wear it down my back, in fact," she concluded with a grin, tossing those diabolical hairpins this way and that until heavy blonde curls lay against her shoulders. She shook her head, sending the curls into luxurious, wanton disarray and causing the little terrier to set up a shrill yapping. "He really is gone, isn't he?"

Boynton just winked and went out the door.

Marisol sat back against the cushions. This was the first moment she'd had alone to think, without the numbing effects of the physician's possets, her brother's restless diatribes on Arvid's moral turpitude, or her aunt's fretting over what was to become of them if the child Marisol carried was a girl. The duchess laughed to find herself wondering whose prayers were more fervent, Aunt Tess's or Boynton's.

She didn't care which, boy or girl, just that this baby be healthy—and safe. No one could wish ill of a daughter, now that Arvid himself was gone. He'd have been furious, of course, to be cheated of his heir. He'd threatened often enough those first years of their marriage to cut her off without a farthing if she proved to be barren. But they would manage, Marisol swore. She, Aunt Tess, and the little girl could live in a cottage somewhere on the sale of Marisol's jewels, those that were not entailed, of course. Arvid had been intent on his duchess presenting the right impression to the ton; she had no say in their selection or when he took which piece from the vault for her to wear, but the gems were hers. If the income was not enough to purchase a pair of colors for Foster, she'd have to let him enlist as a common soldier. That was what he'd begged for this past year, when they both realized Arvid was not going to fulfill his promise. Serving on the line was more dangerous, and beneath the dignity of the Marquis of Laughton, but Foster was brave enough and dedicated enough to rise through the ranks on his own merits. Others had made their own successful careers this harder way. Foster would have to; Marisol vowed that she would not sell herself again.

Arvid was dead. She tried not to think of what he looked like when they carried him in, all the blood and gore. She recalled instead how he appeared when she first met him, an older, sophisticated man-about-town to her wide-eyed debutante naiveté. He offered a fortune, one of the highest positions in the land outside of royalty, and security—everything people told her she wanted in a husband. That wasn't quite all Marisol had wanted in a husband, in fact, but those same people told

Marisol she'd be a fool to look any further than the polished and poised duke.

He was patient, he was gratifyingly attentive, and she had no choice.

Why hadn't *they* told her he was arrogant and cruel, petty and dishonorable? Likely because she had no choice.

Arvid planned the wedding; Arvid selected her gown, her attendants, and her lady's maid. Marisol had not been permitted to make an important decision on her own since her "I do" in church three years ago, until her "I am going home" speech yesterday. And deciding to wear her hair loose today. No man would ever have that power over her again, she vowed. No man would demean her, abuse her, or threaten her family. Arvid really was dead.

Luncheon was a strained affair, and not just because of the empty chair at the head of the table. Arvid's brother took a step toward it, and Marisol's brother growled. Boynton inspected Foster's thrown-together ensemble and carelessly tied neckcloth through his quizzing glass and offered to recommend a tailor. At which Foster offered to rearrange Boynton's nose. At which Aunt Tess kicked her nephew under the table and hissed: "You gossoon, he might just be the next duke."

At which Marisol asked Mr. Dimm if he had any luck with the papers in the safe.

Jeremiah put down his spoon. Turtle soup, by George! Wait till he told his sister Cora. "You was right about them gaming slips, Your Grace. His Grace held vouchers from half the gentlemen in London, looks like. Thing is, most times a swell can't pay his bets he puts a hole through his own brain, not someone else's."

"That's called honor, my dear sir," Boynton drawled.

"How would you know?" Foster demanded from across the table.

"But you are going to investigate the names, aren't you?" Marisol wanted to know, *and* wanted to distract her two other male guests. Aunt Tess had recovered sufficiently from her nervous indisposition to join them for the meal, but she was too busy feeding Max tidbits under the table to be of much help, if she even heard.

Dimm swallowed a mouthful of something that looked like a tadpole swimming upstream through a sea of white paste. Not bad. He thought of the miles he'd have to cover to interview half the names on his list. Not good. "Yes, Your Grace, me or my associates will go have a chat with all of them. Except the prime minister, I reckon."

"Good grief, never tell me he owed Arvid money!"

Jeremiah nodded, scraping some thick sauce off the next dish so he could see what was beneath. Beef? Bedamned if the toffs didn't buy such cheap cuts of beef they had to hide it!

Meanwhile Foster was asking what was to become of those outstanding debts.

"If Arvid had owed anyone, the estate would be expected to pay," Boynton stated. "So the estate should collect," he added hopefully.

Remembering his own father's burgeoning obligations, passed down to him, Foster sneered. Before he could make a cutting remark, Marisol intervened again. "I'm sure the solicitors will tell us what is correct. I, for one, would be more than willing to forgive any debts."

"Might be for the best," Dimm commented, looking askance at the smallest little chicken he'd ever seen, set in a ring of peas and beans on the plate in front of him. He was supposed to get the meat off those tiny bones without picking the blasted thing up in his hands? Not in this lifetime! He pushed it aside and took up a forkful of vegetables, then noticed that they were all waiting for him to explain.

The Runner slid a deck of cards out of his pocket onto the table. "These was in the wall safe along with the jewels. Fuzzed."

"What's that?" Miss Laughton asked.

"Shaved, ma'am. It's a crooked deck. I ain't saying yes, and I ain't saying no, but those gambling wins might of been dishonorably come by."

Foster and Boynton were both eagerly reaching out for the deck. Marisol won, picking up the cards and handing them to the butler with instructions to see the things burned before they brought more dishonor to the house of Pendenning or Laughton. The butler handed the pack to the footman outside the door, who was the real winner, until he was caught out and stabbed by a very sore loser. But that was another story.

Marisol was discussing the coming journey, leaving Dimm in peace to enjoy the next course, until the footman whispered in his ear that he was supposed to dip his fingers, not drink the stuff.

"When you make the arrangements with the stables, Foster, figure on one less passenger. My maid Tyson has decided she'd rather stay on in London."

Dimm came to attention, missing the pastry tray altogether. "Kind of sudden like, ain't her decision?"

"Well, the whole move is rather sudden," said the duchess. "I admit to being a trifle discomfited by her timing, but I do understand Tyson's position. Her family is here in London, for one thing, and I really do not need a fancy dresser in my condition, for another. Tyson feels her talents would be wasted, what with the baby, and mourning, and country entertainments."

"Deuced disloyal, if you ask me," Foster grumbled.

"I do believe she has a *tendre* for Purvis, Arvid's man, and that's the real reason she wants to stay behind. There's no purpose for him to travel to

Berkshire, naturally. I said I would write them both recommendations."

"I still say it's dashed inconvenient and inconsiderate. I mean, there's no time to find a suitable replacement, and you should have a maid with you for the journey at least, in case you need anything."

"The trip to Berkshire cannot take long, even at the pace the physician insists I keep. And you forget, dearest, that Aunt Tess and I were used to doing for ourselves. We'll manage."

"Especially if you wear your hair in that charming new style," Boynton put in, drawing attention to the simple black ribbon keeping Marisol's long hair off her face. Foster looked thunderous, seeking the insult in the fop's words, but Marisol just smiled and went back to peeling an apple.

Gor'blimey, Dimm thought, it's a wonder they don't starve!

"I have the answer to the problem, dear," Miss Laughton addressed her niece, after feeding the terrier half a pork chop. A pork chop! Dimm griped to himself. Now where in hell did she come by an ordinary, unembellished pork chop? He felt like challenging the rugrat for it.

"Really, it's the perfect solution. You send a note next door and hire Lady Armbruster's abigail. Obviously she is looking for a position."

Marisol almost choked on a thin slice of cheese. "Really, Aunt Tess, I do not think I could be comfortable with my dead husband's dead mistress's maid bringing my chocolate in the mornings."

"Happens I have a daughter looking for work, Your Grace," Dimm offered, shoveling cheese and fruit onto his plate before the footman could remove the serving dish. "She used to be an apprentice seamstress but her eyes were going bad and her husband didn't want her working none. But he's off with the army now and she's lonely and bored. Might answer both problems."

"And it might get you an informant in the household," Marisol congratulated, raising her glass to him. "But since I have nothing to hide, it might serve. Send your daughter to me this afternoon and we'll see if we suit." She stood to leave the table. The men, perforce, stood. And the footmen cleared away the plates. Dimm sighed.

Chapter Five

$\mathcal{A}$ tart had fallen to the floor. Jeremiah beat the little dog to it and was munching the thing on his way out of Denning House. It was coming on to rain, naturally, so he paused in the doorway to raise the collar of his overcoat. He'd learned a lot this noontime, but not much of it having to do with the case.

He was trying to decide whether to go to Lincoln's Inn Fields to try to winkle the terms of the will out of Stenross, Stenross, and Dinkerly—as in who would have benefited most from the duke's passing—or to return to the gentlemen's clubs and start raising the hackles of half the nobs in town by discussing their gaming debts. Debts of honor, the nodcocks called them, and the toffs didn't usually pay them off with a ball of lead. Still, an investigator's job was to turn over every rock and see what crawled out. Jeremiah nodded. Had to remember to tell young Gabriel that one.

Then a horseman galloped up on a tall bay horse all flecked with mud, and drew to a halt in a splash of water. Likewise spattered, the rider dismounted,

44

tossed the reins to a groom who ran out, and strode two at a time up the stairs to the covered entrance to Denning House, where Dimm was still standing.

"Have you found the killer?" the Earl of Kimbrough demanded when he saw the Runner in the doorway.

"No, milord, but I'm working on it."

"No, you are not, by Jupiter," his lordship snapped back. "You are standing around wasting time, eating sweets and trying to keep your toes dry. You would not last long in the army, mister, nor in my employ."

"No, sir," Dimm found himself murmuring, almost tempted to salute, except the rest of the tart was in his saluting hand, and he wasn't in the army anymore.

"Blast, then it's even more important I see the female. Here," he said, turning to the butler who had come to the door. The earl handed over a card, one corner carefully turned down to show he had called in person. "Tell Her Grace it is important that I see her."

"I am sorry, my lord, Her Grace is not receiving." The butler looked up, subtly trying to draw attention to the hatchments over the door, as if Kimbrough were unaware this was a house of mourning.

"Dash it, she has to see me! Tell her it's crucial. Tell her it's about her husband."

"Her Grace is resting, my lord. Perhaps you'd do better to discuss your information with Mr. Dimm here, who is handling the investigation."

The earl's curled lip spoke eloquently of his opinion of the Runner's investigation. "Just tell her I absolutely must see her."

When the butler moved off, shaking his head, Kimbrough paced the narrow hallway. "Blister it," he muttered, "she'll send back a polite refusal. A slight indisposition, dash it, or a headache. Yes, I'd wager on the headache. By Jupiter, the baggage is not going to put me off." He stormed down the hallway after the butler, dripping raindrops onto the Turkey runner.

Now Jeremiah Dimm would have given his eye-teeth to hear the conversation between these two folks what swore they never set their peepers on each other. He did the next best thing, giving some of his nibs's silver to the footman on duty in the hall. In exchange he was led to the room adjoining Her Grace's Chinese parlor. The connecting door wasn't too thick, the keyhole wasn't too low, and the bonbons in a little dish weren't too filling.

One day her husband was murdered, almost in his lover's arms. The next day her maid gave notice. What else could go wrong?

"Carlinn, Lord Kimbrough, requests an audience, Your Grace. Pardon me for disturbing your rest, Your Grace, but he insists it is—"

"He insists it is a matter of life and death," an angry voice bellowed from directly behind the very upper servant.

The stately butler's face took on a pained expression, to be caught so derelict in his duty as to permit an unwanted guest to intrude on his mistress's privacy. Then he noted again the height and breadth of his lordship's imposing physique and the thunderous scowl on his dark visage. The butler beat a hasty, not-so-dignified retreat. His mistress's privacy be damned. She was leaving for the country tomorrow anyway. She'd find plenty of privacy among the cabbages and turnips.

Marisol looked up from her reclining position, and up some more. So this was Kimbrough. Indeed he was larger than life, just like the tales of his heroics. She thought he might have been attractive, had his thick brows not been furrowed and his mouth not been turned down in a frown of disapproval. He did not have Arvid's classic features or Boynton's elegance, of course, and certainly not Foster's boyish good looks, but, yes, he was handsome. Marisol was sure many a young girl would be sighing over that cleft chin, those intense brown eyes and weathered cheeks, did he show his phiz in Town. No wonder they called him the Elusive Earl. Debutantes and their mamas would be falling all over themselves to get to him if he participated in the Season.

Of course, Marisol herself did not appreciate such rugged features, such oversized virility. Nor did she appreciate mud on her Oriental carpet, nor being stared at so rudely. She struggled to a sitting position and cleared her throat.

Kimbrough jerked back to attention. Gads, for the first time in his life he wished he carried one of those foppish quizzing glasses to give the jade a set-down for her inspection of his person. He hadn't missed the curled lip at his muddied boots or the haughty lift to her eyebrow at his buckskins. Then she'd raised her nose—not the dainty little turned-up affair he admired in a female—as if he'd brought the smell of the stable in with him. Even if he had, she was an arrogant piece of goods with the bold look of a strumpet. Why, she was not the Diamond he'd been expecting at all. Her dress was less than elegant, and her blonde hair was loose like a wanton's. Of course, circumstances were such that lapses could be excused, and those sky blue eyes, he noted objectively, were undoubtedly her best feature.

What Carlinn couldn't tear his eyes from, however, what Marisol caught him guiltily absorbed in, was the sheer bulk of the duchess. Zounds, he'd seen dead cows in the hot Spanish sun less bloated. He hadn't realized she was this close to term or he might have reconsidered his approach. As it was, he was forced to apologize. "Forgive me for staring, Your Grace. I, ah . . ."

"Yes," she interrupted with a slight lift to the corners of her mouth. "I have never understood why they call it a delicate condition myself. As you can see, there is nothing whatsoever delicate about it."

Instead of smiling in return, Kimbrough frowned even more. He took a step closer, and Marisol reached for the bell on the table at her side. At his step, however, Max the terrier started barking and tearing around, snapping at the earl's scuffed boots.

"Hell and tarnation," Carlinn swore. He bent down, grabbed the dog, and lifted Max to eye level. All four feet paddling in the air as if one of the dragons from the Chinese tapestry had come to life and was breathing fire at his nubby little tail, Max whined. Marisol was about to demand the dog's release when Lord Kimbrough declared, "You, sir, are an embarrassment to the entire canine family. Now behave yourself or I shall lock you in one of those lacquered cabinets."

He lowered the dog and Max ran to hide under Marisol's skirts, trembling. "How dare you frighten my dog!" she exclaimed, forgetting for the moment that Max was actually Aunt Tess's pet and a nuisance to boot.

"A real dog wouldn't need to be frightened," he snapped back, "but it's all of a piece." He waved his arm around at the exotic furnishings, as if they met his standards as poorly as Max or Marisol herself. Well, she'd had enough. Enough of some angry gentleman forcing himself into her presence and then doing his best to intimidate her. By heaven, she was not going to permit this . . . this ruffian to frighten her.

"Get out, sirrah! I did not invite you, and I do not wish to see you. I demand you leave at once!"

"Not until I've had my say, I won't, so don't you get on your high horse with me, Duchess. It won't wash."

"How dare you! You barge into a lady's drawing room without permission—into a house of mourning, I might add—wearing mud and buckskins like some . . . some—"

"Country rustic? Gentleman farmer? Honest Berkshire landowner? I'm not surprised you cannot recognize the breed, ma'am."

"And I am not surprised you stay away from Town if these are your manners! How dare you come to my own house and insult me!"

"And how dare you involve me in your sordid little scandals? My family has never been tainted with such filth before and wouldn't be now, if not for you and the London rumor mills. Thank heaven my parents are not alive to see how low you and your kind have brought our good name. But what about my sister, Duchess? Have you considered anyone else in this? My sister will make her come-out next year, if her reputation is not already so besmirched by your scandal that no hostess will invite her anywhere and no man will offer for her."

Outraged, Marisol sputtered. "My? My scandal? I involved you? My husband was murdered, and you were the last person known to have words with him! You threatened him. Scores of witnesses heard you."

"Denning was a bounder."

"He was my husband!"

"My regrets, ma'am."

Marisol gasped. "Why, you— Here you are, spouting some fustian about finding your name in the muck, when you thrust yourself uninvited into the presence of an unchaperoned female. A recently unmarried female, I might add! For all I know you killed Arvid and you've come to continue your bloody path."

"Don't be absurd, Duchess. Not even gapeseeds from the hinterlands go around seducing or strangling pregnant women."

He looked as though he might wish to do the latter, though, so Marisol demanded, "Then why in the name of all that's holy *have* you come?"

Kimbrough drew a folded sheet of newsprint out of his inner pocket and tossed it down on the table beside Marisol. "I have come because of this," he said with a snarl, "and a demand that you insist they print a retraction."

The man was mad, Marisol decided, as she unfolded the paper. That was all there was for it; he was a Bedlamite. That he thought she could get a journal to issue an apology for a scandalous cartoon proved it. The drawing showed the interior of a coach where an *enceinte* woman and a large gentleman both held pistols on an entwined couple on the opposite seat. The caption read: "After you, my dear."

"This?" Marisol asked in disbelief. "This is what has you so up in the boughs? It's not even a good likeness."

"Devil take the likeness! I don't even know you, ma'am, and I resent being pictured with you in this filthy thing. You must go— No, you can write the newspaper at once, demanding they recant."

"What, after you walked past that platoon of journalists on the street outside? Or were you so burning with righteous indignation that you did not notice the ragtag group out there with sharpened pencils? Shall I parade down to Fleet Street and sob to an editor that I don't count any large gentlemen among my associates, or did you mean the one I had tea with this afternoon?"

Kimbrough ran his hand through his hair. "Blast!"

Marisol felt no sympathy for his chagrin. "Indeed. Not only would I be made to look more a fool than any cartoon could ever do, but I would destroy whatever credibility I possess at this moment. I cannot begin to imagine what Mr. Dimm would be thinking, after I told him we had never met. I thank you for casting doubts upon my honor, sirrah!"

"Honor? What would a Pendenning know about honor?"

The duchess was very much afraid that if she did have a pistol right then, she would use it. Eyes narrowed to slits, voice low and harsh, she told him again to get out. "For you are the rudest man of my acquaintance, and having been intimately acquainted with Arvid Pendenning, that is saying a great deal."

"I suppose that last was uncalled for," he conceded, pointedly eyeing the chair she had not offered. She still did not, so he paced to the mantel and examined a Ming dog there, while Marisol held her breath that the clumsy oaf would not drop the priceless porcelain. "So what are you doing about this bumblebroth?" he finally turned and asked.

"I am not confessing to Arvid's murder, if that is your aim, no matter how it might suit you, my lord earl. Instead I am assisting Mr. Dimm to the best of my ability and opening my house to him both here and in Berkshire, so he might follow *all* his leads."

Her emphasis on the *all* left Carlinn in no doubt that the duchess considered him the prime suspect in Berkshire. He swore under his breath as he stomped back and forth in front of Marisol's couch until she was growing seasick. 'Twould be useless to ask him to desist, she felt. If he wouldn't obey a direct order to leave, he wasn't likely to care about her queasiness. Either the lunatic would exhaust himself with that furious pacing—Lord knew she was growing tired watching—or he'd wear a hole in her lovely Oriental carpet, or she'd cast up her accounts. Marisol was wondering which was likely to come first when he muttered, "Botheration. This is getting me nowhere." He came to a stop across from her and impatiently asked, "Duchess, who controls the Pendenning lands now? Is it you? That caper-merchant Boynton? The solicitors?"

With great satisfaction at his frustration, Marisol was able to reply that she honestly did not know how things were left. "But knowing Arvid, they will be as awkward as possible. You shall just have to wait on the reading of the will with the rest of us, and on the birth of my child, I should suppose. You might join your prayers for a girl to Boynton's, for I am sure he'll sell off every unentailed parcel to finance his gambling."

Then Marisol clamped a hand over her mouth. In her anger at this addlepated bumpkin, she'd forgotten he could be a murderer. If that acreage meant so much to Kimbrough that he'd kill Arvid over it, what was another tiny life? Especially after she'd practically promised that Boynton would be easier to deal with. She put her other hand on her stomach.

Carlinn didn't miss the protective gesture, nor the fear in her eyes, and he cursed again. He was furious that a pregnant woman was afraid of him, even more furious that she'd believe him a killer. "Dash it, ma'am," he shouted, "I do not murder innocent women and children. I did not even murder your husband! I cannot say I am sorry someone else did, but the fact is that I did not."

"How do I know that? You come in here in a rant and expect me to change public opinion. You follow no form of social conduct I've ever heard of. How do I know what you are capable of?"

"And how do I know you didn't kill the bounder yourself over some trinket or other?" he retorted.

"Trinket?" Marisol shrieked, pushed past her endurance. "You think I would kill my own husband over a pearl necklace or something? Was Lady Armbruster a trinket? Is my child's welfare a trinket?" she yelled, pushing mightily to get her ungainly body out of the cushions so she could be more on a level with this hulking clunch. Max ran to hide under the couch.

Seeing her struggle, Kimbrough naturally offered her his assistance. She put her right hand in his and said "Thank you" when she'd attained her footing. Then she hauled back with that same right hand and slapped him across the face so hard even the powerful earl reeled back. Or perhaps it was the surprise.

"My husband lies dead upstairs," the duchess was crying, "his mistress next door. I have been accused of murder by an odd little man in a red vest. My maid has given notice, and I am fat. But you . . . you are the worst of the lot!" She sank back to the sofa, her face in her hands, sobbing. "And now I have struck a man to whom I've never even been introduced!"

The earl held out his handkerchief and tried to speak past the dust of contrition in his throat. "Carlinn Kimbrough, ma'am, at your, ah, service."

Jeremiah Dimm wished he'd stayed in the dining room searching out more fallen pastries. He could have heard the whole conversation from there, so loud were these two, and without having to put his ear to any door. Then again, that red handprint on the stiff-rumped earl's cheek, even outlined by the tiny keyhole, sure warmed the cockles of the Runner's heart. Didn't help the case none, a' course, Dimm realized, but salute *that*, you sanctimonious prig!

Chapter Six

$\mathcal{A}$rvid had been an indifferent traveler, restless, uncomfortable, impatient of delays. His child looked to follow in Arvid's unsettled path. No matter the finest sprung carriage, the slowest pace, the most careful avoidance of ruts in the road, the baby made Marisol's journey a misery, the same as Arvid would have done. At least the baby didn't get nasty and belligerent; neither did Arvid, for once, bouncing along in his ornately carved casket in the special funeral carriage up ahead. Boynton traveled next in his own coach with his valet and a mountain of valises, and the baggage wagon came after, with Mr. Dimm crammed between wardrobe trunks, delicacies from the London markets, household items from her own old home that the duchess did not wish to leave behind, and all the trappings she'd been gathering for the arrival of her child.

Dimm's daughter rode in the spacious crested carriage with Marisol and her aunt, thank goodness, for Sarah turned out to be a marvel with biscuits and peppermints and distracting chatter about her own large family and Ned Turner, the soldiering husband she wrote to every day.

Aunt Tess managed to sleep for most of the journey, her knitting fallen in her lap. Marisol was green with envy ... or something. She was also jealous of her brother, who had chosen to ride alongside, or ahead, or on short cross-country excursions. That was the first thing she was going to do after the baby, Marisol vowed, ride with the wind down tree-shaded lanes, taking her jumps flying. The baby protested the flying part, too, so she sighed and pictured quiet strolls through the castle's rose gardens. Of course, that was in the spring, and who knew where any of them would be when the flowers bloomed? Except Arvid, of course.

Gardens, flowers, country rides, fresh air. It took Marisol a day and a night to recover from the journey before she could recall why she'd been so desperate to get to Berkshire in the first place. Then it took less than half an hour of raw, cold rain, winter-barren landscapes, and the drafty old barn of a relic, for reality to return with a thud. The thud of the dowager's cane, to be exact.

Arvid's mother had not moved to the Dower House on Marisol's marriage. There was no need, the older Duchess Denning had decided, since Arvid intended to spend as little time away from London as possible, and his mother was such an admirable manager of the estate and the household. She managed Arvid, didn't she?

The dowager obviously intended to keep on managing: assigning bedchambers, announcing dinner hours, selecting the hymns for Arvid's service and new curtains for the nursery. She punctuated each of her pronouncements with raps of her ebony cane on the marble floors that sent tremors through Marisol's aching head. The noise also set Max into a frenzy of yipping and lunging, so the dowager ordered the little dog banished to Aunt Tess's room, which offended that lady so much she chose to take her dinner upstairs on a tray. Marisol was too spent to argue.

At least there was no confrontation over the bed-chambers. The dowager had moved to the recently renovated east wing when Arvid brought home his bride, so Marisol still occupied the duchess's suite, with its ill-fitted casement windows, antiquated furnishings, and resident pigeons outside in the battlements.

Dinner was another matter. The first night Marisol walked into the dining room on her brother's arm to see that Boynton sat at the head of the table and the dowager at the foot.

"Boynton is head of the family now, Marisol," the dowager declared, ignoring Marisol's own seniority, of however short duration. Marisol decided she was not as well recovered from the journey as she thought. She'd do better with dinner on a tray in her room also.

The next morning Marisol ordered a round table. She was willing to compromise, not buckle under to her mother-in-law's dictatorship. When the butler and housekeeper looked toward each other, and then allowed as how they'd best consult with Her Grace, Marisol reminded them that *she* was also Her Grace, for now, and possibly for years into the future. A round table it would be. Not for the state dining room, of course, but for the smaller room where the family ate. That night the dowager took dinner in *her* rooms. Unfortunately for Marisol's appetite, this left the younger widow alone with her brother and brother-in-law, who sniped at each other throughout. The funeral tomorrow would be a relief.

The man from Bow Street was finding his stay in Berkshire a real treat. He'd decided to put up at the inn in Pennington after being consigned to the stables by that nasty piece of work at the Castle, once Her Grace, Lady Marisol, that is, took to her bed. He hired himself a gig and called in at the pubs and farmsteads. Over hearty ales and fresh-baked breads, the locals were happy enough to talk about the gentry. Their "betters," they said with smiles and raised mugs.

No one had a good word to say about the late duke and less to say about the next, should it turn out to be that coxcomb Boynton. No one could think of anyone nearby with a reason to kill Duke Arvid, though, excepting that he was a miser, a lecher, and a snob. As far as absentee landlords went, that was the finest kind. He never came near Pennington much, so he never bothered them much.

Boynton scared the locals worse. Where Arvid had tried to make the most profit off his lands, Boynton could just wager the Pendenning holdings away, and with them the future of everyone in the little community of Pennington. The villagers were mostly agreed that if they had to have their lives in the hands of a gambler and they had their druthers, they'd pick a winner over a loser every time.

The young duchess and her babe were unknown factors to the country folk, and much would depend on who got named trustee for the little duke, if it be a boy, and if she got hanged.

Then there was Lord Kimbrough. No one hereabouts would hear a word against the earl. Could he commit cold-blooded murder? The vicar's wife would tie her garters on the main street first. Kimbrough was fair, generous, and not above having a pint or two with the lads after a hard day's work. Now *that* was a real gentleman.

Lord Kimbrough even made a point of finding Dimm at his inn and inviting the Runner to dinner one evening. A real dinner it was, too, not a batch of those pawky little bits of things swimming in sauces. The earl served an honest haunch of venison, mutton, and beef, with potatoes and turnips and peas, and no footman to scoop the platters away before a man had his fill. Kimbrough didn't get to that size and strength eating no lark's tongues, Dimm reflected contentedly. Besides, the Runner had already wangled a position in his lordship's stables for his younger boy, who had a real touch with horses. And he was in a fair way to landing a living for Cherry's brother, who was currently ministering to the lost souls of London's slums, at Dimm's expense. And that was all before dessert. Too bad that funeral was tomorrow.

Lord Kimbrough decided to attend the funeral after all. He wasn't going to at first, not to pay respects to a man he despised. But he was keenly aware of his responsibilities and knew that as magistrate, neighbor, fellow nobleman, and bordering landowner, by rights he should go. He wouldn't want to be thought lacking in courtesy to the duchess, either. Both duchesses, he amended. Besides, he didn't want anyone suggesting he stayed away because of a guilty conscience. He had absolutely nothing to feel guilty about, Carlinn told himself, at least nothing to do with Denning's murder. Making a recent widow cry, driving to tears a woman who was breeding, that was another matter. And then fleeing! Cow-handed and chickenhearted both!

His guilt must have shown, for even the amiable Dimm looked at him queerly, almost as if the Runner knew what a clumsy oaf Carlinn had been.

So he was going to Arvid Pendenning's last rites. There might even be some satisfaction seeing the bastard put in the ground he cared so little about. And, too, he had Dimm beside him, so he could help identify anyone else come to gloat. It was Dimm who pointed out the duchess's young brother, acting as one of the pallbearers. Laughton had the same fair coloring and the same patrician nose. With a little maturity and a bit of country cooking, the lad might be pleasant looking, as opposed to the sister. Carlinn recalled the duchess as looking aged beyond her twenty-one years and as if she'd been eating for two for all twenty-one of them. She wasn't present, of course, but would be waiting at the Castle with the other women to receive those wishing to express their condolences.

Kimbrough did not so wish. He'd done his duty to Arvid's memory, having sat through the Castle's private chaplain's droning attempt to find something nice to say about the blighter. Then he'd stood in the biting cold at the Pendenning burial grounds while the chaplain gave it a final go.

There were three distinct groups of mourners, Kimbrough noted as his mind wandered. One batch consisted of more relieved noblemen seen in one place than since Fou-Fou La Rue burned her journals. These were the men Dimm wanted identified, Arvid's gulls come to see if their notes were being called in. Then there were enough tallow-faced Captain Sharps to fleece every lamb in Berkshire. Boynton's friends, he supposed, come to support him in his grief—and to stake their claims to his future riches. The third group, a small gathering of tenants and local citizenry, stayed well away from the Londoners.

It was these last whose hands Kimbrough first shook when the cleric finally ran down. Then he moved among the knights, barons, and honorables, introducing Dimm when he could. Dimm in turn introduced him to young Laughton, who was pathetically glad of the opportunity, having little in common with any of the three disparate groups except his antipathy toward the deceased. On hearing the earl's name, Foster developed an instant case of hero worship for the retired army officer and begged Kimbrough to accompany the funeral party back to the Castle for refreshments.

Carlinn was torn. He'd satisfied the conventions; now he wanted to put this whole sorry mess behind him. But the boy was a pigeon among these wolves, especially with the fiery temper gossip said he had. Leaving the young marquis alone would be like sending a raw recruit out to the front line. Kimbrough couldn't do it, even if the bantling was one of the other murder suspects. He'd only have been defending his sibling. Kimbrough could understand that; he'd skewer anyone who offered harm to his own sister. So he accepted. And managed to get through half the curses he'd learned in the cavalry by the time a footman relieved him of his coat and gloves at Denning Castle.

Many of the grave-side mourners had refused Boynton's invitation to partake of the Castle's hospitality in favor of starting the trip back to London before the day was too advanced. Others chose to toast Arvid at a nearby tavern, where they might also get up a game of cards or two. The working people mostly went back to their farms and businesses. The company was thin, therefore, when Kimbrough and Dimm entered the large drawing room.

To one side gathered Boynton and his cronies, sampling Arvid's wine cellar. Kimbrough nodded. He'd just seen most of those fellows. Near the enormous fireplace the dowager held court, accepting sympathy from the local matrons, the squire's wife, and the mayor's sister, all her bosom bows among the neighboring gentry. The earl bowed and murmured something about being sorry. He was sorry he wasn't out riding his new chestnut stallion. But the dowager nodded and preened that the highest ranking gentleman in the shire—temporarily, naturally—had graced her son's obsequies. It was fitting, of course, but one never knew about Kimbrough. She ignored the Runner's presence entirely.

And finally, in a window embrasure across the vast room, sat Arvid's widow, her brother, and an older woman. They might have been lepers for all the attention paid them. A lesser woman might have retreated, taken to her rooms, but the duchess sat straight in her chair, chin raised. She was all in black, with a black lace veily thing on her head like those Spanish mantillas he'd seen on the Peninsula. Her hair was still down, loosely tied at the back of her neck. She had bottom, Carlinn had to give her that. And dignity.

"Coventry, that's what it is," Dimm whispered as they crossed the Aubusson expanse. "The dowager's got all the old biddies on her side, swearing the chit was responsible for Denning's death. If she didn't aim the pistol herself, according to the old besom, then it were the rackety brother. And it were the young duchess what forced Arvid to a life of sin in the first place."

"She couldn't conceive of Boynton being guilty?"

"No more'n you could picture your right hand up and cutting off your left. No, they got the gel drawn and quartered. She'll be an exile out here, iffen the dowager has her way. A' course, they'll all have to change their tunes when the baby's born, iffen it turns out to be the next duke. Or pay the piper. But that's months away."

"Do I detect a note of sympathy for Denning's doxy? I thought you chaps were supposed to be objective."

"I got daughters her age," Dimm said with a shrug, pausing to relieve a passing footman of a handful of toast squares spread with goose liver and fish eggs. "And her life couldn't of been easy, what I hear."

"She married him for his money and the title. That's what she got."

Dimm clucked his tongue. "Were things all that black and white, I'd be plumb out of a job."

There was no way she could get out of the room before he got to her. Heavens, there was no way she could get out of this chair in that amount of time. Unless the floor should open and swallow her up, she'd have to face the man she'd slapped. He'd deserved it, of course, barging into her drawing room like some ravening beast, but a lady should never lower herself to acting the fishwife, no matter the provocation. And then turning into a watering pot in front of a perfect stranger! At least he'd been gentleman enough to hand over his handkerchief and then leave before she disgraced herself further. Why did the barbarian have to show his second effort at proper conduct on this of all days?

He even looked more civilized. His clothes were well tailored if not absolutely bang up to the mark, without a single crease, spatter, or scent of the stables. His hair was combed, his eyes weren't shooting sparks, and his hands were wrapped around a wineglass instead of her throat. She should be safe.

"Marisol, have you met the Earl of Kimbrough?" Foster asked, eagerly drawing Carlinn closer to the little grouping.

"We've never been formally introduced," Kimbrough said before she could reply. "How do you do, Your Grace? May I take this opportunity to express my deepest regrets?"

Foster looked at him in astonishment and even Aunt Tess wondered aloud, "What's that? Did he say he was sorry Arvid was dead?"

He hadn't. He'd correctly apologized for their last meeting, Marisol understood. She nodded her head. "Thank you. This is a difficult time for all of us."

"Too kind," he murmured. There was more he wished to say, but not in front of her family and the Bow Street Runner. Dimm must have some skill in detection, for he winked at the earl and drew Laughton to the side with a question about one of Boynton's set.

"What's that?" Aunt Tess asked. "I hope they bring back some of those grilled oysters."

Speaking softly for once, and with a smile that quite transformed his face from passably attractive to positively stunning, he amazed Marisol further by apologizing more fully. Arvid had never apologized for anything, ever.

"I have no excuse for my actions," Kimbrough was saying, "except that I am used to being in control, Your Grace—of my circumstances, of my tongue, of my temper. Mostly of my privacy. But everything had gone beyond my control that day. I was thrust willy-nilly into a public spectacle of the type I most deplore. Still, I should never have taken my frustrations out on you. I sincerely apologize."

"And I am sure I would never have subjected you to such an ill-mannered, emotional display were I not suffering the same upset. So I believe we are even, my lord, unless, of course, you were the one who murdered my husband."

"Witch," he muttered even lower.

"What's that? They're playing whist? In a house of mourning? Why, I never!"

A proper twenty minutes later, the earl and the investigator took their leave.

While they waited for his curricle to be brought 'round Carlinn asked, "Did you discover anything new?"

Dimm pondered a moment. "Not much, less'n you count a partiality for lobster patties."

Chapter Seven

*H*is nibs at Bow Street wasn't happy. No fresh scandal had rocked London, so the newspapers were still gnawing on the Denning case. With the principals out of town and no new facts coming to light, the editors were crying privileged treatment for the privileged class. Whitewash, they called it, with no one being brought to account. More like no vulgar headlines to sell more newspapers.

The reporters would lose interest soon enough, soon as there was some war news or a new sensation in the ton, some marchioness running off with her footman or something. Till then, his nibs wasn't happy. And when the boss wasn't happy, no one was happy, least of all Jeremiah Dimm, who was wearing out his shoe leather again, trying to dig up more evidence.

"But you can't just make facts. They is like rocks; you can find them, you can uncover them, but only time and nature can make one of the confounded things."

He went back over his notes. He retraced the paths on that fatal day of the brother, the neighbor, the wife's brother. He carefully checked the background of all Denning's associates, and he talked to the servants again at the duke's house. Her Grace's maid was staying with her mother, he learned, and the valet, Purvis, was helping to pack His Grace's belongings between visits to the employment agencies.

Dimm saw for himself all the reports that said no one had come to Lord Armbruster's love nest, not in a week of round-the-clock surveillance, so he went next door to Armbruster House, which was also draped in black, with its knocker off the door.

Lord Armbruster was still up north delivering his wife's body to her people in Cumberland, where he might convince some prelate she'd taken an accidental overdose of laudanum. There had been no reason to hold him in London any more than there'd been reason to detain the duchess or any of the others, despite the scandal sheets crying leniency for the aristocracy. Blast, you'd think this were France or something, Dimm considered, crossing that bit of roadway between the houses where Denning had met his Maker. Or unmaker. Deuce take it, the crime happened in the middle of the afternoon. Someone should have seen something! Or heard the shot.

"Oh no," Armbruster's butler contradicted him. "Our walls are very thick. His lordship would not want to hear the sounds of traffic or street vendors, don't you know. And then there was Lady Armbruster screaming. Of course that might have been after, but if before, we wouldn't have heard the shot, during. No, no one here knows anything."

But someone did. Lady Armbruster's maid was just finishing packing all of the dead woman's clothing into boxes when Dimm found her.

"You didn't happen to come by any suicide note, did you?" he asked for the eighth or ninth time, having searched for one himself before traveling to Berkshire. He had found enough writing in Lady

Armbruster's hand to know she hadn't sent the message to the duchess, unless she disguised her writing, of course, but a farewell note would have been Christmas and a promotion and lobster patties, all rolled into one. Especially if the lady had confessed to killing her lover before taking her own life.

"No, she were too sleepy to do any writing," the maid told him. "Right from the first. I didn't see her when she got up to take the rest of the bottle, but she couldn't of been thinking right, now could she? And just look at this mess." The maid waved her arms around the room. "And my lord intends to give it all to the poorhouse; he doesn't want to see any of it again."

"You mean he's not letting you have her clothes?"

Dimm interpreted her petulance aright, for the maid replied, "No, the bastard blames me for leaving the bottle with her. As if that's any of my job. And he's not even going to give me a good reference, he says. So what am I supposed to do now, I ask you?" She crammed a satin gown into a glove-sized space in the box. "I don't suppose you're on terms with Her Grace next door to put in a good word for me, are you? I heard Tyson didn't want to go to the country."

"The duchess already hired a new maid when I saw her in Berkshire." He didn't say it was his own daughter. "But maybe they won't suit. You never know."

"Well, here," she said, handing him a brightly colored shawl. "You take this, in case you hear of anything."

"I'm not sure . . ." he began.

"Oh, go on, his lordship owes me something, he does. I mean, I did try to stop Lady Armbruster from taking that first dose, I did. I told her right off that it wasn't good for the baby."

Dimm knew what to do with the pretty shawl; his widowed sister Cora who kept house for him and all their relations would look a treat in it. He wasn't so sure about this new bit of information. So he took his theories with him back to Berkshire, just about the time the will was going to be read.

"A baby? How sad." Marisol could not find it in her heart to feel sorry for the woman who had thrown her life away over a tawdry affair. But the poor, innocent baby was another matter. "But why?" she asked the Runner, as if Mr. Dimm would have the answers.

He was the one asking the questions, though. "I was hoping you could tell me, Your Grace. Did she say anything to you? Did your husband mention anything?"

"Goodness, Mr. Dimm, surely you know the spouse is always the last to find out about these things. Besides, Arvid hardly told me when he was leaving town for house parties and such. He'd never discuss more personal matters with a mere wife. But are you so sure the child was Arvid's? Did the maid say so?"

"No, twice. But why else would Lady Armbruster carry on about being ruined?"

"I wonder if Nessie were not simply mentally unbalanced. Why couldn't she just have passed the child off as Armbruster's? Ladies do it all the time. Ah, that is, I have heard such things happen." Embarrassed to have blurted such a scandalous statement—her aunt would have the vapors if she heard—Marisol offered the Runner more tea. "And do have another macaroon, Mr. Dimm. I am going to and I hate to eat alone. It makes me feel like a glutton, but I am always hungry."

Jeremiah was happy to humor a woman in such an interesting condition. As they nibbled away, though, he still pursued his line of inquiry. "Knowing Lady Armbruster was breeding, Your Grace, would you say she'd be more or less like to up and shoot the duke?"

"Killing Arvid wouldn't make Nessie any more or less *enceinte*. Of course, Arvid might have been threatening to tell her husband. I wouldn't put blackmail past him," she confided over another slice of poppyseed cake. "But they did not seem to be arguing when I saw them in the carriage."

"No, Your Grace, I didn't suppose they was." He took another gooseberry tart to help swallow the disappointment.

Lord Kimbrough was another disappointment. "I can't stand all those sweet things," he'd explained, but Dimm assured him the thick slices of bread and butter were more than adequate. The discouragement came when the earl said he did not believe either of the Armbrusters committed the crime.

"Nerissa Armbruster was your typically hysterical female. She would have fainted at the sight of all that blood. More so if she was in a delicate way." Carlinn burned his tongue, thinking of what the duchess had said about that euphemism, instead of sipping the hot tea carefully.

"Then what about his lordship? He finds out his wife is presenting him with a token of another man's affections, he's like to be a tad overset."

"But why should Armbruster kill Denning? He'd have done better to kill his whoring wife. Oh, I know you'll hear how these indiscretions are politely accepted in the ton, but that's after a man has his heir. Armbruster didn't, after—what? Five, six years of marriage. He does have cousins and such, I know, and I am sure he'd rather they step into his shoes than Denning's bastard. Besides, you said that maid had no way of knowing if Armbruster even knew his wife was breeding, much less who fathered the brat."

"It's a mess, all right," Dimm lamented. "I suppose all the Quality has to fret about who inherits, like this Denning argle-bargle. At least poor folks don't have that headache. By the way, my lord, who's your heir?"

Kimbrough put his cup down with a thump. "I have a cousin in Bath." A middle-aged, hypochondriac bachelor, but Dimm needn't know that. "And I am only seven-and-twenty, after all. Plenty of time to worry about the succession."

"Denning was only thirty-nine. Don't suppose he meant to cock up his toes yet either."

"By George, you're full of cheer today, Dimm. But buck up, maybe something will come out of the reading of the will this afternoon. Best have another cup of tea and some more to eat; the dowager's as cheeseparing as Arvid ever was."

"What's that man doing here?" the dowager demanded, banging her cane up and down on the Axminster carpet in the Castle's library. No one knew whether she meant the earl or the Runner.

Marisol thought Lord Kimbrough must be at the reading in his capacity as local magistrate, but Mr. Stenross, the second Mr. Stenross of Stenross, Stenross, and Dinkerly, the family's solicitors, announced that he had invited the earl on business pertaining to the will. The dowager's scowl deepened, as did Lord Kimbrough's. Mr. Dimm mumbled something about Crown investigation and took a position toward the rear wall, well out of the dowager's way.

"Shall I send for the servants now?" Marisol asked.

Mr. Stenross cleared his throat and shuffled his papers on the desk. "That, ah, will not be necessary."

By this everyone understood that Arvid had not provided for his long-term retainers, which boded ill for any lingering hopes that he might have had a generous moment while contemplating eternity. Aunt Tess reached for Marisol's hand. Foster put a hand on her shoulder, from where he stood behind his sister's chair.

Mr. Stenross seemed to feel elucidation was in order, as if anyone in the room needed a lesson in Arvid's mean, clutchfisted character.

"His Grace felt that the servants were being well compensated for their labors," Mr. Stenross explained uncomfortably. "Since none were due for retirement, he did not feel it necessary to provide pensions at this time."

"Yes, yes, man, we know he didn't intend to die just yet," Boynton said, forgetting to drawl. "Get on with it."

Mr. Stenross cleared his throat again and reshuffled his papers. "Getting on with it" was clearly beneath his dignity. Boynton moaned and Foster tightened his fingers on Marisol's shoulder.

"I must advise you that His Grace was very careful of his will, revising his codicils regularly. This document was meant to be an interim will, created for the purpose of expressing His Grace's wishes, should the sex of his progeny not be determined at the time of his demise."

"You mean he wrote a new will when Marisol got pregnant?" Foster asked, then flushed at his own outburst.

"Exactly." Mr. Stenross settled a pair of spectacles on his nose and began reading: " 'Being the last will and testament of Arvid Alexander Pendenning, Sixth Duke of Denning, Baron of Denton,' et cetera, et cetera. I shall skip over the technical paragraphs, but a copy of the document will be left here for your perusal, that there be no doubts of its authenticity or legality." He cleared his throat again. " 'To my mother who has been living at Denning Castle instead of the Dower House, conserving her own funds, I leave the annuity established under my father's will.' "

The dowager slumped in her chair and groaned.

Boynton tossed her a vinaigrette and leaned forward. "Go on, go on."

" 'Likewise, my brother already receives a sufficient allowance. Had he higher income, he would game deeper.' "

"Bastard!" Boynton shouted.

Mr. Stenross looked up.

"I didn't mean you. He can't do that, can he, if I'm his heir?"

The solicitor frowned. "These terms are conditional on the outcome of Her Grace's delivery, naturally." He turned back to the papers. " 'To my wife, Marisol Laughton Pendenning, I leave the sum of ten thousand pounds, should she fail to carry the infant to term or have a stillbirth, leaving me without issue.' "

Marisol gritted her teeth. Trust Arvid to consider every horrifying possibility. But they could live on ten thousand pounds, with the sale of her jewelry. She patted Aunt Tess's hand.

"Should my wife be delivered of a female child, I leave her ten thousand pounds a year until my daughter marries or reaches her majority, at which time the said daughter is to receive a dowry of fifty thousand pounds. The aforementioned annuity also terminates at my wife's remarriage.' "

Aunt Tess let go of Marisol's fingers in order to wipe her eyes. "I was so afraid he'd let us starve if you didn't provide the heir."

Mr. Stenross glared at her for the interruption. "Yes, the heir. Under both of the above conditions, His Grace's brother would inherit by law the title and all entailed property, including but not limited to Denning House in London, Denning Castle, Berkshire, the hunting box in Leicester, holdings in Jamaica, their incomes and earnings."

Boynton smiled, and even the dowager perked up, until Mr. Stenross went on. "I tried to advise His Grace concerning the disbursement of the unentailed property but the duke was adamant. The bank accounts, real estate investments, consols, et cetera, were his to do with as he wished."

"Yes, but we all know that's where the real wealth lies. Who gets it?" Boynton almost shredded the lace at his cuffs, in his excitement.

" 'If I die with no posthumous heir, neither my wife nor my brother is to have a farthing of the unentailed property,' " Mr. Stenross recited, disapproval evident in his voice, " 'which is to be used instead to establish a home for unwed mothers.' "

Boynton fainted dead away, falling off his chair at his mother's feet. Mr. Stenross's reading had to be suspended, which was a good thing since Marisol was tempted beyond reason to pick up the dowager's cane and beat Lord Kimbrough about the head to stop him from laughing so hard.

Chapter Eight

The reading continued, Boynton having been revived and fortified with several glasses of Arvid's finest claret. The earl and Mr. Dimm must have needed fortification also, for they partook just as liberally. Marisol wished that someone had offered her more than the tea she shared with her aunt and Mr. Stenross, to keep her hands from shaking so.

Mr. Stenross wiped his spectacles, cleared his throat a number of times, surveyed his audience to make sure he had their full attention, as if anyone might doze off during the disposition of Arvid's enormous fortune. He found his place and read: " 'If the child my legally wedded wife now carries is a male, my wife receives fifty thousand pounds in her own name, free and clear, to be used for her personal needs as well as those of her family. She is furthermore entitled to the income from the aforesaid unentailed property until our son comes of age to manage these holdings or until she remarries, whichever comes first.' " Mr. Stenross looked up as Foster let out a loud cheer. "The next clause establishes the firm of Stenross, Stenross, and Dinkerly as trustees for this property, since the holdings are extensive and also since Her Grace is an underage female."

Boynton, reclining on a sofa, managed to find a glimmer of hope there. "But that's all to do with the loose change. What about the entailed estate and all of its income? I mean, m'nevvy will need a guardian, won't he? Not even m'brother would be so havey-cavey as to leave it all in the hands of a slip of a girl and a pack of fusty old solicitors."

"Precisely. His Grace was very concerned about that very thing, that the will could be overturned on those grounds." Mr. Stenross was old enough to ignore Boynton's eruption, not fusty enough to let it slide. "Or that the estate might fall into unscrupulous hands. Therefore His Grace named a guardian"—Boynton adjusted his neckcloth; Foster stood to attention—"which is why I have asked Lord Kimbrough to attend today's reading. Due to Her Grace's young age and the infancy of the hypothetical posthumous heir, His Grace has named Carlinn Kimberly, Earl of Kimbrough, to stand as guardian to his minor son and administrator of the entailment."

"What?"

"That's outrageous!"

"I won't stand for it!"

"How could he?"

Marisol got Mr. Stenross's attention first. "Sir," she said, hating the quaver she heard in her own voice, "this must not be. I refuse to have this ... stranger in charge of my son, having any say-so in his rearing."

"I am sorry, Your Grace, but you cannot refuse what was written into His Grace's will, nor would it be in your interests to contest this clause. By law, a female cannot own property or stand as guardian to an underage child. The law looks the other way at times, but not in the case of an estate of this size, when the infant has such standing among the

74

nobility. The courts would appoint a guardian in any case, and you might find their selection even less to your taste."

Marisol found that hard to imagine. Her disagreement must have shown on her face, for Mr. Stenross continued: "With his reputation no court could find Lord Kimbrough an unfit guardian. I looked into it myself, at His Grace's request. He was insistent that certain parties not find grounds to overturn the will."

One of those parties was even now finishing off the bottle of claret.

Marisol twisted her handkerchief. There had to be a way out, besides having a girl child. "But his lordship knows nothing about children. He's not even married."

"And you know nothing about managing estates, Your Grace, begging your pardon."

"I cannot believe even Arvid could be so stupid as to pick a . . ."

Before she could think of anything terrible enough to describe her feelings for the brute, Kimbrough pushed himself away from the wall next to Mr. Dimm and strode up to the desk.

"The duchess might not be able to refuse myself as guardian, but I can and do. I refuse the offer. I never wanted anything to do with that reprobate Denning, and I want less to do with his ramshackle retinue. This hobble has naught to do with me, and I am leaving."

Mr. Stenross stopped him with a few quiet words before the earl could fling open the library door. "In return for your acceptance of the guardianship, His Grace signed over the deed to that parcel of land in dispute." Mr. Stenross held up a piece of parchment. "He conceded that the rechanneling of the water altered the boundaries, so the new land cannot be part of the entailment. Pending, of course, your overseeing the welfare of his son."

"Damn and blast!" Carlinn swore, hitting his fist

against the doorframe. "The makebait must have known I couldn't refuse, not with my people getting flooded out every rainstorm."

The solicitor was going on as if the earl's capitulation was never in question. "In answer to your question, Lord Boynton, concerning the interim period—"

"Interim be damned," Boynton shouted again. "I want to know what's to happen in the meantime! That whelp isn't due till when, Duchess?"

Marisol quietly replied, "After the first of the year."

Boynton's creditors were waiting on his doorstep at the Albany. "So what are we supposed to do in the meantime, besides sit around watching the egg hatch?"

"Everything is to continue as before, with expenses to be paid from the estate, overseen by myself." He anticipated Boynton's next question by saying, "There are also provisions for if the child does not survive to reach majority—"

"Stop it!" Marisol cried, putting her hands over her ears. "I do not want to hear those things! The child is not even born yet. How can you be discussing its death?"

"My apologies, Your Grace. Of course such details do not need to be mentioned at this time. I wished merely to illustrate that His Grace was very thorough."

"His Grace was a bounder of the first degree!" Boynton angrily declared. "Cutting out his own brother."

"No, it's all her fault," the dowager screamed, getting to her feet and waving her cane in Marisol's direction. "You two-faced slut! Arvid's mealy-mouthed, complacent little bride, all the while plotting behind his back. Yes, you and your lover here, plotting how to get rid of him and keep everything for yourselves." She stepped toward Marisol, still

76

brandishing the cane. "You'll never get away with—"

"That will be enough, Your Grace." Kimbrough stood over the dowager and removed the cane from her hand, snapping it across his knee as if it were so much kindling. "There. My first job as guardian of the possible future duke. Your son was a cur and a scoundrel from childhood. I remember the hell he raised in the neighborhood when I was yet a schoolboy. Instead of blaming the duchess, rather blame yourself for raising him to believe he was above the law, above the dictates of polite society or moral conscience. If I have anything to do with the next duke—and, Duchess, I mean to have as little as possible, so you can stop shredding your handkerchief—the boy will learn his responsibilities as well as his rights. He'll find out what Arvid never understood: that he is not better than anyone else because he is Denning. He will be born hosed and shod, but he will have to earn respect."

The dowager took to her rooms; Boynton took to the bottle. Mr. Dimm was closeted with Mr. Stenross, going over those sections of the duke's will that Marisol had not wished to hear.

"Just what you could of figured," Dimm muttered. Obviously it was what Boynton figured, too, since his lordship hadn't bothered to stay to look at those passages. "The bastard cuts everyone off if the heir dies. The widow gets whatever's left of her fifty thousand, and Boynton gets the title and what goes with it, and not a groat more."

"And the home for unwed mothers gets the rest. Very commendable, I'm sure."

"That must be lawyer talk for spiteful, eh? That dirty dish didn't have a charitable bone in his body. Devil take it, though, none of this is getting me a better motive. And you say no one else was privy to the contents of the will anyways, right?"

"Are you questioning the integrity of my office?"

"Clerks has been known to take bribes." Although the ones at Stenross, Stenross, and Dinkerly hadn't, when Dimm sought to read the will aforetimes. Of course, 'twere always possible he hadn't offered enough of the ready.

Mr. Stenross was folding the papers back into their portfolio. He drew himself up and firmly stated: "The only way anyone could have known the contents of His Grace's will was if His Grace had so informed him. Or her."

"And judging by the shock we seen just now, no one had an inkling, or they were deuced fine actors." Which was all of a piece, since this whole hubble-bubble was enough of a farce to get billing at Drury Lane.

Since he had brought the Runner in his curricle, Lord Kimbrough was left to wait with the duchess and her aunt, awkwardly aware they'd be wishing him to Jericho. The aunt had moved closer to the fireplace with her knitting, booties this time. Blue ones. The duchess rang for tea.

"Thank you for coming to my assistance," Marisol said when he had been served, then rushed into her major concern: "Shall you truly leave me to raise my son?"

"Unless I see reason to interfere. I have a life of my own, you know. Managing my own estate is time-consuming enough, without having to worry over Denning's, much less the grooming of his heir." Carlinn vowed he wasn't going to get involved in the brat's upbringing. He wasn't going to let any Town belle dump her responsibilities off on his shoulders so she could resume her gay life in London, doing the social rounds.

"Thank you again," she said in relief, although he'd not offered any favors that he could see. "Isn't it odd that I'd be thought capable of rearing a daughter, but not a son?"

"Odd? Not at all. A boy needs a man's influence."

Marisol was silent, wondering what kind of influence her husband might have been. What if the child turned out to be like Arvid, even without his presence? She put down her plate, her appetite having flown, and pleated the fabric of her gown with nervous fingers.

And a woman needs a man, Carlinn thought when she went quiet. The jade was most likely thinking of the poor sod she'd snabble next to keep her in jewels and furs. Fifty thousand pounds and a proven breeder ought to put the duchess in contention, even if the high-nosed shrew had the tongue of a Billingsgate fishmonger. Of course, she'd have to get back her figure and her looks, or she'd frighten off the heartiest *parti*. Then again, he mused, perhaps she'd just take herself and her booty back to Town and set herself up as a dashing widow, going from dance partner to bed partner in the twinkle of a diamond bracelet. Yes, that was more likely, considering she'd already put off mourning for Denning, and him barely cold in the ground.

Marisol noticed when Kimbrough's brown eyes focused on her hands and the blue kerseymere material between them. She smoothed out her skirts and adjusted the black shawl at her elbows. "I only had three mourning gowns made up," she found herself explaining. Why she had to justify her wardrobe to this lumpkin in corduroy coat and unstarched cravat Marisol did not know, but she went on: "It seemed such a waste to order more for just the next month or two, when I'll hardly be seeing anyone anyway. Besides, it does annoy the dowager no end." She smiled then, and Carlinn suspected there might be dimples beneath the puffed chipmunk cheeks; something must have earned her the title of Incomparable.

He smiled back. Encouraged to try to make friends with the man who might have such impact in her son's life, she joked, "I decided to leave some black fabric for other widows, since my gowns take so much yardage."

Marisol was pleased to see a twinkle come to his eyes, and Carlinn was convinced that, yes, they were definitely dimples. "Now that you mention it, Duchess, are you sure you won't have twins? That would cause havoc with all the betting."

"Goodness, I'd better not. Arvid didn't make provision for that, did he? But the physician said no. I wish—" she began, but did not finish.

"For twins?"

"No, I wish no one cared whether my child is a boy or a girl, that I wasn't on exhibit like some empress giving birth to the royal heir. I wish no one else's future depended on my poor innocent babe."

She looked perilously close to tears again, Kimbrough thought in dismay. He quickly said, "Is the dowager causing you any difficulty? I heard her viperish tongue. Shall I go slay more dragons? Consider it part of my duty."

Marisol tried to smile. He really was being quite nice. "There is no need for such gallantry yet, my lord. Everything is awaiting the big event. If I have a boy, Her Grace will move to the Dower House, if I have to pay for the refurbishing myself. I'll pension off her servants and hire my own, who will owe me their loyalty. And if I have a girl, I shall simply leave. Another month or two of the dowager's unpleasantness won't matter. But there *is* something you can do, now that you were kind enough to offer."

Carlinn almost bit his own tongue off. Lud, what was coming next? Confound the woman and her blasted tears! He nodded, indicating that she should go on, but his lowered brow and clenched jaw were not encouraging.

"It's not a very large dragon, my lord, just that my brother and my brother-in-law are continually at daggers drawn. The situation will get worse as the bad weather keeps Foster in the house more, and his debts keep Boynton from returning to London. Their brangling cuts up my peace worse than the dowager ever does, for I don't dare leave the two of them alone together. Do you think you could spend some time with Foster, perhaps help him pick a regiment? Now that I know we can afford the colors Arvid promised him, Foster will have something to do, and will not feel so dependent."

"He needs schooling, the way he rushed out of here."

"He is feeling his youth. He could have been named guardian, were he older. And he should have been able to manage an estate, if ours hadn't been lost. Mostly I believe he holds himself responsible that we are all at Arvid's mercy, or lack thereof. He needs reassurance and advice, not Boynton's constant sniping. And he looks up to you."

"That's what comes of being so big."

"And humble, too. But you said yourself that a boy needs a man's influence."

His wayward tongue be double damned! Rolled up horse, foot, and gun. "I can see I'll have to weigh my every word around you, Duchess. But yes, if it will set your mind at ease, I will see what I can do. Might even put him to work exercising my old cavalry charger to shake the fidgets out of both of them. Old Beau is eating his head off, wondering what we're doing chasing foxes when we're supposed to be chasing Frenchies."

"Thank you. I know Foster will be thrilled, and I would appreciate it. And perhaps your sister might like to call while you are off drilling your new troops. I'd enjoy the company." She didn't say that the loneliness was almost unbearable, what with the dowager turning all the local women against her. She'd not had one visitor in the entire week since the funeral.

Carlinn picked a speck of lint off his sleeve. "I am afraid my sister is taking her new duties as chatelaine very seriously now that she is home from school. She is busy with menus and such, since she'll be having friends come to stay for the holidays."

"I see. Later, then, after the baby." Marisol saw, all right. She saw that this lummox didn't want his precious sister associating with the Coach Widow. The prig. So much for being her friend. "I doubt I'll feel like entertaining company anyway, so do not feel obliged to call, my lord. But thank you for coming. I am sure you will be notified if and when your services as guardian will be needed. Good day."

She had dismissed him! The Earl of Kimbrough found himself cooling his heels in the drafty hall of Denning Castle, his mouth hanging open. First she used dimples to soften him up, then tears to manipulate him into nursemaiding her scapegrace brother, then she showed him the door! That arrogant bitch!

Dimm was worried about the thunderclouds. Not the ones obscuring the sun, but the ones on Lord Kimbrough's face. The earl was driving the horses like all the hounds of hell were nipping at his heels, putting distance between him and Denning Castle. Or Denning's widow.

"If it's the dowager's words what has you so blue-deviled, pay them no never mind. I didn't take them to heart, so there's no reason for you to. The idea of you plotting with the duchess don't hold water."

"The idea of me throttling her does! She's the most infuriating female I've ever met, looking down her nose at anyone who doesn't take snuff with one hand. Hah!"

"Seems down to earth to me, for a gentry moll. Puts out a nice tea. Watch that there hay wagon, guv."

Kimbrough paid no attention to Dimm's words, either about Her Grace or the lumbering cart they passed with a scant inch to spare. "I don't know how I'm to maintain any degree of civility with her for minutes on end," the earl fumed, "and I'm looking at twenty-one years till the boy is grown. It's a life sentence!"

"But think of all the good you can do for the folks hereabouts if you get to manage that property. You said yourself Denning didn't take care of his people. Didn't even have a sawbones to look after them. Which reminds me, I have a nevvy at home what set out to medical school in Edinburgh. One year left of studies, he's got, but the money's run out. I'd wager he'd be willing to pledge his services for, say, five years, in exchange for his tuition. What do you think?"

"Done." The earl took the next corner on two wheels. "Hell and damnation, I'd almost rather the child be a girl. I'm sure I could buy that piece of land from the home for unwed mothers. Blast! If she lets a bunch of lightskirts come to Pennington, I'll murder her for sure."

"It's not as if Her Grace has any say in the matter, my lord. You might try praying though. By the bye, that brother-in-law of mine we talked of, the one in collars, is ready to move into that vicarage you mentioned. His wife and young 'uns is that excited to be getting out of the city." And out of Dimm's house.

His lordship grunted and flicked his whip over the horses' backs for more speed. Dimm held on with both hands. "What you need is a wife, milord."

"Why, do you just happen to have one of those stashed in your attics, too?"

"Not 'zactly, and you'd do better to keep your eyes on the road than sending me black looks like that."

"Oh, did you mean I need a woman's refining touch? Hah! That's just what I need on top of everything else, someone to nag about the polish on my boots or the smell of my cigar or the way I drive my cattle. I mean, a scandal and a murder charge and that aggravating female aren't enough? You'd saddle me with a prunes-and-prisms wife besides?"

"Devil a bit, guv. But you ain't thinking clearly, milord. Women die in childbirth all the time. Then there's always milk fever. What happens if Her Grace sticks her spoon in the wall any time these next five or ten years? You're stuck with a infant, your lordship, all on your own."

For the first time in twelve years, Carlinn put the curricle in the ditch.

Chapter Nine

$\mathcal{K}$imbrough kept his promise about Foster. He was a man of his word, Marisol conceded, whatever else she might think of his stiff-rumped earlship. And she thought of him more than was good for her or the baby, since his very name made her blood boil. Every enthusiastic encomium pouring from her brother's mouth grated against her nerves when she remembered how Kimbrough had denied her his sister's acquaintance. As if she'd contaminate the girl, for heaven's sake! He'd behaved like a doyenne pulling her skirts away from a mud puddle. And that sanctimonious snob was to be in charge of her son? No wonder she was in the doldrums.

The weather did not help, being raw and gray when it wasn't raw and rainy. Walks were more torture than pleasure. The wintery chill outside was nothing to the dowager's attitude inside, and the lack of congenial company was driving Marisol to distraction. She tried to keep busy renovating an apartment in the north tower, with Mr. Stenross's approval. The historic ducal suite was no place for a child and too drafty for its mother. But even that work was proceeding for the most part without the duchess, since the smell of paint made her queasy and the hammering of paneling gave her the headache. She only had to approve swatches of fabric from books and choose desks and chairs brought down from the attics for her inspection, there being no way she could navigate those steep steps and narrow aisles.

After that, there were only so many books she could read, letters she could write, little caps she could sew, comments about the weather she could shout to Aunt Tess to fill her days. She was reduced to playing with Max, for pity's sake!

For all that she was bored to flinders without his company, Marisol did not begrudge her brother his new interest. Kimbrough kept Foster busy and excited, sending him home physically exhausted, enough so that Boynton's acerbic comments at dinner fell on ears suddenly as deaf as Aunt Tess's, to Marisol's relief.

She was also relieved that the earl had taken her hint and not called, the high-handed, pompous prude. He was so worried about what people would say, it was laughable. Why, he fled the London social scene to avoid the gabble-grinders, she'd heard, burying himself in the country like a turnip putting down roots, the noddy. As if anyone's opinion mattered, not even his high-and-mighty lordship's. She did not care a bit that he didn't call for weeks after the reading of the will; it just showed what a rude, boorish clodpole he was. Of course, she heard about the carriage accident from her maid, but Foster assured her it was nothing.

Foster was too impressed by his hero to mention that Carlinn—they were on a first-name basis now—was suffering from abrasions and cracked ribs. Real men didn't whimper about their injuries. Besides, Foster would never let it be known that Carlinn was anything less than a top-of-the-trees whip. There had to have been ice on the road that evening. All Marisol knew was that the earl was letting Foster tool his curricle and pair—and bang-up bits of blood they were, too, according to her brother—and exercise his Thoroughbreds.

"And he's even writing his old commander about me. Cavalry, don't you know," Foster chattered happily. "Carlinn says that's the only way to go, especially for a chap hoping to win advancement in the field. Carlinn says I might hear shortly if there's an aide-de-camp position open."

Marisol was sick unto death of hearing what Carlinn said, but she smiled for Foster's sake. The rustic earl might be stiff and dull, without an ounce of cultured refinement in him, but at least he was steady. He wouldn't lead Foster into bad habits, like Boynton kept trying to do, daring the younger man into rash wagers. Since they were all pockets to let until the final disbursement of funds, nothing came of it, but Marisol could only be that much more appreciative of the earl's influence.

Boynton kept to his rooms for the most part . . . and to the bottle. When he wasn't in the stables trying to fleece the grooms of their wages, Arvid's brother and his shifty-eyed valet experimented with new ways of tying neckcloths. Occasionally he challenged Marisol to a hand of piquet for imaginary sums. They gave up on billiards when Marisol couldn't get close enough to the table.

The dowager, meanwhile, was suffering pangs of indecision. On the one hand, her daughter-in-law was a fallen woman, a pariah, and a murderess, deserving only of the cut direct. That's what she'd convinced her friends, so none of her cronies called. On the other hand, Marisol might be the mother of the next duke, controlling Denning Castle and all of its inhabitants. What to do? The dowager's decision was made easier by the lack of company she also felt. She couldn't accept invitations for dinner parties and cards, not after making a to-do about the trollop's lack of proper mourning, and the local matrons were hesitant about calling. They didn't want to get in the middle of the two duchesses either. So the dowager was forced to give Marisol grudging acceptance, to have a fourth at whist.

The Bow Street Runner was recovering from his concussion nicely. Just the occasional headache now, thank you, but a chap couldn't be too careful with head wounds, don't you know. He was staying on at the inn at the earl's expense, naturally, with two pretty chambermaids at his beck and call. This left the proprietor of the Three Feathers a shade shorthanded, so he agreed to give Dimm's niece a trial. Changing sheets at a country inn mightn't be precisely what Dimm would have chosen for the girl, but Suky was a pretty little thing with a head on her shoulders. If she didn't nab herself a handsome young farmer or such, his name wasn't Jeremiah Dimm. 'Sides, he told himself, it wasn't like she'd have any chance of getting into trouble, not with her strapping big cousin working in Lord Kimbrough's stables, another cousin fixed as the duchess's abigail, and her other uncle right now setting up as vicar one town over.

Dimm was doing just fine, keeping to his bed. A nice, slow recovery suited him to a cow's thumb. It didn't suit his nibs in London. Not by half. One week later Dimm's boss sent for the Runner and demanded results.

"I don't care who you arrest, just arrest someone. Charge the wife, by George—she had the most to gain just getting rid of that dastard. She'll never hang for it anyway, so there'll be no harm done."

" 'Cept the real killer will have got off easy. I can't do it, sir, sorry."

"Then somebody else! Surely you must have a prime suspect in mind. They are up in arms over this at Whitehall, that a nobleman can be gunned down in broad daylight and we cannot find the killer. Doesn't look good on our record, does it, Dimm?"

"No, sir."

"Good. Then what shall I tell the reporters?"

"Well, they all has alibis so thin you can poke a stick through them, but that Lord Armbruster won't name his. Man has something to hide, or I miss my guess."

"No, no, it couldn't have been Lord Armbruster. In fact, those men you had watching his flat in Half Moon Street have been reassigned. Waste of tax-payers' money, don't you know." His nibs shuffled some papers, without meeting Dimm's eyes.

"Begging your pardon, sir, but who gave that there order?"

"The prime minister himself, if you must know. So go find another suspect. Get on with it, man."

Jeremiah got on with it. He parked his son Gabriel in a carriage across the way from Armbruster's love nest. The boy had to learn surveillance work, didn't he?

"Facts is like rocks, my boy. The deeper they try to hide, the harder you got to dig."

The earl was licking his wounds. My word, he kept berating himself, how had he ever come to do such a corkbrained thing? Tipping over his carriage like the merest whipster. He deserved to suffer!

It was that woman's fault. Marisol Pendenning brought out the worst in him, that was all. He despised the way she put on airs, looking down on him as though he were lower than that foolish dog Max. She even talked to the mutt in warmer tones than she used to him. And no matter that she was the spoiled pet of a superficial society, she usually succeeded in making him feel like an unmannerly lout. Hell and tarnation, how was he going to face her now, with half his face rubbed raw from the accident? With his ribs strapped tight, he couldn't even make her a proper bow. Oh, how the witch would laugh at his comeuppance.

Unless he didn't come to call. Carlinn decided he'd rather she think him a craven than a clunch. Let her highness believe he stayed away because she'd disdained his company. That was better than the truth.

If he couldn't stop by to see how she did in that mausoleum of a castle, which he'd do for any neighbor in difficulty, at least he could keep his word about seeing to the brother. The boy was downright handy, in fact, cheerfully playing the role of carriage driver so the earl could get around the countryside on his estate business. Of course, young Laughton handled the ribbons like a novice, jolting Carlinn's aching ribs over every rut and ridge in the road.

Staying home was worse, for then he had to put up with Cousin Winifred's fussing over him. What the hell did Cousin Winifred—his father's cousin, actually—think lavender water was going to do for a busted rib? Or a posset? Or a mustard plaster, or any of the hundred other nostrums she tried to press on him?

His sister Bettina was worse, going into strong hysterics every time she saw his battered and bruised face. She was already nervous over her first house party, even if her guests were only three schoolmates and their mamas interrupting their journeys home for the holidays for a fortnight's visit. Those three matrons were crucial to her Season next year, Tina had confided, for without a mother of her own, and Cousin Winifred having lived in the country so long, she quite depended on the patronage of her friends' mamas to make the right connections.

In other words, an advantageous marriage. Gads, Carlinn asked himself, when had his sweet little sister turned into a conniving manipulator? When she approached womanhood, he answered his own question. Hair up, skirts down, gentlemen beware.

And her friends were worse, when they finally arrived. Giggling, simpering, batting their eyelashes and waving their fans around hard enough to make the candles flicker—and for him, a battered hulk of a gentleman farmer! He could see the calculating gleams in the mothers' eyes, too, assessing the furnishings at the Hall, the number of bedrooms, the quality of the food. They must have researched his income down to the last shilling; now they were calculating their chicks' chances. Carlinn was titled, wealthy, and unmarried, ergo he was fair game! Blast it, he felt like the fox with the hounds on his heels, and in his own house.

And Dimm thought he ought to get married! What, should he pick a bride from one of these chattering schoolgirls? He'd rather have four more broken ribs. The chits were as silly as peahens, his sister included, with more hair than wit. Blushes, yes, giggles aplenty. They possessed the usual insufficient talent to entertain but not enough sense to know it, and not a jot of intelligent conversation between the four of them. Gowns and beaux and next year's parties: that was the extent of their interests, and their mothers', their older sisters', and their ape-leader aunts' interests.

Jeremiah, when he went to bring the Runner some oranges from the hothouse, was sure they'd ripen with age. The chits, not the oranges. Carlinn was of the opinion that the town bronze they'd get next year would just add a superficial covering to superficial minds. Instead of being unspoiled schoolgirls, they'd have all the affectations of acknowledged beauties. He couldn't even think of picking a bride from the ranks of those . . . those incipient Coach Widows!

Mantraps in training, Foster's cow-handed driving, Aunt Winifred's coddling, Dimm's knowing chuckles, and a face that could scare birds out of trees—they were all too much to bear. Besides, he had another problem.

It was one thing to have young Laughton driving his curricle and running tame in his stable; it was quite another thing to invite him inside the house when there was a gaggle of susceptible young females in residence. Carlinn felt for the lad, really he did, and a wealthy wife could ease his way immeasurably. But these ninnyhammers were Kimbrough's guests. Their families trusted him to see they were not introduced to any scandal-ridden young scapegrace without a feather to fly with. Carlinn found himself making excuses to see less of the boy, steeling himself against Foster's wounded-pup expression.

Then Dimm announced he was being called back to London. Still feeling guilty over the older man's injury, Carlinn had the knacky idea of conveying the Runner into Town in style, in his own well-sprung traveling carriage. Of course, he and Foster would have to go along to make sure Mr. Dimm did not suffer any relapse. Carlinn could do some shopping—Christmas was just around the corner—and take the opportunity to introduce the young marquis to friends at the War Office.

A brilliant idea, the earl congratulated himself. He should have had it a sennight ago before the first of those plaguey females arrived. Of course, a week ago he couldn't have managed the stairs at the Pulteney, much less the carriage ride to Town. Still, it was a capital notion, if it was all right with Foster's sister.

Foster was so excited Marisol couldn't help but agree to the plan. He swore they'd be back in a week.

"Carlinn has to be back to see off his sister's houseguests. Bunch of hoydenish little schoolgirls, I gather. That's why he's running away. All the more lucky for me. I mean, Kimbrough putting in a good word for me will assure I get a quick posting and a crack regiment!"

So she kissed him goodbye, made sure he had her list of Christmas shopping commissions in his pocket, and wished him Godspeed. Then she went back inside and told herself how happy she was for Foster. Her beloved brother had a friend, he could get away from this oppressive atmosphere for a week, he was getting to go shopping, and he could go bounding down the steps so Lord Kimbrough didn't have to leave his cattle standing. If Foster weren't her brother, she would have hated him.

The little party arrived back at Denning Castle two days early. Foster did not bound up the stairs; he was half-carried into the hall between Lord Kimbrough and a young man in uniform. When Marisol got to the entry hall, the earl was helping Foster out of his greatcoat.

Both of Foster's eyes were swollen shut, his nose was covered in sticking plaster, and his lips were cracked and bloodied.

"My God," Marisol cried. "What have you done to him?" Then she started beating Lord Kimbrough about the head with the nearest thing to hand, which happened to be the slipper she was embroidering for Foster's Christmas present. "Wasn't killing my husband enough?"

Foster moaned. "Told you she wouldn't kick up a dust, didn't I?"

Chapter Ten

"*C*ut line, Mar," Foster gasped painfully through his split lips. "Not Carlinn. Lord Kimbrough wouldn't . . ." He took a sip from the flask the earl held to his mouth. Then Foster tipped his head back so he could look at Marisol through the slits of his eyes. " 'Sides, you work yourself into a swivet, you're going to drop the brat here in the hall."

Marisol was mortified at her brother's blunt speech, which drew Lord Kimbrough's startled glance to her enormously distended midsection, prodigiously more swollen than even the last time he'd seen her. Marisol felt all the more like a hot-air balloon with the crowd watching the inflating process. Blushing furiously, she tore her eyes off her brother and noticed Lord Kimbrough's face for the first time; his cheek and jaw were all discolored, too.

"I'm sorry." She lowered her hand that was still holding the slipper, embroidery threads trailing. "I never should have said what I did. I wasn't thinking, but—" She paused. "Never tell me you had another coach accident."

"No, blast it!" Carlinn shouted, still reeling from her attack. The woman actually continued to believe him capable of murder. Why, he hadn't suspected her in ages, not after getting to know her and her brother. She was imperious, and loyal, and something of a spitfire, but not a killer. Carlinn could picture her going at Arvid with a shoe, not a loaded pistol. How could she still suspect him?

Foster groaned. The earl gave him another sip from the flask. "He'll be more comfortable in his bed. I'll help him up the stairs, then we'll talk."

Marisol wanted to assist, but Foster's weight, those steep stairs—"Don't be a nodcock, Duchess. Your footman can show us the way." He put one of Foster's arms over his shoulder; the young man in army uniform took the other. "Oh, yes, I forgot. This is Joshua Dimm. He's another of Dimm's sons. Joshua was thinking of running off to join the army, to Mr. Dimm's regret and his family's sorrow. So we signed him on as Foster's batman, which should keep him from being cannon fodder. Joshua was invaluable on the trip home."

"Well then, thank you, Joshua, and welcome to Denning Castle. We are in your debt, it seems."

Joshua blushed and bobbed his head. He couldn't very well bow with Foster sagging in his arms. "Think nothing on it, Your Grace. I know my way around a sickroom. That's what comes of having a houseful of relatives and a cousin studying medicine. We'll have him right as a trivet afore the cat can lick her ear."

Marisol sent a message to the kitchens to prepare restorative broths, gruel, invalid foods—and a hearty tea. She was too anxious to wait for the earl's return downstairs, so she ate half the delicacies without him and had to send for more when he got to the parlor.

Carlinn sank exhausted into the chair she offered and gratefully accepted a cup of tea, but he declined further refreshment after he watched the duchess spread strawberry jam on a watercress sandwich.

"I apologize again," she said, oblivious of his fascinated gaze. "You have been kind to Foster, I know, and would not have hurt him. I can only plead a . . . a difficult time and beg your forgiveness."

Carlinn had always heard that women in the duchess's condition needed to be humored. He wouldn't point out, for instance, that most people did not put lemon, milk, sugar, and butter in their tea. The duchess, however, had no one to cater to her whims and relieve her fears. Carlinn did not count that doddery aunt or that dragon of a mother-in-law. And a fine lot of support she'd get from that man-milliner Boynton. He couldn't even support his gaming habit.

No, he shouldn't have taken Foster away, the earl realized now, as Her Grace sugared a cucumber sandwich. He swallowed and looked away. He definitely shouldn't have brought the boy home in this condition, giving her such a shock. And heaven only knew what would happen when he had to give her worse news, trying to explain what occurred in London. She was watching him now with those big blue eyes, waiting for him to begin. Oh hell, he should have told her he'd overturned another carriage.

"I took Foster to visit some friends of mine in the Home Guard," he began, "in case he wanted to change his mind about a cavalry unit. I thought you might rest easier with him staying on English soil."

Marisol nodded. Truly, the man could be thoughtful, when he thought about it.

"Foster met some acquaintances at the barracks and went off with them while I had dinner with an old comrade of mine. I thought he'd find more entertainment with the officers his own age, or I would have kept him with me."

"But he is a young man, not a child in leading strings. It was never your responsibility to look after him twenty-four hours a day."

"But I was supposed to be a good influence, remember? I should have guessed they would . . . At any rate, the sprigs did some heavy drinking."

"As young men are wont to do," she interrupted as the butler came in to ask if there was anything else Her Grace wished. "Yes, I'd absolutely adore some strawberries and clotted cream, please, Jeffers."

The butler bowed and withdrew, as if there was some way on this green earth he was going to produce fresh strawberries in December.

The duchess turned back to Kimbrough. "I'm sorry, my lord. You were feeling badly that the boys were in their cups. What happened then?"

Carlinn straightened his sleeve. "Then one of the others asked about the murder. I'm sorry, but it seems your name was mentioned in an insulting manner, and Foster felt he had to defend you."

"I see." She sat quietly thinking, and Carlinn did not disturb her for a time.

"He incapacitated half a platoon, if that's any consolation," he finally said, "and impressed a lot of the officers with his courage. He'll do well in the army."

"If he lives long enough to join up. He cannot go around brawling every time my name is mentioned." She pushed her cup away and reached for her handkerchief.

Kimbrough heard a sniffle, then another. He jumped to his feet. "Confound you, woman, don't you dare cry!"

Marisol looked up. He was towering over her, scowling fiercely. "Is that an order, sir?"

"Yes, blast it! I mean, no, of course not. Just don't. Please. It's, ah, not good for the baby." He grabbed up a dish of bonbons. "Here, try these."

She dabbed at her eyes. "Thank you, I am all right now. You say Foster is not badly injured?"

"The medico in London assured me nothing's broken, except his nose."

"Is it bad?"

"Nothing to worry about. In fact," the earl went on, relieved to have weathered the storm, "he'll most likely look better—not so snooty, if you know what I mean."

Marisol didn't. Foster had the Laughton Nose, the same one she had. She frowned.

Kimbrough hurried on: "He'll be uncomfortable for a time, and less than pretty to look at, but he'll make a full recovery. The surgeon says your brother's got a hard head."

"I could have told him that! Mayhap some good will come of this, though, if Foster learns not to jump into battle."

"At least not without a regiment to back him up."

The butler returned then with a dish of what appeared to be strawberry preserves atop a vanilla cake, the whole thing covered in dollops of thickened cream. "Cook sent this up, Your Grace, with her compliments. She apologizes, but it is the best she can do at this time."

The earl's mouth watered, seeing the extra dish and fork on the platter. Then the duchess sent it back! "I am sorry, Jeffers, I seem to have lost my appetite. You'd better eat it, lest Cook's nose get out of joint."

"Very well, Your Grace," Jeffers said. He bowed and left.

Marisol sat and twisted her hands in her lap. "Did Mr. Dimm have any news? That's the only way I can see this nightmare ending."

"No, more's the pity. You are right; none of us can relax until the crime is solved. Dimm was going on about facts being as slippery as eels the last time I saw him."

"Eels! I wonder if Cook has any pickled eels."

* * *

The earl called at Denning Castle twice that week before Christmas to see how Foster was faring. The marquis looked as if a carriage had rolled over him, but he was physically fit, and bored. Both times Kimbrough called, the duchess was resting in her chambers.

"The stairs, don't you know," Foster confided over the game of chess Kimbrough had offered by way of entertainment.

"Then I'll ask you to convey my greetings of the season to Her Grace now."

"Oh, we'll most likely see you at church Christmas Eve. The old girl is determined to get there. The dowager's chaplain is all well and good for saying grace and such, Marisol says, but it won't seem like Christmas if we don't go to services in the dark. I mean, you'd never know it was the holiday season around here at all. No greenery, no gewgaws, no kissing bough, no parties."

Foster was fondly recalling Christmases of his boyhood when the family was flush, even the elegant decorations that had prevailed at Denning's London town house in previous years.

Carlinn meanwhile was thinking that young Laughton might have been describing Kimbrough Hall, where every evergreen for miles around had been denuded of branches, every surface was covered with some berry or bow or porcelain cherub, and every neighbor, villager, and tenant was welcomed for carols and wassail. Every neighbor but the Denning ménage, who were in mourning, thank goodness. He moved a rook.

"Mourning, don't you know." Foster was unnecessarily explaining the lack of gaiety. "The dowager swears that even a single wreath would show disrespect for Arvid's memory." Foster made his move, then said, "That's just like Arvid, finding some way to ruin everyone's Christmas."

"If he can't enjoy the holiday, no one should, eh?"

"That's Arvid to the core. Not that Marisol isn't doing what she can, behind the dowager's back, of course."

"Of course."

Foster looked up at the other's dry tone. "She just made sure there was some mistletoe for the servants' hall, mincemeat pies, and a Christmas pudding, so all the tweenies and scullery maids can make their wishes. She made sure there were toys for all the tenants' children for Boxing Day. Nothing disrespectful or dishonest."

"Stubble it, bantling. I wasn't accusing the duchess of being anything more than strong-willed."

Foster's face reddened, not an attractive sight mixed with the purple and yellow. "Pardon. I shouldn't be so sensitive, I suppose."

"No, you shouldn't. The duchess is well able to defend herself when she needs." He studied the board.

Foster thought of Arvid again and dropped the piece he'd been about to move. "Sorry." Then he thought of Boynton and grinned, which hurt his split lips. "Ouch! But you should have seen Marisol light into that coxcomb Pendenning over the Yule log. She went on how the well-being of the whole house of Pendenning hinged on his going out to find a log that would burn till Twelfth Night. She said she didn't care who was duke, but her child wasn't going to suffer because Boynton was too lazy to help the servants find a suitable log. He was head of the household, no matter how temporarily, and he better start acting like it!"

Mulling over his move, Kimbrough allowed as how he'd dragged a huge tree limb home, too. "Silly superstition, but the house of Kimbrough should prosper, too."

"You should have seen Marisol carrying on. And you should have seen Boynton after, with his nose all red and his hands dirty. What a sight. But we do have a Yule log ready to be brought in when we get back from church Christmas Eve. The dowager disapproves, of course. She says we should worship here because we're in mourning and Marisol is too, ah . . ."

"Big with child?" Kimbrough supplied, declaring checkmate. "So naturally your sister is more determined than ever to get in the bumpy carriage and travel through the cold, dark night to a little unheated church. Why am I not surprised?"

The group from Denning Castle was not at midnight services after all. Lord Kimbrough drove his own party home, oversaw the lighting of the Yule log, and toasted everyone's health in wassail. Then he rode over in the direction of Denning Castle to see if anything was amiss.

That fancy London *accoucheur*'s timing, that's what was amiss. Half a mile away Kimbrough could see the castle on its hill, lights in half the windows, grooms riding off in every direction.

Foster nearly threw himself into the earl's arms in relief. "Thank heaven you've come. Marisol has been brought to bed two weeks early. The nearest physician is drunk with Christmas cheer, the next closest is down with influenza, and the local midwife is visiting her daughter in Oxford. I'm at my wit's end."

"You must be, if you're glad *I'm* here. Jupiter, what in the world do you propose I do? I mean, if it were a mare I'd have a go at the thing." He shrugged. "Surely one of the women . . ."

Foster poured the earl a drink with shaking hands. "My aunt's never had a baby. Neither has Marisol's abigail, the cook, or the housekeeper. The dowager had four, but forty years ago."

"I'm sure they still do things the same way." Carlinn tried to be reassuring, but found his own hand starting to tremble.

"That's what I said, but Marisol won't let the old bat near her, nor any of the local matrons like

Squire's wife. She says the dowager and her friends won't care if the baby dies, if it's a boy. She's out of her head, but maybe she has a point. I don't know. Lud, what am I going to do with her talking about dying and all?"

Foster looked as frightened as any green recruit facing the artillery for the first time. Kimbrough felt as if he'd already been shelled. Retreat wasn't possible, so he tried a delaying maneuver. "What have you done so far?"

"Well, Sarah, that's Marisol's abigail, sent for her aunt at the vicarage. That's Dimm's sister-in-law, and she's got three or four brats, I don't remember what Sarah said."

"Aha, that's the ticket. We only have to hold out till the reinforcements arrive! And Mrs. Vicar Hambley has four children. I saw them at church not two hours ago. She'll know what to do."

Foster was beyond rational thought. That was his sister upstairs, cursing her dead husband. "But what if Mrs. Hambley doesn't come in time?"

"Don't even think about it, lad. What else have you done?"

"Well, I sent for Dimm, too. Marisol might be dicked in the nob about someone trying to hurt the baby, but I had to humor her. He won't get here till tomorrow anyway."

"Rear guard never hurt. What else?"

"We put water on to boil. Everyone knows to do that much. And he"—Foster jerked his head toward the corner of the room where Boynton sat—"made another bowl of wassail."

"Excellent, excellent. Nothing like firing up the troops. So now all we do is wait. That's the hardest part of any campaign, the waiting. And there's one other thing a good soldier does before battle: He prays like the devil."

Upstairs a different kind of war was being waged. Marisol was trying to evict the dowager from her chambers, and the dowager was refusing to leave.

"If you can believe I'd harm my own grandson, I can believe you'd be so low as to switch babies to save your own skin. I am staying right here until I see that child with my own eyes."

Marisol was midway through swearing that she'd not let the baby come while her mother-in-law was in the room, when Mrs. Hambley calmly arrived and took over. First she rolled up her sleeves. "See? Nary a bairn stashed anywhere, Your Grace," she addressed the older woman. "And me a vicar's wife besides. I'd never have truck with such havey-cavey doings. What comes is God's will, and that's that, so you can go downstairs and keep the men-folks from drinking themselves stupid or you can sit in that corner out of the way quiet-like." Next she washed her hands and turned to Marisol. "While we get to work instead of this argle-bargle. And you save your energy for the baby, Your Grace, for from the size of him—or her—it's going to be a handful."

So Marisol stopped fretting about the dowager and concentrated instead on hoping that bastard Arvid burned in hell for doing this to her.

Downstairs the men paced. Then Foster dozed off in a chair and Boynton slipped in and out of a drunken stupor on the sofa. The Earl of Kimbrough found himself pacing alone, which made him so angry he paced harder and faster. What the bloody hell was he doing here anyway, and why was he the one staying up all night worrying over Arvid Pendenning's relicts? He'd just go on home. They could send a messenger.

Then a door slammed upstairs. Foster sat up with a jerk. More doors opened and closed. A woman screamed. Boynton got himself over to the nearly empty wassail bowl and started to pour out a cup. They all heard the next scream; they all bypassed the punch bowl and headed for the whiskey decanter.

There was one more scream and then, when at least two of the men were ready to tear their own hearts out if it would help, came the unmistakable sound of a new life welcoming the dawn of Christmas morning.

Boynton and Foster trailed Kimbrough into the vast, echoing marble hall. They stood there, staring up, for what seemed like hours more.

"For the love of God," Boynton shouted up the stairs, "what is it?"

There was one more shriek, a long, loud, high-pitched moan actually, the unmistakable sound of the dowager pulling her hair out.

Chapter Eleven

The earl paid a duty call two days later. The baby was his ward and all. He brought flowers from the Hall's conservatory for the duchess and a silver rattle he'd picked up in London for the occasion for the baby. It seemed the thing to do. He'd leave his offerings with the butler, play a game of chess with Foster, and be on his way, duty done.

Except the duchess wanted to see him. Upstairs, in her newly refurbished chambers. Carlinn found himself adjusting his neckcloth as he followed Jeffers up the stairs.

Marisol was propped up against the pillows of the large, sun-filled room. But the sun was not shining this day. Instead, the room was painted a soft lemony yellow and had flowered bed coverings and drapes so it reminded him of spring. The duchess wore a robe of amber velvet, buttoned to her chin, and a jonquil ribbon was threaded through the long blonde braid that lay over her shoulder. She looked weary and wan, but happier than he had ever seen her.

Nodding briefly at his arrival, the duchess turned her rapt gaze back to the bundle by her side.

"I wanted you to meet your ward, my lord," she said softly. "It's a boy."

"Yes, so I'd heard," Carlinn replied dryly. He could still hear Foster's whoops reverberating in his ears and the unpleasant sound of Boynton grinding his teeth into nubs. Then there had been the servants' cheers, the ringing of church bells, the messengers sent off to London, Boynton drumming his feet on the carpet. The day after Christmas brought Mr. Stenross with papers to sign, Foster with inquiries about his commission, foxed Boynton to be fished out of the village pond. You might say the earl had heard.

"And he's the most beautiful boy in the whole world," the duchess cooed. "Come look."

Lord Kimbrough took a cautious step closer to the bed. "Very nice, I'm sure. Congratulations."

"Silly, you can't see his face from there. Come closer."

She was right; the child looked like a pile of rags from this distance. He went up to the bed. It still looked like a pile of rags. Then the duchess peeled away a layer or two of wrappings. My word, he thought, he'd seen more appealing specimens crawl out from under a log! Worst of all, the red and wrinkled creature seemed already to possess the Laughton Nose. Great heaven, was that to be his job, too, to see that the child's nose got broken before he reached manhood? The duchess was looking up expectantly.

Carlinn coughed. "Er, handsome indeed. Fine big boy, I understand." That's what the aunt had said, that he was a strapping lad despite coming into the world two weeks early. To the earl the infant looked only slightly larger than a newborn foxhound pup, and not nearly as charming. He must have said the right thing, however, for the duchess was smiling blissfully.

"Have you, ah, selected a name for him?" the earl asked, rather than trying to come up with more Spanish coin. "I, ah, bought him a gift, but it needs to be monogrammed." He held out the tissue-wrapped parcel. Her maid took the flowers to put into a vase and drew a chair next to the bed for him. So much for a brief duty call.

Marisol uncovered the silver rattle. "How kind. Nolly will love it when he is a little older."

"Nolly? I know I said I wouldn't interfere, ma'am, but you really can't send your son through life with a name like Nolly. Why, he wouldn't survive public school."

"I know that, my lord. I'm not a total peagoose, you know. His name is Noel, for being born on Christmas day, but we can call him Nolly until he's bigger. The dowager is furious, of course."

"Of course. I suppose she thought the babe should be named after Arvid?"

"Yes, so that his memory would live on. As if I wanted any reminder of Arvid! I only pray Nolly has nothing of his father in him."

Nolly would have done better with Arvid's nose, Kimbrough decided, but he kept that thought to himself.

"The dowager then suggested, no, she *demanded* that I name him after the fifth duke, her husband Ajax. Everyone says Arvid's father was a worse scoundrel than Arvid ever managed to be. And Foster already bears our father's name. So it's Noel, for the holidays, that he should find joy and hope. Noel Alistaire Laughton Pendenning, seventh Duke of Denning. There's more, but all those titles and such can wait."

"I daresay. So is the dowager resigned, now that she has such a, er, fine grandson?"

"Oh no, we've already had words. I refuse to hire a wet nurse, you see, and she considers that unladylike and indecent." She looked up at him, challenging him to make a comment.

Kimbrough hadn't come through two years on the Peninsula without knowing when to keep his head down. He just nodded.

"And she thinks Nolly should be in the nursery."

Again she was daring him to exert his authority. "Ah, isn't that where infants usually go?"

"What, when he's so tiny and needs me so often? Why should he be alone, or with strangers, or worse, with that old woman who nursed Boynton?"

"Heaven forfend. For all we know, she's the one who first wrapped that coxcomb in puce swaddling clothes."

"You're teasing, but I am not. The woman is as deaf as Aunt Tess. What if Nolly were hungry or hurt?"

"Quite. But how will you manage?"

"Very well, thank you. Women have been caring for their own babies for centuries now, don't you know?"

"But they haven't been duchesses, I'd swear. Soon you'll have this great barn to manage, the dowager to dislodge. And you need your rest."

She nodded, tucking the baby back in his blankets. "My maid Sarah is a gem, for one thing. I cannot even imagine asking Tyson—she was my dresser in London—to help change Nolly's diapers. Tyson hated babies. And Sarah has a sister at home who is wonderful with children. Rebecca helped care for all of Vicar Hambley's brood and is now seeking a position, according to Mr. Dimm. We'll do fine until she arrives in a day or two."

"Oh, then you've seen Dimm?" He studied the tassel on his Hessians, wondering how much the Runner or Foster had said about the latest contretemps. He hoped the news hadn't upset the duchess; there was still childbed fever to be wary against. She didn't look ailing, just tired as she nuzzled the top of the infant's head.

She said, "Yes, Mr. Dimm called yesterday afternoon. Isn't it wonderful?"

"Wonderful? That Mr. Dimm called?"

"No, about the shooting. I don't mean that it's very wonderful for Lord Ashcroft, of course, or his family, but I didn't do it!"

It was too late; the fever had already affected her brain. "Pardon?"

"Don't be so buffleheaded. Your neighbor, Lord Ashcroft, was shot in his carriage on his way to Squire's house Christmas morning. And there is not a soul in England who can possibly accuse me of committing the crime. Isn't that fine?"

"Of all the addlepated ideas . . . It was a robbery gone bad, that's all. Ashcroft was only nicked. Nothing to do with you or Arvid or anything."

"Then why was Mr. Dimm asking Foster if he'd gone straight to bed after the baby was born? And asking Boynton if he'd gone directly to the village to get castaway?"

"Because as magistrate I asked him to assist our local constable, whose major investigation prior to this was finding whose cow ran through Widow Greenfield's front garden. Lud knows why I asked Dimm to help with the detective work, he's done so poorly with Arvid's murder, but I did. And he was asking us questions because he wanted to know if we saw anything that morning, that's all."

"Us? Weren't you home either?"

"No, I was keeping vigil here with your other suspects. Then I went home, across the fields, seeing no one. I let myself into my house, seeing no one, and slept alone in my bed until my sister woke me up to open Christmas presents. No alibi." He crossed his arms over his chest and glared.

"Oh. Well, as you say, it must have been a robbery. And Foster is too excited about his army career, and I told Boynton I'd pay his debts if the child was a boy, so there is no motive." She took her eyes off the baby long enough to notice his dark look. "And you are too well breeched, of course."

Kimbrough got to his feet. "Thank you, I think.

I'll just be going along then. There is a crime to investigate, don't you know, and I am magistrate."

She missed the sarcasm, staring again at the baby in her arms. "You know," she said, "I really could kill someone, I think. I mean, I used to believe I would never do such a thing. But now, with Nolly to protect, I do think I could." She looked up, and a cold, hard expression came over her face. "You might be Nolly's guardian, but I swear, if you ever harm a hair on his head, I'll—"

"Nolly doesn't have a hair on his head, you baconbrained Bedlamite! And I am not a murderer, a brute, or a child molester! What do you think, I'll have Nolly drawn and quartered if he soils his nappy?"

The infant started to cry. Marisol drew him closer. "Look at you, you're shouting! If you can shout at a tiny baby, you can do anything!"

"I am not shouting at the baby, madam; I am shouting at you!" Carlinn lowered his voice to a mere window-rattling whisper. "And yes, you aggravate my temper past bearing, but that's all, do you hear me? That's all! I can be angry without committing mayhem, Duchess. Lud knows you are pushing me to the limits, but I am not a violent man!" He stomped to the door. "Once and for all, I am not a murderer! And your child is not—" He was going to say "not beautiful," but the sight of her rocking the infant, whispering to him, made Carlinn regret even intending the slight. "Your child is not in any danger."

"Deuce take it, the woman is afraid of me!"

"Don't fatch yourself, my lord," Dimm consoled him, over a glass of the finest cognac it had ever been the Runner's pleasure to sip. "Females is unpredictable. They be especially changeable in Her Grace's condition, like with the tides. They got their humors, their moods."

"Yes, but that woman's moods are all bad! And

it's not just now, either. She's always been afraid of me."

"If you think on it, mayhap she has cause." Dimm held the stemmed goblet up to the fire's light, admiring the color of the spirits the way his lordship was doing, but not for too long before having another sip. "Figger this. For all she's a duchess, Her Grace is a weak little dab of a thing what couldn't protect herself from a flea. You're a big, imposing bloke what does shout some." He held up a hand before the earl could protest. "I know, my lord. You be used to yelling at the troops to make sure they heard you—to be obeyed. But she ain't no soldier."

"You make me sound like Attila the Hun. I'm a gentleman, confound it!"

"I can't say as that holds much weight with Her Grace neither. Look what examples of the breed she's known so far. That brother's just an unlicked cub with a quick fuse, but he'd use his fists afore his tongue every time. The father was a decent enough sort, from his rep, but he lost the family holdings so Her Grace had to take the highest bidder, Denning. Violent man, His Grace. No, don't surprise me none if she fears men."

"You're saying he— No, I don't want to know." Kimbrough swirled the cognac in its crystal. "That bastard."

"I'll drink to that." So he did, and the earl poured another glass for both of them. His lordship lit a cheroot, and Dimm had his pipe going, his feet propped on a hassock. Heaven couldn't match this, he figured, then begged his dead wife's pardon, God love her. As dusk fell, so did the level of the bottle. Dimm contemplated his host, sprawled in his leather chair, still glowering over his visit with Lady Marisol.

"A woman like that needs a man with a gentle touch, like a filly what's been broke to bridle too rough. Otherwise that filly won't let any man near her. Unrideable, don't you know."

"What, you think the duchess will never marry again?" In Kimbrough's experience, all women married again and again, given the chance.

"Hard to say. She won't have to, with her income, that's for sure. And it's just as sure that she'll have men buzzing around her like bees to a flower iffen she seems interested. Once she goes out and about, she could have her pick."

"Yes, of every loose screw in England."

"She be young, beautiful, and rich. What more could a decent chap want?"

"Your particular filly's got a dashed odd kick to her gallop. No discriminating gent's going to fall for those big blue eyes and forget the rest."

"No? It happens every day. Plenty."

"Not in the ton, it doesn't. And she won't marry any fortune hunter either, if I have my say."

"But you don't have any say-so, begging your pardon, milord. You be the boy's guardian, not Her Grace's."

"Exactly, and she's not taking my ward away to live with any basket scrambler."

Dimm whistled. "I see some rough sailing ahead, I do. Wouldn't want to be in the room when you tell Her Grace she can't marry where she wants this time around, if she wants."

"Nonsense. I wouldn't discuss it with her; I'd just warn the flat off. I'd be doing the skirter a favor anyway. Her Grace would make a hell of a wife." He got up to put another log on the fire.

Dimm shook his head. "I don't know why you two rub sparks off each other. Onct I got to know her, I found Her Grace a real lady. Loyal, quick-witted, pretty as a picture."

"A picture of a battleship in full sail, you mean. No, the woman I wed will be sleek. None of this running to fat, after. And she'll be biddable, by George, without all those moods and megrims."

"Been thinking of taking a wife then, have you?" Dimm wanted to know.

"I've been thinking of Arvid's going off so suddenly, that's what. And Lord Ashcroft getting shot. Something like that could happen to anyone."

"Uh-huh. If there be one thing certain, it's that life ain't."

"And then there's my sister and that blasted presentation. I can't like depending on acquaintances to chaperone her properly. A well-bred, socially acceptable wife could get Bettina fired off in style."

"No saying but what the right wife can ease a man's burdens. So you want one as won't ruffle your feathers, won't get snubbed by them hostesses at Almack's, and won't be real expensive to feed?"

Carlinn raised his glass in salute of the Runner's perspicacity. "That sounds ideal."

That sounded about like taking a broom to bed to Dimm, but he asked, "Where are you going to find this nonesuch, guv? Iffen you don't mind my asking."

Kimbrough waved the other man's demurral aside. They were old friends by now, he and the Runner, sharing cognac, sharing confidences. Less likely comradeships had formed, though at this precise moment he couldn't quite recall when. "My bride? She won't be in London, that's a sure bet. I don't want any polished Diamond who'll be as cold as a stone in bed and hard as a rock to m'sister and m'friends on the farms. And no spinster that didn't take, of course. None of those stammering debs will do or I'd have to bear-lead two chits through a Season. A country girl wouldn't have the enteer either, so no milkmaids for me."

"That do narrow the field some. Not too old, not too young, not from the country, not from the City. No wonder you ain't legshackled yet."

"Ah, ye of little faith. Such a paragon does indeed exist. My cousin Winifred's goddaughter is currently a leading light in Bath society, where she resides taking care of her ailing mother. Good sign, don't you know, when a chit knows her duty. She had a London Season three years ago and two offers since then as far as Cousin Winifred knows, so she's no ape-leader. Not an Incomparable, but not an antidote. That's the kind of woman I have in mind, one with a sense of responsibility who won't land me in the briars every step."

"And is she thin enough? Better yet, how plump is her ma? You can allus tell what kind of pup you're getting by looking at the kennel."

"Lady Sherville has kept her figure," was all the earl vouchsafed. Lady Sherville was as thin as a rail. Her daughter, unfortunately, was as flat-chested as a boy. Miss Edelia Sherville was well bred, well mannered, well connected, even well dowered. A man couldn't have everything.

"Well? When are you going to offer for the gel?"

Chapter Twelve

$\mathcal{A}$ man couldn't just rush into these things. Mortality might beckon and all but, dash it, a fellow had other responsibilities, too.

Now that the streambed land was his, Lord Kimbrough had to see about reclaiming those flooded fields. He had to consult with specialists, hire engineers, order equipment, and sign on work crews before he could think of leaving the project in the hands of his steward.

Then there was the steward for the Denning lands. The fellow seemed honest and capable, but the property and people were not in good heart. Arvid had been a harsh master, and a clutchfisted landlord. Both the steward and Kimbrough agreed improvements were long past due, but the earl didn't know the other man well enough to trust him with the decisions. Kimbrough was therefore obliged to meet with him nearly daily, to visit the fields to see conditions for himself, and to call on the tenants to hear their complaints, which were numerous and well founded.

Everywhere he looked, everyone he spoke to, gave

more evidence of Arvid's villainy and venery. The people, tenant farmers and villagers alike, were excited about the infant, but mostly they were pitifully eager to welcome a right 'un like the Earl of Kimbrough as liege. So Carlinn had to stop and toast the new duke with homemade wine or ale or cider at every farmstead and cottage, reassuring Arvid's people that *he* wasn't going to be an absentee manager. So he couldn't very well just hare off to Bath for the winter so soon after that.

Kimbrough also had to make sure that young Laughton was granted his commission, now that Foster was recovered enough from his injuries and the dibs were in tune. A few quick trips to London would see the deed accomplished, but Carlinn wasn't about to take his eyes off the feisty lad until he had him in uniform and under orders to abstain from brawling. Of course, then Foster and his batman Joshua needed to be outfitted and mounted. The earl couldn't send his ward's uncle and Dimm's boy off to war on Arvid's old break-downs, could he? Tattersall's was full of park-prads and highbred cattle that would bolt at the first sound of cannonfire. Luckily there were horse fairs in Berkshire.

There were also robberies in Berkshire. Lord Ashcroft's attacker struck another time, again only wounding his victim, another solitary gentleman driving alone in his carriage. The highwayman got away with a heavy purse, but left behind a good description of himself and his horse. The local constable, Mr. Dimm, and his lordship were all on the lookout. As magistrate, the earl felt it his duty to oversee the inquiry.

No, there was no hurry to get to Bath. Miss Edelia Sherville and her flat chest had gone all these years without being snatched up by some other lucky beau; she could wait a month or two. The earl told himself that Miss Sherville's lack of projection had nothing to do with his delay. He wanted a slender wife, didn't he? Besides, there was nothing wrong with Miss Sherville that an infant or two couldn't cure.

And the weather was bad.

Winter raged outside, and a storm blew through Denning Castle. Marisol was cleaning house. *Her* house. Foster went off to London. Boynton, his debts paid and his allowance increased, followed the Regent's set to Brighton. The dowager kept to her wing of the castle with joint pain, her nose in particular being out of joint. And Marisol lined up every last servant in the place, from butler to potboy.

"This castle and everything in it," she told the assembled staff, "now belongs to His Grace, the seventh Duke of Denning. The household, therefore, will function for His Grace's comfort and convenience, as I see fit. If there are any of you who take issue with this, please leave now so that we may avoid any future unpleasantness. For understand this," she pronounced, her chin lifted, her voice raised so the smallest scullery maid could hear in the back, "I will tolerate no insubordination. No disrespect toward my son, myself, my family, nor those I have hired to care for us. No disloyalty, no dereliction of duty to the duke, no disregard for his safety. Nothing. Is that understood?"

She waited to hear murmurs of assent. "Very well. I do not know my mother-in-law's plans at this moment, since she is ill with a sore throat."

"From eating too much crow," a voice in the rear of the ranks called out, and was hushed.

"If she chooses to take up residence in the Dower House, those of you who wish may apply to her for positions there. If she remains, she is also part of the duke's family and as such is entitled to the same respect. No more, and no less."

Not even the bootblack had to be told what that meant: Lady Marisol was in charge, plain and simple. Just for insurance, Marisol added, "Anyone who is less than loyal to the interests of His Grace shall have me to answer to. And the Earl of Kimbrough."

Marisol hated having to invoke the earl's name, but he was Nolly's guardian, after all. Let him be handy for something, even if it was striking terror into the hearts of recalcitrant retainers. She dismissed the staff.

Then every cupboard was turned out, every sheet inspected for mending. Unused rooms were shut off, and important chambers were restored and polished to a fare-thee-well. The castle's structure was inspected and made sound, eliminating drafts, smoking chimneys, and loose roofing tiles. Historic artifacts were catalogued and stored, or displayed out of reach as Marisol and the staff tried to think ahead.

The duchess was everywhere—the new duchess, that is. The old duchess stayed in her rooms suffering from back pain. She wanted to be back in command.

Lady Marisol, as she was called to avoid confusion, ran upstairs and down, from the attic to the cellars, with a hundred stops between. Sometimes she raced up and down the stairs to reach Nolly at his first whimper, but sometimes she just used those steep marble steps for the exercise. Besides the weather being too inclement for outdoor activities, Marisol needed to be within reach of her son at a moment's notice. Furthermore, she was determined to have her shape back before the spring, and the light muslins she so enjoyed. So she also ordered fewer courses served at dinner.

The dowager made her excuses from the table. A headache, this time, from banging it against the wall.

And Nolly thrived. How could he not, under his mother's adoration? He had his aunt Tess's knitted bonnets, booties, and blankets to keep him warm; Dimm's daughter Rebecca to see him clean and dry;

Her Grace's maid Sarah to listen for his cries; and Mrs. Vicar Hambley to lend advice and admiration. And of course Nolly had the smiles and pats and coos of a castleful of people dependent on him for their very livelihoods.

The only thing His Little Grace was missing—not that he suffered from the lack—was his grandmother's affection, for she was too ill. It was heart trouble. She didn't have one.

No peacock in his full plumage ever strutted as proudly as Foster in his brand-new scarlet regimentals.

"Oh dear," Marisol cried as she watched her beloved brother practice walking without tripping on his scabbard, "however am I going to let you go?" Foster wasn't just a little boy playing at soldier anymore; he was really going to go off to war this time, with real swords, real pistols.

"Don't be a gudgeon," he told her in that fond way brothers have. "You can't stop me now. 'Sides, it was you gave me the chance to go and make something of myself in the first place. Arvid never would have, by Jupiter. I'd still be like a dog begging for crumbs at his table. That's the way he wanted it, don't you know."

She knew that, but she also knew how much she was going to miss her brother, how much she was going to worry about him. Marisol wouldn't make Foster carry the burden of her anxieties, though, so she only told him how proud Nolly was going to be with a hero for an uncle.

"There," Foster teased. "I knew you couldn't keep the brat out of the conversation for two minutes! See, you won't miss me a whit, now that you've got Nolly to fuss over. Why, you've hardly noticed me this past month." He fondly chucked the sleeping baby under the chin.

"Not true!" Well, only partly true.

When Foster's orders had come, Marisol scheduled Nolly's christening for the week before her brother was to meet his troop ship, so he could stand as godfather. Aunt Tess would be godmother.

Marisol had sent out invitations to the ceremony at Reverend Hambley's little church and the reception at Denning Castle after, without much response. Still, she spent more time over her toilette than she had in ages. Sarah had transformed one of her old gowns for the occasion, trimming a lavender taffeta into half-mourning, with black ribbons and black rouleau at the hem. The maid had loosely coiled the duchess's thick blonde hair under a black ruched bonnet that trailed a long black veil, and both the bonnet and the gown's bodice were embellished with clusters of silk violets. Black gloves completed the outfit, which should have satisfied any but the highest sticklers. Since none of them had bothered responding to her invitation, Marisol was unconcerned. She felt almost attractive again.

They'd come to the church early, so she might feed Nolly in the little vestry in hopes that he'd sleep through the ceremony. Now she sat waiting, watching the church fill with a few of the tenants, a handful of servants, and the Reverend Hambley's brood. There were more of Jeremiah Dimm's relations here than there were of Nolly's, she calculated. So be it. These were the people who mattered, the ones who cared about her son.

Then Lord Kimbrough arrived. Marisol told herself she shouldn't have been surprised. Nolly was the earl's ward, after all, and Kimbrough was nothing if not punctilious about his duties. The earl had even dressed for the occasion, in Bath superfine and dove gray pantaloons. He was just too large a man for elegance, Marisol decided, but he did look bang up to the mark, as Foster would have said. Except for the frown, of course. Lord Kimbrough's scowls were nothing new to Marisol, but she did wonder if perhaps he was up in the boughs this time because she'd selected Foster to be godfather. The guardianship was enough for one man, she'd decided.

As Foster went out to shake the earl's hand, Marisol realized Kimbrough's forbidding countenance had nothing to do with her, for once. He was aggravated beyond bearing, she could tell from her place in the tiny chamber, at the necessity of introducing Foster to his family. Marisol's handsome scamp of a brother was making his formal bows over the hands of the earl's older cousin and his younger sister. His impressionable younger sister. The stunning little brunette was staring up at Foster, fading bruises and all, with open-mouthed admiration. The earl bustled her off into a pew, glaring.

Marisol grinned. Hoist with your own petard, my stiff-necked lord.

Her attention swung back to the door, through which a knot of gaily decorated gentlemen entered, laughing and comparing times for the journey. Boynton had come and brought some of his friends. "M'nevvy's christening, don't you know," she heard him tell Lord Kimbrough. "Couldn't miss it, so we made it into a race. I won a monkey on Cordell's grays. Use some of the flimsies to buy the boy a gift, don't you know. Can't imagine what he'd need now, of course, so I'll set the blunt aside for when he's ready for a pony, what?"

Ponies would grow wings if Boynton had that money when Nolly was old enough to ride, and everyone knew it. Even his friends all laughed. "No matter," Boynton said good-naturedly, "Prinny sent a gift. Youngest duke in the land, don't you know. Doubt it's paid for either, now I think on't. But it's the thought that matters, what?"

"What's he saying?" Aunt Tess asked, next to Marisol in the side room.

"Boynton's telling everyone that the Prince Regent sent a gift to Nolly."

"How lovely. Unless it's a portrait of himself. That's what he sent Lady Harrowsmith. She had to hang it in the infant's room, of course. The child had nightmares for years."

"It's the thought that counts," Marisol found herself repeating as another commotion at the doorway caught her attention.

Bugles should have been playing a fanfare. At the very least, a superior butler should have stood at the opposite end of a red carpet announcing the new arrival. No, the Regent hadn't decided to attend in person after all. The dowager had.

She swept in on her chaplain's arm, dressed head to toe in flowing black crepe. She accepted her son Boynton's kiss on the cheek and the other gentlemen's bows with a dismissing wave of her hand as she sailed toward the front pew. When Lord Kimbrough's sister swept her a deep curtsy as she passed, the dowager paused and patted the girl's hand. "Practice," was all she said. Even from her viewing place Marisol could see the girl's lower lip begin to tremble. Then Foster strolled by, retrieving one of the scarfs Her Grace had dropped, and winked at Bettina. The sun came out again on her face.

Oh dear, he isn't going to be happy, was all Marisol had time to think, before carriage after carriage deposited passengers at the steps of the little church. Where the dowager led, her fellow gorgons followed. And where those bejewelled, beturbanned, and befurred bastions of local society went, their husbands, sons, and daughters followed, willy-nilly.

Marisol quickly conferred with Sarah, who stepped outside with a message for their coachman, who sent a rider back to the Castle to warn Cook, who almost had apoplexy, that so many more guests were coming.

Then it was time. Marisol handed little Noel Alistaire Laughton Pendenning to his godparents

122

and wept as Vicar Hambley said the prayers over him.

Nolly behaved, Foster stopped grinning at Lady Bettina, and the dowager nodded.

Later, everyone complimented Marisol on her beautiful baby, the refurbishing of the Castle, and the excellent refreshments. If some of the company privately found some of the offerings plain fare, Marisol was not surprised. Cook had excelled, but many of the dishes had been prepared for the servants' celebration later. The duchess promised them a better party tomorrow—and a bonus.

The excellent wines from Arvid's cellars compensated for the refreshments and kept the gathering in high spirits. None were higher than the dowager's as she held court in the Queen Anne drawing room, her grandson in her lap. Nolly's long white lace gown draped over the black crepe of her mourning. It was the gown Arvid and Boynton had worn, she told everyone, and their father and his before that. Of course, none of them had been such a fine boy as Noel.

And Marisol tried to hold back her tears some more, until Lord Kimbrough quietly handed her a handkerchief.

"Those better be tears of happiness," he commanded, but turning her so that his broad back shielded her from curious eyes.

"Yes, thank you. And thank you for coming. It was a wonderful day."

"I am happy for you," he told her, and meant it. This woman could send him into a rage with the curl of her lip, and her tears could turn his knees to blanc mange, but he truly was happy to see her on terms with her in-laws, accepted in the local society, and content. Yes, it was a good day, a happy occasion. Carlinn would have been more than satisfied, had it not been for the sight of his baby sister hanging on Foster Laughton's sleeve.

Blast! It was even more important that he get to

Bath. If Bettina fell for the first scarlet uniform she saw, it was time and past to see her Out. Why, he could even take her to Bath for a month or two, to get her feet wet in those smaller circles where enough of the Quality congregated for the winter. That's the ticket! He could go first to find accommodations and look things over, so to speak. That way it wouldn't be so obvious that he was looking over Miss Sherville. He needed a wife, he told himself. Bettina needed the example of a mature, responsible lady like Miss Edelia Sherville. He'd do it. As soon as the highwayman was caught.

Chapter Thirteen

The apprehension of the robber became even more crucial. One of Boynton's friends was set upon after leaving the christening party. The thief got away, and Sir Oswald returned to Denning Castle late that night, shaken and considerably lighter in the purse. Sir Oswald accepted Marisol's offer of a guest chamber for the night and her assurance that, since he was a guest of the Castle, the Castle would make good his loss. Sir Oswald did not protest as much as he ought, Foster felt, but there was no escaping the evidence of a bullet hole through the man's curly-brimmed beaver. While Rebecca, Nolly's nursemaid, offered to brew a special tisane for Sir Oswald, Marisol and Foster waited downstairs for the constable from the village, Dimm from the inn, and the magistrate from Kimbrough Hall.

Carlinn had just gone to bed, so he threw on his shirt and breeches and an old pair of boots and followed the messenger back to the Castle.

Sir Oswald's profile of the highwayman matched the previous description, but still did not match any of the known local miscreants: for the most part poachers, inebriates, and dealers in goods without excise stamps. This little section of Berkshire countryside was not known as a hotbed of crime, Lord Kimbrough tried to reassure the duchess.

"At least not until we Londoners arrived," Marisol replied, offering the earl sherry in the parlor after his interview with Sir Oswald and his later conference with Dimm and the constable. They had decided the night was too advanced to look for clues in the dark; they'd meet in the morning where Sir Oswald had been waylaid, but without much hope of success.

"I could see it on the faces of those ladies today," Marisol went on, "underneath their politeness. Thank goodness Foster will be on his way Tuesday. No one can accuse him of anything untoward."

Foster was pouring the drinks. He still wore his uniform, unbuttoned, and he ran a hand through his hair. "Dash it, I'm sorry to be going. I'd like to help in the hunt, find the dastard, and stop this infernal gabble-grinding."

"You'd do better to concentrate on stopping the Corsican, bantling," Kimbrough told the younger man, which brought a grin to Foster's lips.

Marisol could not be so easily diverted. She lay awake fretting after the earl left and the house had settled down, and that was how she came to hear the noise next door, in Nolly's room.

Marisol reached for a light, and knocked a book off the night table in her fumbling. She heard a muttered curse, then a cry from Rebecca, and a door closing. To hell with a candle, Marisol thought, flying to her son, calling his name loudly enough to wake everyone but Aunt Tess and the dowager in the far tower.

By the time the duchess reached the makeshift nursery, Rebecca was sitting up in bed, rubbing her eyes. Nolly was wailing, the nursery lamp was still glowing, and no one was in sight.

"I thought, that is, I couldn't be sure, Your Grace. I thought someone shook my shoulder, but I could have been dreaming, and then there was a noise."

Then there was a lot of noise, as Foster and servants came running. No one had seen anything.

They sent for Lord Kimbrough and Dimm.

The earl had been dreaming, and not pleasantly. Even in his sleep he knew he should be dreaming of Edelia Sherville. Life with her would be a sailboat ride on a tranquil day, everything smooth and peaceful, nothing to disturb the proper course. Instead his dreams found him tangled in the sails of a sinking ship in the middle of a raging gale, with a full-bodied siren with flowing gold locks beckoning him onto the rocky shoals. "Damn it," he cursed, waking in a sweat with his sheets strangling him, "that blasted woman has even invaded my dreams."

But it wasn't any blue-eyed siren calling him to his doom: it was his valet, with another urgent message from the Castle.

The shirt, the breeches, the boots, the same sleepy groom saddling a horse.

This time the duchess was in her own dishabille, a blue dressing gown buttoned over a lace-collared white lawn nightgown and a silly lace bonnet tied under her chin. And this time she was not merely fretful; she was frantic.

"The highwayman was in Nolly's room, I tell you! You have to do something!"

"Perhaps you had too much champagne this afternoon, Duchess, and that sherry on top of it led your dreams—" Since his own dreams had been far-fetched but all too vivid, he could well believe hers might be, too.

"I was not dreaming, I tell you. Someone was in

my son's room! And no, I do not believe in ghosts, before you ask me that absurdity."

"But the servants found no one, you said, and the maid wasn't certain. Your nerves have been overset and—"

"I am not a hysterical woman, so do not patronize me, my lord. There is a gunman loose, maybe two counting Arvid's murderer, and I want him found. Them. Whichever one was in Nolly's room. This is your province, Lord Kimbrough, so I demand you do something!"

Foster was upset, too. "Can't like to think about going off like this, leaving my sister all unprotected, with no man in the house unless you count that caper-merchant Boynton. I mean, what if the fellow is a madman?"

"Boynton? Are you accusing Boynton of being a Bedlamite?" He turned to Marisol. "Do you still consider your brother-in-law a suspect in Arvid's murder, trying to do away with his nephew now so he might succeed to the title?"

Marisol twitched at the belt of her robe. "I don't know what to think anymore. Boynton seemed thrilled with a raise in his allowance and a fresh start. I'd rather suspect your highwayman."

Kimbrough was pacing. He stopped and pounded on the mantel. "Begging your pardon, Duchess, and I swear I am not being patronizing, but what in bloody hell do you think a cove on the bridle lay was doing in the nipper's room?"

"Excuse me?"

"I apologize. Let me rephrase that. Why, if someone was in your son's room, do you think it was the highwayman?"

"Someone *was* in my son's room, and your highwayman has been going around robbing and shooting, that's why."

What kind of logic was that? He tried again. "But wouldn't the robber have gone after the silver plate or your jewels?"

Foster nodded. "He's got a point there, sis."

"There are white slavers and things. Gypsies steal children all the time."

"Not in Berkshire, they don't, Duchess. And if anyone wanted a child that badly, he could go to a hundred orphanages and poorhouses. No, I cannot believe this was the same man at all."

"He could have been trying to kidnap Nolly to hold him for ransom. I'd have paid anything to get him back. Everyone must have known that!" Marisol was starting to look damp-eyed, and her voice was quivering. Foster patted her hand.

"Please, Duchess, try not to get hys—ah, upset." Kimbrough might as well have asked the sun not to rise, which he could see it doing out the window just now.

"Don't get upset? What kind of unfeeling brute are you?"

"Now, sis, coming it too strong. His lordship's trying to be helpful."

"No, he's trying to shut me up so he can go back to sleep in his nice, warm, *safe* bed. How can I not be upset, I ask you, when someone might hurt my son? With Foster going off to war, he's the only thing I've got, the only child I'm likely ever to have."

"Don't make this a Cheltenham tragedy, ma'am," Carlinn said in exasperation. "Nothing is going to happen to your son, and you're bound to have a whole houseful of kiddies if you want."

She sniffed. "What, do you think any decent man would marry me now, after Arvid's scandal?"

Well, Carlinn wouldn't, but . . . "Of course, Duchess. You're young, well bred, wealthy."

"Of course, we mustn't forget the fortune," she snapped, having read his answer on Kimbrough's face, the puffed-up, prudish peer. "As if I would wed some down-at-heels fortune hunter. But none of this is pertinent to the matter, my lord. What are you going to do about the intruder in Nolly's room?"

First he suggested she have that yappy little dog Max sleep in the room to act as a warning device. Then he sent a message to Dimm, asking him if he knew an experienced bodyguard who would patrol the house and grounds. Those measures seemed to relieve Foster some, enabling him to resume packing while Kimbrough interviewed the servants again.

They all seemed genuinely distressed that anyone might think of harming the young master or upsetting the mistress, but they had no clues to offer. So he went to speak to Sir Oswald once more before the other's departure, in case the robbery victim recalled any helpful details. He did.

"About that little taradiddle last night ... Didn't mean to frighten the girl, don't you know."

"The girl?"

"The nursemaid, the one who brought me the tisane. Thought she was extending an invite, don't you know. Didn't mean to set the house on its ear."

"You didn't mean to—? Why, you—!"

If Sir Oswald was shaken by the robbery, it was nothing to being shaken by the Earl of Kimbrough. The earl had the man off the ground and dangling by his shirt collar. Sir Oswald swore to leave the Castle, Berkshire, England, anything the earl wanted.

Kimbrough wanted all that plus an apology to the nursemaid and to Duchess Denning, and he wore a complacent grin while he watched the man grovel. Foster grinned, too, after he planted the man a facer and tossed him out the door. But the duchess didn't grin. She didn't even thank the earl. She merely took one look at his smirk of self-satisfaction and reminded him that the sun was up and there was still a murderous highwayman loose in his lordship's domain. Then she went back to bed.

Thunderation! Must he always appear no-account to the blasted female? And what should he care if the duchess thought him rude, arrogant, and incompetent? He cared. And so what if she nonsensically feared for her child's safety and even more foolishly feared him? So he'd do his damnedest to wipe that look of terror from her face, that's what. No woman should be afraid, Kimbrough told himself, not of her husband, not of strangers, certainly not of a bumbling blockhead like himself. Why, the code of chivalry honoring womankind ran so deep in his blood he might have been one of those wretched knights strewn around Denning Castle, clanking along in metal inexpressibles.

Obviously, what he had to do to restore a bit of luster to his armor was capture that thatchgallows on the high toby. There were no usable tracks to follow, no new directions to pursue, which only left setting a trap as a viable course. The makebait liked to prey on gentlemen traveling alone after dark, so the earl and Dimm decided that that's what he'd get.

They planned the trap for that very evening. Since the moon would be full, the highwayman was sure to be at his craft. Before going home for some much-needed rest in anticipation of a long night, Lord Kimbrough returned to Denning Castle. He only thought to relieve Her Grace's mind, he told himself. She would be happy to know that a plan was under way to capture the thief, and pleased that Dimm's son Gabriel, the one in training to be a Runner, was already on his way to safeguard the little duke. Dimm thought it would be good training for the lad, who was familiar with infants, and good for the baby to hear a deep voice now and again.

"Gor'blimey, little chap's being fawned on by five women at least. With that brother of Her Grace's gone, he'll need someone to teach him how to toss a ball and spin a hoop."

When the earl had last seen His Grace at the christening, Master Noel had needed nothing more than sour milk mopped off his chin. But if it eased the duchess's mind, one more Dimm on hand made no difference to Lord Kimbrough.

Marisol was indeed pleased that Nolly would have an armed guard by the end of the week. She was not quite as pleased with the earl's plan to act as bait for the robber. In fact, the approval, trust, and respect Carlinn thought to see in her eyes for once was missing altogether. In her eyes instead were enough fireworks to light up Vauxhall Gardens.

"No, not even you can be so chowderheaded, my lord," she said, fists clenched at her side. She didn't even offer him tea, she was so angry. "Then again, you must have been the gudgeon, for Mr. Dimm would never have devised such a reckless scheme. I am surprised he agreed to go along with it at all."

Dimm's agreement was hard-won, but Lord Kimbrough was not about to give the irate duchess more ammunition. "I thought you wanted me to apprehend the felon," he noted instead.

"Yes, to capture him, not offer him your head on a silver platter!" she shouted. "It's too dangerous, you jackanapes! Can't you see that, or are you so puffed up in your own conceit that you cannot comprehend an armed and desperate man winning out over the Earl of Kimbrough?"

"What, never say you are worried over me? And here I thought you'd be happy to see me gone."

"Don't be ridiculous," she said, puncturing what vanity the earl had left. "I am concerned for Nolly's sake only. What, pray, happens to him if the gentleman of the road does not behave in a gentlemanly fashion? What if he shoots you first, for instance, and then asks for your purse? What good is Dimm hiding in some bushes going to be then? And what good to my son are you going to be dead? The court will appoint another guardian, most likely Boynton. He is the Prince's friend, for heaven's sake. And you know what he is, what he'd do to

Nolly's estate." She crossed her arms over her now-heaving chest and pronounced, "You cannot do it."

Carlinn tore his eyes from that same generous bosom. "Dash it, Duchess, you cannot tell me what to do. You are not my wife, b'God."

"Heaven be praised for that mercy! And I pity the poor woman who takes on that thankless task. Of course, a wife might remind you of your responsibilities more."

Carlinn crossed his arms, too, more so he wouldn't be tempted to shake her than anything else. "You go too far, Duchess. I have made allowances for your sex, for your condition, even for the uncomfortable position you found yourself in with a virtual stranger thrust into your affairs. I have even tried to make excuses for your shrewish tongue. But I have *never* needed to be reminded of my duties, which is why I will not permit you to dictate my behavior, and why I will not permit a criminal to prey at will on my neighbors."

Marisol stormed over to the parlor door and threw it open hard enough to rock the panel on its hinges. "So you'll ride into danger with your pride for protection like any insolent, footloose bachelor. What about your responsibilities to Nolly, my lord? To your sister? You are even more of a jackass than I thought."

She left in a swirl of silk. The earl shook his head, wondering if that was the sound of the door slamming or the sound of his brains rattling loose in his skull. And here he'd thought she'd appreciate his efforts.

Lord Kimbrough and Jeremiah Dimm went ahead with the plan that night despite Her Grace's objections. The earl drove his curricle up and down the highways and country lanes, humming unconcernedly, while Dimm lay covered with a carriage blanket at his feet, pistol in hand.

It was a good plan, Carlinn told himself, not

reckless or devil-may-care. He cared very much to stay alive, thank you. He'd even sent reservations to the Ship Inn in Bath, so confident of the future was he. As Carlinn tooled his pair up a tree-lined lane, the perfect place for an ambush, he wondered how soon after his arrival in Bath he could call on Miss Sherville without being too obvious. He'd have a letter from Cousin Winifred, of course, her godmother, but it wouldn't do to raise expectations in her mama's hopeful breast until he was certain.

Fortunately the highwayman did not choose that particular spot to make his move for, unfortunately, that hopeful breast brought to mind not Miss Sherville's inadequate one, but the devilish duchess's milk-filled, rounded, mounded abundancy. The carriage hit a rut and Dimm cursed. Lud, the sooner he was wed the better.

The highwayman did not choose any other roadway Kimbrough drove that night either. It was a good idea, driving around with a lantern on his curricle like some perverse Diogenes seeking a dishonest man, but it didn't work. Nor did the earl's efforts to keep Duchess Denning out of his dreams when he finally sought his bed after midnight.

Chapter Fourteen

*T*he urgent message came at three in the morning. There had been another incident at Denning Castle. With a scant two hours' sleep in two days, and that interrupted by extremely disturbing dreams, the earl could not generate the fever pitch of excitement he used to feel riding into battle. He didn't bother with a neckcloth or a waistcoat or a hairbrush. He just went. Lord Kimbrough was not in prime twig for more alarms.

Neither was Marisol. Her thoughts all night had been filled with images of the earl's bride, whoever she turned out to be, the poor dear. He'd bully her and shout at her and insist on having his pigheaded way about everything. The woman would be miserable, unless she admired broad shoulders and a firm jaw and a dedication to duty as immovable as a mountain, the widgeon.

Marisol pummeled her pillow. At least there was something she could force to her will. Of course, the pillow fought back, making lumps and hollows that kept her from a deep sleep. Tossing restlessly, she was easily roused by a slight noise next door. She waited to hear if it was Nolly stirring, or Rebecca checking on him, or even Max sounding an alarm. She heard nothing, and was about to drift back to sleep, chiding herself for a peagoose, wasting precious sleep time when Nolly would be up soon enough.

Then she did hear another noise: the sound of a door shutting.

"And don't tell me my imagination was working overtime, my lord," she told Kimbrough, "for someone was there. They knew enough to give Max a lamb chop to keep him quiet, and if I hadn't screamed, who knows what would have happened?"

Her scream had woken the baby, of course, and the weary servants who had to be up in a few hours, and Foster, who was to leave after breakfast. Even Boynton dashed to the rescue in his nightshirt, his hair in curl-papers. They found nothing but the lamb chop to signal an intruder.

The earl had the staff go outside with lanterns, looking for tracks under windows, signs of forced entry, anything. He made each one account for his or her time, then made them swear on the Bible they hadn't come next or nigh the infant. Then he ordered wine for the duchess; she must be more disturbed than he thought, for she didn't even rip up at him over his high-handed treatment of her servants. She merely amended his order to tea, with brandy for the gentlemen. Marisol was so pale, with purplish shadows under her eyes, her voice so subdued, that the earl almost forgave her for another night's missed rest.

What a damnable coil! Foster was in anguish over leaving in the midst of a family crisis. The young man's sense of honor couldn't permit him to abandon his sister in time of need, but he had his orders. Boynton, on the other hand, was packing to get out of this madhouse as soon as his valet could manage. Between the infant's caterwauling and his sister-in-law's fits and starts, a gent couldn't get his beauty sleep. Marisol meanwhile was asking the butler to find Arvid's hunting rifle. Lud, that was all they needed, Carlinn thought: a hysterical woman with a loaded weapon. She was wound so tight she'd likely shoot a crackling log in the hearth or a branch scraping along the window. Or him, for not protecting the infant.

Kimbrough could see the accusation in her eyes: He'd been out having a lovely drive around the countryside while some heinous malefactor was attempting to make off with her baby. He rubbed his eyes and tried to stifle a yawn. The sooner Dimm's son got here, the better.

Servants lit a fire in the parlor, the child was put back to sleep with a weary nursemaid, and Max was taken outside to be dosed with salts in case the lamb chop was poisoned. The footman who got that job was almost as aggravated with the earl as the duchess was. The servant couldn't show it, of course; Her Grace could. She practically ignored Kimbrough's presence while they waited for Mr. Dimm and the tea tray, as if she regretted sending for the nobleman and his useless suggestions.

Marisol was indeed avoiding looking at Lord Kimbrough who, with his unbuttoned shirt and ruffled hair, was looking barbaric and heroic and sleepy. His poor wife would have to look at that broad, hairy chest every night, if she was lucky. Marisol blushed at her own thoughts and dragged her mind back to Nolly. Maybe she should take him into her own bed? Nolly, she reminded herself, Nolly. At this rate her son was never going to reside in the nursery the dowager was so busily refurbishing for him. He'd never ride the rocking horse or play with the tin soldiers, for he'd have to be walled around with armed guards. But she would not weep. No, not a drop, at least until she was alone in her room, Nolly under one arm and a rifle under the other. Marisol made herself be strong for Foster, so he could go off and follow his own dream. And she had to show the earl she was no milk-and-water miss. She tucked a wayward curl back under her nightcap and poured out the tea as if she were entertaining Princess Lieven and Sally Jersey at an afternoon call.

The earl had to admire the chit's backbone. But how could she sit there so calmly when he was at his wit's end wondering what was to be done? Not that he thought the child was in any real danger; if someone truly wished the boy harm, there had been plenty of opportunities. He wondered if the duchess would feel safer at Kimbrough Hall. He could move her, infant, nursemaids, aunt, and all, but would he get any sleep whatsoever, knowing she was a few doors away? Botheration. Besides, he couldn't promise to keep her safe and then scamper off to Bath. What kind of watchdog would that be?

"A watchdog, that's what you need," he declared. "Not a barking lap-sitter like Max, but a real trained guard dog. The kind that stays out watching after sheep and cattle, defending them from wolves. Looking after one small baby can only be, well, child's play to a protective breed like that."

Marisol was dubious. A large, unkempt herd dog in Nolly's room? Besides, there hadn't been wolves in England in ages; she'd worry more the animal would swallow the baby. But Foster was nodding eagerly and the earl was going on, excited to have a plan of action. This plan seemed as harebrained as his notion of trapping the bandit, but Marisol didn't say anything. He meant well, and she didn't actually have to get the dog, so she nodded.

Then Kimbrough said, "Don't worry, I'll take care of finding just the perfect animal myself."

Before Marisol could voice her objections, Aunt Tess wandered in, a frilly mobcap askew on her gray hair. She frowned at her niece. "I saw all the lights, dears. Don't you think it is a trifle late for company?"

"This isn't a social call, Aunt Tess," Marisol explained, pouring a cup of tea for the older woman and speaking loudly. "I didn't want to wake you to another frightening event, but there has been another intruder in Nolly's room. Please don't be upset, Aunt Tess, but someone gave Max some food to keep him quiet. We don't think it was poisoned, but . . ."

"Poisoned?" Her aunt blinked. "Oh no, Cook would never leave poisoned food out on the table. Why, one of the servants might eat it. Much better to put the lamb chop on the floor behind the cupboard if you wish to kill rats. But I thought cheese . . ."

"Aunt Tess, you knew Max ate a lamb chop?"

"Of course, dear. Didn't I tell you Cook leaves a snack out for me? I don't sleep well at night. Old bones, don't you know. So I often take myself to the kitchen for some warm milk or whatever Cook leaves out. Tonight I thought Max was doing such a good job, he deserved a treat, too. And I did want to check on dear Nolly in case he needed another blanket. I thought he might like a lullaby or something, so you could sleep longer. You've been looking so tired, dear. But he was sleeping soundly, precious darling, so I tiptoed out."

"And you didn't hear me scream?"

Aunt Tess was stirring her tea. "What's that, dear?"

So Carlinn drove his curricle home as another dawn was breaking. He was exhausted, emotionally drained, confused by the feelings that warred in him. That's when the highwayman struck, of course.

The first shot startled the horses into rearing and kicking. Kimbrough had all he could do to keep the curricle upright. He certainly couldn't remove a hand from the ribbons to reach for his pistol in his greatcoat pocket. He fought the horses to a standstill, as per instructions.

"That's right, guv'nor, keep them steady. Hands on the reins where I can see them." The masked horseman rode over, a second pistol aimed straight at Carlinn's heart. "Now real slow, throw down your purse. And if you think to reach for a gun instead, you better be thinking fast, for I can't miss at this range."

It wasn't worth the gamble. He didn't have much money with him at any rate, and the thief already had his weapon cocked. Carlinn did as directed.

"Hell's fires!" the bandit cursed when he felt the lightness of Kimbrough's purse. "And not even a stickpin or a watch fob to pay for my time. Damn it!"

For a moment Carlinn feared being murdered for disappointing a deuced footpad. "Sorry," he said. "If I'd known your intentions, I would have been better prepared."

"I'm sure you would have, guv'nor. The local militia and a small cannon, eh?"

"No, just my pistol at the ready. I misdoubt you'd be so brazen were this a fair fight."

The highwayman laughed harshly. "Life ain't fair, m'lord, or haven't you heard?" With that he slapped the flank of the carriage horse nearest him, sending the curricle on another mad dash. He rode off into the woods while the earl struggled to halt the plunging team. If Kimbrough hadn't been a consummate fiddler, he'd never have brought the bays under control so quickly, nor managed to turn them in time to see which direction the rider had taken.

The dastard had gotten away with Carlinn's small purse and with a large portion of his pride, but he hadn't gotten clean away this time. The presunrise air was cold and frost lay on the ground, frost that kept a perfect set of hoofprints riding through the woods. When the earl had the horses calmed, he stepped down from the curricle, tied the bays to a bush to nibble, and followed those receding marks until he had a good idea where the bandit was heading.

This was his land they were on now, and Carlinn knew every inch and every abandoned gamekeeper's cottage. If he was mad before, he was outraged now; the maggot was using Kimbrough land for his hideout. Carlinn did not let his anger blind him to reason, however, so he went back to the curricle rather than going after the cutthroat on foot with only one round in his pistol. He drove home and changed his curricle for a fast horse, enlisted his stable staff, and sent riders off to fetch Dimm and Foster.

They all met at the marker that divided Kimbrough's property from Denning's, had a short conference, and followed the earl into the woods on foot. Some carried pistols, some pitchforks; all wore tired but determined expressions.

When they saw chimney smoke deep in the forest, the earl deployed his troops to encircle the small cottage he knew was there. "But remember," he whispered, "the man is dangerous. He is a hardened criminal who has nothing to lose now, for he can only hang once. No heroics," he especially warned Foster and his man Joshua, "and no one moves until I give the word."

They all nodded and took up positions surrounding the stone dwelling. The earl alone crept closer, dodging behind tree after tree until he was crouched almost beneath one of the narrow windows at the side of the house. He listened intently, then silently crept forward. He listened again. At last he straightened enough to peek through the window.

The glass was none too clean so he had a hard time making out the interior of the cottage. A bed, a stool, a sink, a cupboard. Then he saw a hand-hewn table, with two pistols lying on it alongside his purse. And finally, in the far corner, he spotted the dangerous, deadly, cold-blooded highwayman. Shaving. Pistol in hand, the earl wormed his way around to the front door, waving his cohorts nearer. When they were close behind him, he reared up, kicked the door in, and tumbled after it, landing next to the table holding the man's weapons, which he swept to the floor.

"Hands up, you son of a bitch."

The bandit, his back to them, slowly raised his hands, dropping the razor he'd been holding. Jeremiah Dimm kicked it away and gathered up the fallen pistols. "Evidence, don't you know," he said, then cleared his throat. "Pardon, milord, but this here's my line." He cleared his throat again and addressed the prisoner's back. "By the power vested in me by His Royal Highness King George, you is hereby arrested in the name of justice. Now turn around, you son of a bitch."

The man slowly turned, hands still in the air, to face at least five gun barrels. His own face, however, was still covered in soap lather.

"Shouldn't he wipe his face first, Da, before you take him in?" Joshua Dimm asked. "I want to see what he looks like."

So did Lord Kimbrough. He tossed the man a towel.

The highwayman scrubbed at his face, then made the earl a mocking bow. "Jack Windham, at your service."

"Windham? That label is on my list somewheres," the senior Dimm declared, reaching into his inner pocket for his notebook.

Foster was staring at the accused, a man not much older than his own twenty years. "Why, I know you. We played cards at Banning's place one night."

"I'm sure I lost. I always do. Do I owe you money,

then?" He jerked his head toward a box on the cupboard. "Help yourself."

Kimbrough's eyes were narrowed. "Windham, eh? Any relation to Lord—"

"My uncle," the man answered quickly, glancing at the crowd of stablehands in the doorway, mouths agape.

"What the bloody hell is any nephew of Lord—" Kimbrough began, to be interrupted by the Bow Street man.

"Aha! I got him now. This here is one of the blokes what lost so heavy to His Grace afore the murder. My man reported that Windham was with a doxy at the time."

"Patsy is a loyal thing, if a tad mercenary. And of course I was one of those whose vouchers Arvid Pendenning held. Why else do you think I would be doing this?"

Kimbrough shook his head. "You've taken to the high toby to pay a gaming debt?"

"Not just a gaming debt. Denning won everything I owned and then took my vowels. Honor was about all I had left, so I had to pay him off." Windham turned back to the tiny mirror and frowned. "I really do need a shave, old man. I don't suppose . . ."

The earl shouted to his back: "Turn and face me, sirrah, and tell me what honor there is in robbing and shooting innocent people!"

"I never meant to shoot Ashcroft, I swear. He threw his whip at me and my horse reared. The gun went off by accident. As for taking up the bridle lay—debtors' prison was a certainty, Tyburn tree was a gamble. I'm a gambler." Windham shrugged. "I thought the family name could stand my death better than my disgrace. And this was the only way I could pay Denning back, or his widow, as it turned out."

"Then I take it you never received Her Grace's note?"

Windham sneered. "Desperate criminals on the hideout seldom get regular mail delivery, my lord."

"Too bad, fool. She cancelled all of Arvid's debts. He cheated."

The highwayman threw the towel to the ground and stomped on it. "Blast! Then you mean I'm going to hang for nothing?"

"Why, no. You are going to hang for highway robbery, assaulting a peer of the realm, and possibly murdering Denning."

"You can't lay that on my dish, and I can prove it. I was on Hounslow Heath at the time, robbing two carriages. You want evidence?" He stepped toward the cupboard, with all the pistols following his move. He tipped the box onto the table and pawed through the contents. "Here's Lord Lithgow's snuffbox; this is Mr. Harriman-Browne's fob."

Dimm chewed on his pencil. "He's right. I remember thinking I was happy to get the Denning case 'stead of the robberies that same day. Still, we got us a confessed criminal."

"What we've got," Lord Kimbrough told the Runner, "is the nephew of one of the most highly placed men in government."

He whispered a name in Dimm's ear that had the older man sighing, "His nibs ain't going to be happy about this 'un a'tall."

Lord Kimbrough turned to Windham. "You say all of the booty is here? All the money you stole?"

"Of course, every shilling. A few more pigeons and I'd have enough to pay back my debt. I don't care that Denning cheated. I do not welsh on my debts to widows and orphans."

"Jackanapes," the earl muttered, feeling very old, very tired. He pulled Dimm out of the tiny house for a conference.

When they returned, Dimm collected the loot to be restored to its owners. Then he set off for London to collect the reward, if he could explain matters to his superior. Lord Kimbrough went home to pack. Then he traveled to Bristol that very morning with Foster and the younger Dimm, along with His Majesty's latest conscript for the Army.

Once he saw the official papers signed, the nodcock's uncle notified, and the ship's anchor raised, Carlinn took a room at an inn and slept for two days. He woke refreshed and reinstilled with a sense of mission. Bath was not far out of his way home. He'd stop and pay his respects to Miss Edelia Sherville. But somewhere between Bristol and Bath, the earl found just what he was looking for. And he couldn't very well call on Miss Sherville with a three-legged Border collie under his arm.

Chapter Fifteen

$\mathcal{M}$ax was in love. The little terrier followed the collie bitch around and did not let her out of his sight. One wave of Sal's tail sent the fluffball flying, so at least Max learned to mind his manners. For her part, Sal seemed to understand instantly what she was supposed to do. Carlinn did not even have to wrap the baby in lambskin, as the shepherd had advised, thank goodness, for he wasn't eager to sell that plan to the duchess.

The shepherd was sad to part with Sal, for he'd raised her from a pup, and her mother, too. But she'd been caught in a poacher's trap, and a three-legged dog was just no good out on the dales with the sheep. The herder hated to put a good dog down, but he was a working man who just couldn't keep a big, hungry animal as a pet. He already had a one-armed brother-in-law.

The deal pleased the sheepman, who went home that much richer, and Kimbrough, who'd convinced himself that making the duchess more comfortable in Berkshire was the right and proper thing for him to do. Somehow his guardianship of the infant overflowed its paper boundaries to include the mother's peace of mind. Carlinn refused to consider how that had come about.

Marisol wasn't sure she was comfortable with the collie at all. Sal was the best-mannered dog the duchess had ever seen, but that was not saying much, considering she was used to Arvid's barely civilized foxhounds or social lapdogs like Max. But Sal was devoted to Nolly. If he cried and no one came soon enough, the dog threw her head back and howled. If anyone entered the room, her hackles rose until Rebecca the nursemaid or Marisol told her "Friend." She knew who was allowed to bring things into the room, and who was allowed to carry the baby away. On her brief excursions away from the baby, to the kitchens or outside, she was restless and whiny, until she could lope with her peculiar gait back to Nolly's room, check the crib, and take up her position in front of the fire.

Marisol couldn't have asked for a better bodyguard for her son, especially with Dimm's son Gabriel to watch over the dog with a pistol at his side, just in case Sal forgot.

The highwayman was captured, Boynton had journeyed to a house party in Kent, and Sal recognized Aunt Tess as a friend. Marisol had nothing to worry about, except her brother, of course, and minor household matters. So unperturbed was the duchess, in fact, that the earl was able to convince her to go on a short outing, especially when he informed her in that blunt way of his that she looked like death on a dish, from lack of healthy outdoor color. They drove in his curricle to visit that flooded parcel of land, so Kimbrough might explain what the engineers had advised. She left Nolly for a whole hour. Even more astonishing, she spent that hour in the earl's company without once coming to cuffs with him.

So she thanked Lord Kimbrough and started getting out and about a little on her own. She didn't accept social invitations, both for Nolly's sake and as a sop to the dowager's mourning. But she did return a few of the local ladies' afternoon calls, she and Aunt Tess. Mostly the duchess enjoyed her brief visits to the child-filled vicarage, where she and Mrs. Hambley discussed the need for a larger school in the district, so girls as well as boys might learn their letters and possibly some skills to better their lives. With the work to be done for such a project, Marisol found that she needed a wet nurse after all. The dowager didn't gloat too much. And Marisol didn't wait too long before telling Sal the dowager was a friend.

Settling in to local life and motherhood, Marisol started thinking of gardens come spring. It was almost here now. The Kimberly ladies called once after the christening, and the London Season was all Bettina wanted to talk about. Marisol wouldn't miss it a bit.

Her letters to Foster were full of Nolly's latest accomplishments, of course, and the doings of the little village of Pennington, and her callers, especially Lady Bettina's wide-eyed fascination with everything to do with London. *"I wish you were here to chat with the girl,"* she wrote, *"since I cannot satisfy her curiosity with any pleasure on my part. London holds no fond memories. Certainly I was never as eager as Lady Bettina for my presentation. Her own brother says he dislikes everything about Town and doesn't want to think about it until he has to face her debut, next year."*

Marisol realized her letters would bore Foster; he hardly knew the Berkshire neighbors, and she didn't even have any London gossip to impart. By the time she got to the newspapers they were weeks out of date.

That's why she was so happy to greet Mr. Dimm when he called after a visit to the vicarage.

"Come to see how my boy Gabriel is doing with the dog and the babe, and if you've heard from that brother of yourn," he told her over a hearty tea, after admiring the baby's growth.

"Your house must seem empty now, with so many of the younger people finding employment here in Berkshire."

"Wouldn't say it was 'zactly lonely, not with my sister still keeping house and the occasional in-law dropping by. Then there's that boy we aren't sure who he goes to." He stacked a cucumber sandwich atop a watercress sandwich and put the whole in his mouth. "But it's getting so I can hear myself think nowadays, and that's no bad thing."

Curiosity made her ask if he had done any more thinking about Arvid's murder, and if people were still talking about her in London.

"I can't tell you 'bout the Quality, by Jupiter, but in my circles, they're talking a mite too much for my comfort. His nibs ain't happy that we've still got an open book on the case."

"Then there's nothing new?"

"Well, there is and there ain't. Jack Windham's alibi holds; so does Lord Armbruster's."

"Oh, you found Armbruster's ladybird?"

"Not 'zactly. I finally found who Lord Armbruster visits at that there love nest, but it ain't going to make a difference in the case."

"His, ah, bit of muslin vouched for him, then?"

"His bit o' muslin wears it for a cravat."

Marisol had to think about that for a minute. She quickly glanced in Aunt Tess's direction to make sure that her innocent aunt was still busy with her knitting. "Oh."

"Worse. Not only wasn't Armbruster not meeting a high-flyer, he was meeting the under secretary of the Exchequer. I figure that's why I was sent on vacation, like. Warned off. Hanging offense, don't you know."

Marisol didn't care about Lord Armbruster's hanging if it wasn't to be for Arvid's murder. "Perhaps that was why Lady Armbruster was so concerned when she found herself breeding."

"Right, Armbruster must of knowed he couldn't be the father. Might've been happy to have an heir, might've been furious. He swears he didn't know. My thinking is she hadn't told him yet, waiting on what Denning said that day. Still, Armbruster didn't kill her or the duke, so we're nowhere, 'cept I'm out of a job if I go near Armbruster again."

Marisol was disappointed, but not terribly so. She never thought quiet Lord Armbruster could have shot anyone. Then again, she never thought quiet Lord Armbruster could have . . .

"Oh, by the by," Dimm was saying, "do you have the address of the mother of that ladies' maid of yourn in London? The servants at Portman Square don't have it. I want to ask her a question or two again. Be surprised what people remembers when they have more time to think."

Marisol shook her head. "No, but the employment agency must. Or else they'll give you her new employer's address. She'll have a position by now, since I wrote her a good reference. Check there, or with Purvis, I suppose. Arvid's valet might know, though he must have a new direction by now, too."

"Not yet. The others say he's talking of emigrating to the colonies. Tired of waiting on swells, they say, but it might just be sour grapes that he ain't found a job."

"I wonder if Lord Kimbrough would consider taking Purvis on. Heaven knows the man looks like he dresses in the dark half the time."

"Been seeing much of his lordship?" Dimm asked casually as he made a selection from the pastry platter. "I called there, but he was out and about."

"No, we don't see much of him these days," Marisol said, angry to hear the petulance in her voice. "That is, I understand the earl is very busy. He is getting things ready so the county can survive his absence for a few weeks when he goes to Bath."

"Bath, eh? Taking the waters, is he?"

"Taking a wife, if gossip is correct. I am surprised you hadn't heard."

Dimm choked on his third macaroon.

Marisol never put much stock in the servants' grapevine, not even the almost infallible Dimm network, but she'd heard this rumor from the earl's own sister.

"He says he's going to see if there's a suitable house to let," Bettina grumbled. "As if I want to go to fusty old Bath. And Carlinn hates it there, too. He had to go once to recover from a wound, and I remember him complaining how there was no company except invalids and old ladies."

"Then why is your brother going, especially when he seems so busy having to oversee Nolly's property in addition to his own?" Marisol felt guilty at all the extra work pushed onto the earl's shoulders, broad though they might be. "He isn't feeling downpin enough to seek a cure or anything, is he? Those broken ribs from the curricle accident have healed, haven't they?"

Bettina laughed. "Carlinn? He's healthy as an ox. You must know he thrives on hard work. No, I'm afraid this latest start of his is my fault. Not exactly my fault, perhaps, but on my account. Carlinn told Cousin Winifred that he wished I had a female relation among the ton to take me in hand before I blotted my copybook."

"I'm sure that's not what he meant. He must have been wishing for someone who knew all the hostesses and all the rules, to take you around. That does make things easier."

"Yes, but then he said it was time he started thinking about setting up his nursery."

All of Marisol's recent warmer feelings for Kimbrough slipped away, leaving a knot of icy disdain behind. She forgot about the dog, and how the earl had helped Foster, and how conscientious he was about the Denning holdings. Kimbrough was going to seek a proper wife, was he? Someone who could produce both Bettina's successful Season and the necessary heirs. He'd most likely line up the eligible females and select the one with the best breeding, the widest hips, and the largest dowry. No, Kimbrough didn't need a wealthy wife, no more than Arvid had. The earl would want a more mature lady so she could chaperone Bettina, but otherwise it was the same. Another poor female would enter another cold, loveless relationship, where her lord and master made sure he got good return for his investment, then went his own way. Perhaps she'd shoot him.

"And then," Bettina was going on, "he asked Cousin Winifred about her goddaughter who lives in Bath. Edelia Sherville; do you know her?"

Marisol smiled. Edelia Sherville wouldn't have to shoot Kimbrough; she'd bore him to death. Yes, the duchess knew Miss Sherville; they had shared a Season. And yes, she was everything proper and correct. She was attractive, accomplished, well connected, and even well dowered, Marisol believed. She was also the most self-consequential person Marisol knew, after Kimbrough himself. What a perfect couple, two perfect jackasses! Truly it would be a match made in heaven; unfortunately they'd be living next door.

Marisol reproved herself for uncharitable thoughts. She didn't know why the thought of Lord Kimbrough's wedding should be distressing; surely the man was entitled to a happy marriage. And if Miss Sherville was his choice, well, Edelia was no green girl being sold on the Marriage Mart. She'd only accept Kimbrough if she wanted an oversized, fusty churl, or if she thought she could reform him. Marisol wished her good luck. She also wished, for Bettina's sake, that the earl had asked his cousin about her goddaughter merely out of curiosity or family feeling.

Carlinn had asked Cousin Winifred about Miss Sherville because he wanted to make sure she hadn't fallen into any bumblebroths or betrothals while he dithered in Berkshire.

"I'm sure I would have heard if she accepted any of her beaux, Carlinn, but what do you mean, has Edelia gotten into any hobbles? She's a lady, Cousin, not a hoyden. Edelia Sherville does *not* fall into scrapes."

Cousin Winifred's emphasis gave him pause, but not enough to change his plans. That was what he wanted: a wife above reproach. He packed, he left instructions with his staff, he held one last conference with the Denning bailiff, he paid his farewells to the duchess.

Marisol was in the morning room when he called, the baby kicking his legs in the air on the sofa next to her, the dog Sal at her feet. Carlinn paused in the doorway to admire the picture they made, the warmth shared between mother and child, the love that made Lady Marisol almost beautiful. Until the butler announced him. Then that mask of hauteur fell over her face. The chin rose, the nose went in the air, the duchess was back. He could almost see the strawberry leaves and ermine. Blister it, the woman changed moods as often as his sister changed her outfits. Today, he could tell, the duchess was as prickly as homespun drawers.

Marisol's greeting was cool, her wishes of Godspeed tepid, and her regards to his family perfunctory. Carlinn got up to leave after ten minutes, refusing tea because of the press of packing. The duchess wrapped the baby in his several blankets and picked him up to walk Kimbrough out. Before they reached the door, however, a huge commotion erupted in the hall beyond, with thuds, clunks, crashes, shrieks, and curses. The earl made to go see.

"No, my lord, please stay here. This is obviously a domestic crisis, and your presence will only embarrass the staff at such an awkward moment. I'll go. Here, you hold Nolly."

And she handed over the baby. Just like that. "But, ma'am, I've never—"

"Then it's time you learned," she said from the doorway.

Carlinn looked down at the pile of blankets in his arms—the child weighed almost nothing—and said, "I cannot believe you'd trust me with him."

"I don't. I trust Sal. Stay, girl. And do not worry, my lord, you'll do fine. Just hold his head up." And she was gone.

Hold his head up? The last time someone said something like that they were talking about an artillery cannon. "'Old 'er 'ead up, boys," some old, grizzled sergeant used to yell, warning the cannon was loaded. Lower the barrel and a live ball was liable to drop out among the troops. My God, he thought, holding the infant farther away from his body, what did the duchess have in mind?

Embarrassed servants be damned, Carlinn started to follow Marisol out the door. Sal had other ideas. Her orders were to stay. Stay she would. The big dog got between Kimbrough and the door. The fur on the back of her neck rose; the lips over the long white fangs lifted.

"Friend," Carlinn called in his cavalry-command voice.

"Grr." Sal marched to a different drummer.

The earl slowly backed up until he felt the sofa behind him. He sat, gingerly cradling the baby. The dog sat, tongue lolling, tail wagging. "Good dog. Good baby."

But the baby wasn't being good. He was starting to screw up his face and turn red. Oh God. Carlinn jumped to his feet and started pacing, three-legged

Sal following with her eyes. The movement calmed the baby some, but his arms and legs were thrashing in the blankets. "Want the coverings off, do you, old chap? Can't blame you. She's got you done up like a straitjacket."

But when he started to place the baby down, Nolly started to cry and Sal started to whimper. Carlinn snatched him up again. Like trying to juggle eggs, the earl tried to unwind the constricting blankets. And keep Nolly's head up. And keep walking, but not toward the door. "And don't drop it, whatever you do," his lordship muttered to himself, wishing he had another hand to wipe the sweat off his forehead. Why did they have to wrap the creature in so many layers? It was deuced warm in here.

Finally the baby was more or less free, except for the death-grip Kimbrough had on him. Nolly turned his face into Carlinn's chest, got a mouthful of blue superfine, and started sucking. "Dear Lord, not that!" He shifted the light weight around, so Nolly was more or less upright, and close enough to get a fold of the earl's neckcloth in his mouth. "No!" Carlinn almost shouted, but caught himself in time when he saw furrows appear on the little brow, making Nolly look like a thoughtful old man. He stuck his thumb in the baby's mouth. "It's the best I can do, old chap. Don't blame me; blame her for leaving you."

Nolly wrapped his hand around the earl's thumb and looked up at him. The gray-blue eyes stared into Lord Kimbrough's brown ones almost assessingly, as if wondering just what kind of guardian he was going to be if he couldn't provide a snack. The earl was mesmerized by that clear stare, the tiny fingers, the downy hair, and petal-smooth skin. The infant smelled of talcum and weighed next to nothing, and frowned his disapproval like the most superior of aristocrats. Like his mother. And he was so soft, like his mother.

Then Nolly spit out the earl's thumb, with a quantity of drool, and smiled up at him.

"As changeable as your mother, too, Your Grace," Carlinn said, grinning back and thinking that he was right to get to Bath. The sooner he offered for Miss Sherville, the sooner he could have one of these all his own. One without that Laughton Nose. And hopefully one that didn't leave a damp streak down his fawn breeches.

Chapter Sixteen

Bath was as awful as he recalled, only worse. This time Kimbrough wasn't recuperating, so he didn't spend his time bathing or resting. Without those activities, there was hardly anything to do, as the clerk at the White Hart informed him. The Pump Room, the Tea Room, the Upper Rooms, the Lower Rooms, the Gardens: That was Bath. Slow walks and promenades, twice-weekly assemblies, once-weekly musicales, card parties. If the pools weren't so crowded with gout-ridden oldsters, he'd go swimming anyway. And Bath was everything he hated about London, only smaller and not so smelly, except at low tide. Here was all that constant bowing and hat-tipping, changing one's clothes by the hour, being surveyed and audited, all without the escape of the gentlemen's clubs.

There were coffee houses, to be sure, but some doddery old windbag was liable to interrupt Kimbrough's newspaper reading to ask his opinion on the latest war news. He didn't know the latest war news; London papers took longer to get here than they did to Berkshire.

On a walk through Sydney Gardens, he was just as likely to be accosted by retired officers as retiring spinsters, women of a certain age, women of uncertain incomes. Were there no youngish gentlemen in the town?

Carlinn's original plan was to happen upon Miss Sherville by luck—and a bribe to the hotel clerk to find which giddy entertainment she'd be enjoying—but he changed his mind. Another day dawdling around would have him complaining of his rheumatics. Besides, who could make tittle-tattle out of a duty call to his cousin's goddaughter?

The six simpering matrons in the Sherville drawing room, that was who. Six pairs of eyes watched him cross the room to the Sherville ladies, to express his cousin Winifred's greetings and regard for Lady Sherville's health.

"Why, 'tis as tiresome as ever, as I'm sure Winifred must know. I just wrote her last week. But I do find the Bath climate salubrious."

Salubrious? Carlinn found the climate about as healthful as the air around that bog he was draining. Right now, in the overheated drawing room, he was finding the atmosphere positively oppressive. Or was that because of the six pairs of watchful eyes? Lud, how he wished he could loosen that blasted neckcloth!

"So what brings you to Bath, Kimbrough? Can't be your health; you're looking disgustingly robust."

He wasn't sure whether to apologize to Lady Sherville or say thank you, so he just explained the mission he'd created.

"Oh no," Miss Sherville exclaimed, "you mustn't bring Miss Kimberly to Bath now. It is the summer which is positively gay for the younger set. The Regent's crowd flocks to Brighton, but families and such come to Bath. Sydney Gardens are at their finest then."

So were his mother's perennial borders. What, should he give up the fishing and riding and the most productive time on the agricultural estates? And why did Edelia's words make him feel old? From what he'd seen, though, Edelia was correct. Tina would be miserable in Bath, where a horseback ride required a day's outing.

From what he'd seen of Miss Sherville, however, he was correct in making Bath his destination. She was lovely in her morning gown of oyster-shell luster, fashionable without being flashy. Every auburn hair was in place on top of her head; there wasn't a single curl to tempt a man to tuck it back. She had a small, slightly rounded nose, thank goodness, and pleasant hazel eyes. Those wide-set eyes bespoke neither a dewy-eyed virgin nor a fiery temptress, but a chaste, clear-gazed maiden who wouldn't play her husband false. She even modestly lowered her eyes under his scrutiny.

His own gaze dropped, then rose. Better not dwell on that distressingly untempting neckline.

The proper twenty minutes for a social call passed quickly, with no interruptions for babies or dogs or importunate relations. His seat was immediately taken by a clerical gentleman who posed a question about last week's sermon, and an ex–India colonel took Miss Sherville's other side with a mention of the war news. Politics and religion; now those were fitting topics for the drawing room, not all that twaddle about fashions and balls his sister was always prattling on about, nor the latest crim. con. stories that surrounded Denning Castle.

Before leaving, he asked if Miss Sherville would walk out with him to give advice on renting a property, in case he decided to take a place for the summer. Which he would do if Berkshire or Hell froze in July, whichever came first. But the six pairs of eyes were nodding and passing their scrutiny over to the two newcomers, so his request must seem plausible.

Miss Sherville highly recommended those residences in the Royal Crescent as the most fashionable. They were also the most closely connected, cheek-by-jowl dwellings he'd seen outside a London slum. They were elegant, of course, and pleasing to the eye, but there was no land! Just the cursed endless hills they were climbing up and down at a snail's pace, to suit the speed of the female in black who trailed behind. Carlinn didn't know if she was a maid or a paid companion, for he'd never been introduced, but Sal could have taken lessons in watchdogging from the old crow.

That night he had a dance with Miss Sherville at the Assembly Rooms. Just one, for she was promised for the rest to a clutch of middle-aged Romeos with pomaded locks, creaking corsets, and snuff-stained fingers. Two were even in wheeled Bath chairs. Kimbrough assessed the competition while doing the pretty by every wallflower and widow in the room; he wasn't worried. He also wasn't tired when the Assembly ended at the stroke of eleven. So he was happy to walk back to his hotel rather than take one of those dratted sedan chairs where the polemen grunted at his weight with every step, hoping for a bigger tip.

The following morning he made one loop of the Pump Room with Miss Sherville on his arm to fetch her mother a glass of the foul waters, before his arm and company were politely but carefully dismissed. In the afternoon, he took one cup of tea before his allotted time was expired. He played one hand of cards with her that night before partners were switched. No, there would not be idle gossip about Edelia Sherville. There would also be no getting closer to the female without a formal declaration.

Damn and blast, he couldn't just propose. He wasn't ready. Besides, a woman expected to be courted. Circumspection was all well and good, but the devil take it if he was going to act the mooncalf under the eyes of every Bath tabby.

But how could he get to know her, to see if they

would suit, if they were never alone? And how many days was the deuced thing going to take before he could go home?

He suggested a ride out of the city. She thought her mother would be delighted for the drive. A shopping expedition? The lending library? Miss Sherville organized a party of her friends, with luncheon at one of the coffee houses. Such conduct would have been considered fast in a girl his sister's age, Edelia confessed, straight-faced, but she considered herself above the most confining social strictures.

Then why the hell wouldn't she step an inch off the path at Sydney Gardens? For heaven's sake, Duchess Denning was willing to sleep with a rifle at her side and thumbed her nose at society by not wearing full mourning. And the duchess drove out with him with no chaperone and entertained him in her nightrail without blushing. Granted, Lady Marisol was a married woman, a mother, a widow, but she couldn't be much older than Edelia Sherville. In fact, she seemed much younger, except in experience. Kimbrough reminded himself that he didn't want an experienced bride, a woman of the world. He wanted just what Miss Edelia Sherville offered: a dignified gentlewoman who understood the proprieties.

Then he reminded himself again. And again the next day.

Never before had Lord Kimbrough appreciated the mayhem that entered his life with the introduction to Duchess Denning. Never before had he received one of her urgent summonses with such delight. Actually the duchess hadn't requested his presence back in Berkshire at all, nor had she suggested the groom ride neck or nothing to deliver the message. She'd just written to inform him of the occurrence, but no one in Bath had to know that.

"I am saddened to have to shorten my visit with nothing settled," he hinted to Miss Sherville, her mother, the six members of the Greek chorus, and the ever-present black-clad dragon. "The rental property, of course. But there is an emergency in Berkshire; a neighbor needs my help. The messenger almost rode his horse into the ground to get to me, so I must leave at once. Thank you for making my stay in Bath so pleasant. Farewell." Miss Sherville permitted him to take her hand and kiss the fingers, which was the closest he'd come to intimacy with the woman in a sennight.

Carlinn left Bath faster than Marisol's messenger had entered it. And happier.

The emergency in Berkshire was that Foster Laughton was home, and a hero. He was wounded, Marisol wrote, but the doctors were optimistic. She hadn't wanted Lord Kimbrough to hear the news elsewhere and be concerned. So he wasn't, and took his time on the return, not pushing his horses, not taking chances with bad weather or muddy roads. Freedom was a heady brew and Carlinn was going to enjoy every last drop.

He supposed the duchess expected him to entertain the lad, or speak to the War Office about a promotion now that Foster had distinguished himself. Perhaps he would.

Or perhaps he'd have the young marquis drawn and quartered.

"Bloody hell," Kimbrough shouted when he saw how matters stood. "Why didn't you tell me to hurry back?"

The duchess slammed the door in his face and went back to the room where Foster lay on a sofa. The baby gurgled over some toys on a blanket on the floor, and Aunt Tess knitted in the corner. Sal kept watch from the hearth, and Max chased a ball of yarn. And there, leaning over the sofa, hanging on the invalid's every word, bringing him lemonade or a cool cloth for his head or a book to be read aloud or a guessing game, was not the nursemaid, not milady's abigail, but Kimbrough's own little sister! Entertain young Laughton be damned! Carlinn would see him entertained in the afterlife, if he didn't stop ogling Bettina's chest when she leaned over that way. And where the deuce was Cousin Winifred? Was ever a man so besieged by rattle-pated females?

Foster, it seemed—and Kimbrough read the newspapers to verify the details—was indeed a hero. His troop ship, in convoy, had caught fire just two days before landing in Lisbon. The fire was not due to any enemy cannonade, but to a carelessly smoking seaman in the munitions cargo hold. Suddenly there was pandemonium aboard the ship, with explosions and burning sails, flying sparks, falling masts.

The captain's dying words were "Abandon ship" so the first mate and half the navy crew did, leaving the army recruits and their few inexperienced officers to fend for themselves. Men were trampled in the stampede for the longboats; others just jumped overboard. Then Foster proved his mettle. He ordered his batman Joshua and the highwayman Jack Windham to stand by the lifeboat lifts, pistols in hand, to make sure the men made an orderly retreat.

Foster, meanwhile, went below, dragging injured naval officers and enlisted men up on deck to be carried to the boats and safety. When everyone he could find in the smoke and flames was away, he had Joshua and Windham launch the remaining boats, manned or not, so the men in the water could be rescued. The three of them rowed and rowed, for hours, it seemed, prying panicked soldiers away from burning debris. Over Joshua's protests, Foster even dove into the water to haul out exhausted swimmers until another of the convoy ships got close enough to send out boats.

All the survivors were taken aboard the second

ship, which proceeded on to Lisbon and the army surgeons. The uninjured and those whose wounds were minor were sent to join their units; the more seriously hurt were left on board and returned straightaway to England. Jack Windham would get his preferment in Portugal; Foster Laughton was a war hero, without his feet ever touching foreign soil.

Now he was home being feted by the neighborhood, as helpless as Nolly, his burned arms and chest swathed in gauze and ointments. Joshua Dimm had been promoted, but sent home to care for his officer, who needed to be fed, dressed, and diverted from his pain and discomfort. Foster's favorite diversion, it seemed, was Bettina Kimberly.

"Damn and blast!" her brother cursed again. "You should have seen the look on the little snirp's face," he told his cousin, who was home with a head cold. That was why she wasn't chaperoning Bettina, although Winifred had thought the duchess, her aunt, and the dowager ample protection from one bedridden soldier. She guessed not, with Cousin Carlinn wearing a hole in the Aubusson carpet with his angry pacing.

"She looked like one of those martyrs in the stained glass windows who's just been told he's going to heaven. Why, I couldn't loosen her from the boy's side with a pry bar. I was right. She needs a firmer hand at the reins." He kept pacing. Cousin Winifred blew her nose, hoping she'd be well enough on the morrow to go visit dear Foster and precious Noel. Carlinn's next words intruded on her thoughts of calves' foot jelly and mustard plasters.

"Your goddaughter Edelia was so helpful to me in Bath, showing me around, introducing me to her friends, that I thought I should repay the favor."

"I'm sure a note would not come amiss. Edelia would never expect anything more. She is a very polite sort of girl."

"Yes, and that's even more reason I thought you

might want to invite her for a visit. She'd be a good influence on Bettina. Show her how to go on, that kind of thing."

Somehow he'd gone from a thank-you note to an invitation while Winifred sneezed. She blinked. "You want me to invite her here?"

"Of course. Nothing out of the ordinary in that; you're her godmama. If I were to extend the invite, naturally tongues would wag, perhaps expectations might even be raised in certain quarters. But it cannot be pleasant for her in that musty old town with those octogenarians for company. And her mother is amply cared for, so Miss Sherville can enjoy a vacation away from the dismal place. Lud knows she deserves one."

"Here? You expect me to invite Edelia Sherville here? In the middle of winter?"

"It's not wintery at all," Carlinn said, ignoring the cold wind that had his ears stinging during the ride home. "Why, it's almost April. Before you know it, there will be flowers, and fishing."

"Fishing? You really think Edelia will enjoy fishing? You did say you had a chance to meet her, didn't you?"

"Puttering around the garden, then, or going for long rides to pick wildflowers. You know, spring in the countryside. What could be more lovely?"

"To Edelia? The assemblies and teas and card parties and musicales her letters are full of."

"Yes, but she must like the country somewhat, mustn't she?" It was time he found out, for he did not intend to spend another day of his time in Bath. London was entirely out of the question. "She does ride, I hope?"

Winifred wiped her nose and tried to recall if Edelia had ever mentioned a horse in her letters. There was that horse-faced Miss Kilborn who visited Bath last month and came away engaged to a dyspeptic viscount. "Bath is very hilly, you know. But yes, Edelia did take her turns in Rotten Row during her Season, I'm sure. You mustn't expect a delicate female like my goddaughter to spend all day in the saddle the way you do though, out and about on the property from morning till night. I expect she wouldn't even approve of Bettina's neck-or-nothing style. Edelia wasn't raised in the country, Cousin, so she is liable to have different interests. I don't think she'll come."

Carlinn thought of the jackstraws who made up Miss Sherville's court, that pasty-faced baronet with the rasping cough, the prosy cleric, or the jug-eared widower with four children. It did not take any great degree of vanity for him to say, "She'll come."

Chapter Seventeen

She came. Edelia Sherville was no country-woman, but she was no fool, either. She was prepared to admire the bucolic beauties, from a distance, of course, and endure. This was her ticket back to London. Oh, how she missed the theater, the opera, the balls, and the shops. Oh, how she cursed her mother's ill health that made their residence in Bath so necessary. Oh, how she regretted not accepting any of those offers that she'd turned down in her first Season, hoping to make a better match in her second.

"Oh, how lovely," she enthused as Lord Kimbrough pointed out the view of the formal gardens from the glass doors in the library. Would she like to stroll there? How silly, but her slippers would be ruined. A ride about the estate later? She had in mind doing a watercolor of the ornamental lake, as seen through her bedroom window. A walk through the home woods searching for the first daffodils? She had promised her mother to practice the pianoforte faithfully.

Edelia was happy to accept Kimbrough's offer of

a drive into the village to visit the shops—until she saw the shops. All three of them, if you didn't count the butcher. But she did enjoy sitting up beside the handsome earl, so expertly tooling his elegant rig down the roads. She'd have enjoyed it more, had there been anyone of distinction to notice their passing instead of the cows and their equally bovine keepers. And the inn, where she'd felt the need for a restorative cup of tea before the return trip, did not even boast a private parlor. Miss Sherville sipped her beverage quickly and downed her sweet roll in haste, before the blacksmith or some such took a seat next to her. Mama would be horrified.

The earl was pleased. "There, you should come out more. The fresh air does wonders for the appetite and puts roses in your cheeks."

Miss Sherville spent the rest of the day in her room applying Denmark Lotion to her skin.

Cousin Winifred also spent a great deal of time in her chambers. Miss Austen's new work having arrived on her difficult goddaughter's heels, Winifred decided to have a relapse, leaving Edelia's entertainment—and chaperonage—to the earl and his sister.

"La, I don't know what Mama would say. Of course I realize manners are less strict in the country, but a girl can never be too careful."

"Miss Sherville, I assure you, you are in no danger of being compromised." Bludgeoned, maybe, not compromised. Perhaps the visit was not a good idea, Carlinn decided, coming at a time when he was too busy to devote himself to Miss Sherville's amusement. Work on the streambed was continuing, as well as the improvements on the Denning properties. And the occasional chess game did seem to get Foster's mind off the pain he was undoubtedly suffering.

The earl's busy schedule and Cousin Winifred's retreat left Edelia more and more in the company of Bettina, whom she considered a hoydenish schoolgirl in the throes of calf-love. Miss Sherville was having nothing of such Turkish treatment, especially when she could turn it to her own advantage.

"Your sister is left to her own devices too much, my lord," she did not hesitate to inform her host, cornering him in his estate office. "A young girl like that needs to be more strictly supervised. Why, she should be preparing her wardrobe for her Season in London, not coming home with her skirts all muddied. I would be happy to lend my advice, if you agree Lady Bettina should pay a visit to Reading to have some new gowns made up."

"Tina knows she has but to send for Madame Molyneaux if she needs anything, and besides, she's not to make her come-out until next fall." He shuffled some papers. She didn't take the hint.

"The fall? Next year?" There went Miss Sherville's hopes for an early wedding. "But never tell me you'll present her at the Little Season? Why, she's old enough to be presented right now."

"I see no reason to rush young girls into these things. Besides, I'm sure some dashing young man will come sweep her off her feet the minute she shows her face at Almack's, and I'm not ready to part with her yet."

No one had swept *her* off her feet, Miss Sherville thought bitterly. Out of sheer spite she told him, "If you are not careful, she will form an entirely unsuitable connection here in the country and she will never make her curtsies at Almack's at all."

"Laughton? No, I am convinced she'll outgrow her infatuation for the boy. Especially if I don't come down the heavy and make him seem like forbidden fruit." That was the duchess's wisdom talking; Carlinn would have tossed his sister into the nearest carriage headed for the Antipodes else. "It's only hero-worship, after all."

"Lieutenant Laughton? The marquis is well

enough, I suppose, now that he's made a mark for himself. Not a feather to fly with, of course. But it's the sister I was referring to. The Coach Widow. Absolutely ineligible."

A pencil snapped in Kimbrough's hands. "She is innocent," was all he said.

"Of the murder, perhaps. But what of the rest? Why, I hear she's not even in full mourning for her dead husband."

"The situation was out of the ordinary." Kimbrough uncomfortably found himself making excuses for the duchess. "And there is the baby to consider. He likes bright colors. Why, you should see him with Mr. Dimm's waistcoat, and these gold buttons of mine were a big hit this . . ."

Miss Sherville's painted-on eyebrows were raised almost to her hairline.

Edelia resumed her attack over luncheon, when Bettina announced she was going to visit at Denning Castle that afternoon. She had promised to read to Lieutenant Foster, she declared, challenging anyone to gainsay her.

"But perhaps Miss Sherville would rather meet some of the other neighbors, Tina." Carlinn tried for diplomacy.

"Then perhaps you should take her, brother dear," his sister shot back, still angry with him over his early words about Foster, even more furious that he and Cousin Winifred were foisting this porcelain princess off on her.

"Maybe we could all go call on Denning Castle tomorrow. You really must see it, Miss Sherville, for it truly is a singular bit of architectural history, with its restored battlements and—"

"No, thank you. I am sorry I must refuse to meet your neighbors, but it is not at all the thing, as I have mentioned. And you, Lady Bettina, would do well to heed my example. A girl cannot be too careful of her reputation if she wishes to have a successful Season. You should guard your name better, for a female is also known by her associates."

Cousin Winifred, who had joined them for luncheon, stepped in before Tina could retort. "I am sure the duchess is unexceptional. My stars, you should see the wonderful work she's doing with the local schools and helping the vicar see to the needy."

"Schools? The needy? The woman is a pariah, a social outcast. Of course she has to bury herself here in the country, busy with good works."

"Marisol is a true lady!" Bettina cried, throwing down her napkin.

Her brother quelled the incipient tantrum with a frown, then he turned his lowering look to Miss Sherville. In a quiet voice, he said, "Denning Castle has suffered enough from gossip and ill will. The Duchess has proved to be an asset to this community, and as such deserves our respect. Foster Laughton is lying wounded in his country's service. But even if she were less of a lady, and her brother a cad, Noel Pendenning is still my ward, requiring my attention to his welfare. Therefore my family"— his eyes moved first to Bettina, then to Cousin Winifred, before coming to rest on Edelia, who was patting her mouth with a serviette—"shall all visit Denning Castle tomorrow, with the duchess's permission, of course. You, Miss Sherville, are welcome to accompany us."

Edelia stalled, folding the napkin into tidy corners. Kimbrough was furious, she could tell, and that little minx Bettina was smirking. Even her own godmother had turned against her. If she didn't pay that call on Denning Castle, she may as well pack her bags and return to Bath. Instead she smiled, showing all her perfect teeth. "La, I do keep forgetting that country standards are not so exacting. I can see you are all won over to poor Marisol's side. Oh, didn't I tell you we were acquainted from our first Season together? Lovely girl. I really must pay my respects now that I am in the vicinity, mustn't I?"

"What's a dog doing here?" Edelia hissed into the ear of the lady next to her on the sofa. All those suits of armor, battle-axes, and maces were off-putting enough, but a big hairy creature that was crippled besides? Edelia's idea of a house dog was more that shaggy little thing dancing around in search of crumbs, not Cerberus guarding the gates of Hades. She sat rigid on her side of the couch, afraid of moving lest she draw the beast's attention to herself.

"What's that?" Miss Laughton asked loudly enough that she—and everyone else—could hear. "What about the dog?"

Lord Kimbrough leaned over. "That's just Sal. She minds the baby. She won't bother you unless you threaten Nolly."

That brought to mind another source of Miss Sherville's discomfort. Babies were to be brought forth, admired, then dismissed. What was this one doing here, at tea? She whispered to the earl, "Why is it not in the nursery?"

"Nolly? Oh, he's our local entertainment, aren't you, my lad?"

The earl plucked the infant out of its mother's arms while Bettina wailed, "Unfair! It was my turn!"

Edelia couldn't believe her eyes; they were nearly fighting over possession of that damp, squirmy article. If that weren't bad enough, on top of the dog, Kimbrough was dangling the child in front of her rose-colored muslin gown, which must already be covered in dog hair.

"Would you like to hold him?" the earl was offering, as if he held the Crown Jewels instead of a grubby brat.

"No. No, thank you." Cute? Edelia had never seen anything less appealing, unless it was the sight of that Lieutenant Laughton, recumbent on the opposite sofa. Edelia couldn't bear to look at him, with his bare patches of raw, red flesh. The least they could do for company was cover him up in more than the bandages and dressing gown he now wore. Miss Sherville turned her eyes away.

Unfortunately they landed on an unprepossessing little man in a red waistcoat and tight-fitting unmentionables. When Kimbrough caught her direction, he explained that Mr. Dimm was with Bow Street, but he was here today to see his son, who had come home from the army with the lieutenant. His son-in-law, married to Lady Marisol's maid, had also been on the hospital ship carrying the wounded home from the Peninsula. Ned Turner was abovestairs now. Another of Dimm's sons, Kimbrough went on with a straight face and a twinkle in his eyes Edelia was too offended to see, was the fellow in the corner with the pistol in his pocket.

Edelia needed all of her upbringing to stifle the scream in her throat. How could Marisol have permitted herself to sink so low, she wondered, turning her parlor into a nursery, a sickroom, a kennel, a thieves' den? Murder was one thing, but such a lapse of proper conduct was quite beyond the pale. And she was sadly off her looks, Edelia was gratified to see, positively blowzy. To think she, Edelia Sherville, had been jealous of the twit for capturing Arvid Pendenning in her first Season.

At least the dowager duchess was there representing good ton, Edelia was relieved to see, and in full mourning, too. Her Grace was acquainted with Miss Sherville's mama and many of the other Bath biddies, so there was news to relate and messages to convey. Edelia could politely ignore the rest of the room's occupants, instead of continuing her previous impolite disdain.

Soon the gathering had divided into other smaller groups. Aunt Tess and Cousin Winifred were vying with the tea tray for Mr. Dimm's attention; Foster and Bettina were engrossed in a book whose title neither of them knew or cared. Rebecca the nursemaid came for the now-sleepy baby, and left accompanied by the big dog and the bodyguard.

Lord Kimbrough asked Marisol to walk apart with him, to discuss a new tenant for one of the vacant cottages, he told the others. When they were at the other end of the room, ostensibly admiring an ancient tapestry on the wall, he apologized for inflicting Miss Sherville on her and her family.

"Think nothing of it, my lord. I assure you, I am more than familiar with Edelia's kind. Be happy the Hambleys did not drop in, children and all. Miss Sherville might never have recovered." She thought he muttered "Too bad," but must have misunderstood. "I suspect she is simply out of her element here. My, ah, casual style is not what she is used to, in Bath or in London."

"About London, Duchess. I'm sorry to have to inform you that you'll have to change your plans about London."

"My plans? I have none that I know of."

He ignored her protests, concentrating on the difficult news he had to impart. "According to Miss Sherville, and I have no reason to doubt she is *au courant* with the current tittle-tattle, word about your lack of mourning is common knowledge, along with tales of Arvid's indiscretions." He stepped closer to the tapestry, examining a section depicting blackamoors leading tigers on leashes. "None of the mess has been forgotten. You will not be received. I was informed by Lady Sherville herself that I was tolerated only because I was a man and could be forgiven my part in the imbroglio. The rumor mill will not deal as kindly with you."

Marisol shook her head, dislodging a curl from its ribbon. "You were tolerated, my lord, because you are a wealthy bachelor peer. I am a wealthy widowed duchess. I would be accepted eventually by all but the highest sticklers, unless they had a son or brother to settle, but thank you for your concern. And I must remember to thank Miss Sherville for hers," she added dryly. "However, I have no intention of putting my luck to the test. I do not plan to go to London anytime soon."

"Of course you do. It's your way of life," he insisted.

"What, leave Nolly and my responsibilities here for the pleasures of Town?"

"That's what every other woman would do." It was certainly what Edelia Sherville would do, and they both knew it.

"Thank you, my lord, for the thought. And I am sure Edelia will be relieved that you consider a true lady most at home in London. But I can only repeat, *this* is my home. I am not Edelia Sherville."

Together their eyes moved across the room to where Edelia was still in conversation with the dowager, still turning her back on the rest of the company as if they were beneath her.

Carlinn couldn't help contrasting the auburn beauty with the blonde at his side. Edelia was perfectly groomed, *point device* in thin, low-cut muslin, and shivering, while Marisol wore a soft dark blue merino with long sleeves and a high collar. She looked warm, comfortable, inviting. He wiped that last thought from his mind and turned back to the tapestry. One tiger was leaping, in the midst of capturing a rabbit for all eternity. Somehow he knew how the rabbit must feel.

"I apologize again. I should have known better."

"What, the Earl of Kimbrough apologizing twice in one day? Unheard of!" She smiled to lighten his mood. "Besides, I might want to go up to Town next year or so, do the shops, the opera, and such. It would be infinitely more comfortable to have Arvid's murder solved and forgotten. It's too bad Dimm cannot find any more clues."

Together they looked toward the trio around the

tea table. "Though I do not know how he expects to uncover any evidence in London when he spends most of his time here in Berkshire flirting with Aunt Tess."

"What, are you matchmaking there, too, Duchess?" Carlinn demanded.

Her smile disappeared. Her chin rose. "That is none of your concern, my lord. You can try to keep your sister from a misalliance, but my aunt and Mr. Dimm are none of your affair."

"My, how easily you fly into the boughs, Duchess." He tapped her nose with one finger. "I was teasing. I meant to save Mr. Dimm for Cousin Winifred."

They shared a laugh, but Carlinn noticed how quickly her smile faded. He thought she must still be troubled over the talk about her reputation. And she was looking tired, he realized, rebuking himself for battening his entire family and difficult guest on her at one time. How could she not be exhausted, looking after Foster, the baby, and the new school? And her maid was no help, with the abigail's husband also needing nursing. "Have you been getting out at all, Duchess, other than your parish work?" he wanted to know.

"What, going to parties and such? Now that would set the county on its ear. I do keep to some kind of mourning, you know."

"Yes, but you are entitled to some pleasure, too. How would you feel about a small dinner party among neighbors at Kimbrough Hall? The adult Hambleys, Squire and his sons, perhaps a few others. No one could find fault with that."

No one but Miss Sherville, who had turned to watch them, obviously impatient with her neglectful escort. Carlinn sincerely believed the duchess needed time away from the infant and the invalid; he also believed it was time he established mastery of his own household. If Miss Sherville did not like his friends . . .

Marisol also looked to Edelia, and felt the other woman's barely concealed loathing. A night out sounded marvelous, but what pleasure could there be in seeing that jealous cat sitting at Kimbrough's right hand?

"Come, your brother can't have all the valor in the family."

But she didn't have to decide. The dinner party was cancelled when the note arrived at Denning Castle. *If you care about Denning's brat,* the message began.

Chapter Eighteen

If you care about Denning's brat, the note read, *leave 200 pounds in Hyde Park at 5 P.M. Tuesday next*. Below was a rough sketch of the park with an arrow to one path, an *x* marking the third bench past an ink blot. No, that must be a landmark of some kind, a big tree or a monument. Marisol could not quite recall that particular footpath; she was more familiar with the carriage ways along Rotten Row. No matter, she'd search out that third bench as if her life depended on it—or Nolly's.

"You'll what?" the earl yelled, not believing his ears. "You'll go pay this cockamamie ransom demand when they don't even have the boy? Are your attics to let, woman?"

"Don't you dare shout at me! And yes, I'll go give them anything they want so they leave us alone."

"Leave you alone? This is only the beginning. If you pay them now, you might as well put them on your payroll! I've never heard a more paperskulled idea. I forbid it!"

"You cannot forbid me anything, my lord. I have my own accounts to draw from."

The earl tore his neckcloth off and threw it to the ground, so he could shout louder, it seemed. "You nimwit, this is not a kidnapping, this is just extortion! You don't pay someone for making threats!"

Marisol jumped to her feet and stood glaring at Lord Kimbrough. "What would you have me do, wait until they harm Nolly, then pay them? Now that is being penny-wise and pound-foolish in the extreme, my lord."

"This has nothing to do with money, for heaven's sake!"

"It has everything to do with money! I have it, and they want it! Two hundred pounds is a small price to pay for my son's safety."

"And that's another thing. What kind of maggoty blackmailer asks for two hundred pounds when they have to know you're worth thousands? You cannot do it."

"I can and must!" She stomped her foot for emphasis. "I'll get that money to Hyde Park with or without your approval."

"That's fine," he said with a sneer. "The duchess is back in command. You'll ignore my advice just to prove your superiority. What will you do, flounce off to London and leave Nolly here unprotected? Then again, you've hardly left him out of your sight for his—what? four months?"

"Nearly five. Some kind of guardian you are," she muttered, "not knowing your ward's age."

"Just so. Nearly five months. So what do you intend, to take him with you to Town? You might as well hand him over to these cockleheaded criminals now, along with his fortune, for there is no way to protect him in London."

"I hadn't thought of that," she said quietly, sitting down again.

Carlinn sat beside her and took her hands in his. "I know, Duchess. You're only thinking with your heart, not your head. But you can't, for Nolly's sake. A threat like this is meant to arouse fear, that's all. If you give in, they've won without doing more than writing a letter. We can keep Nolly safe here; you know we can."

An army of relatives, trusted servants, and dogs surrounded the baby. He was never left unattended by less than two people and one dog. He was never brought into a room without it being checked for lurkers first and never taken outside except in a phalanx of adults. The grounds were patrolled regularly, the village was on the alert for strangers, and Marisol kept her embroidery scissors on a ribbon around her neck. Even Lord Kimbrough had taken to carrying his pistol with him, and Dimm's son Gabriel was never out of shouting distance, with his ready weapon.

"Nolly is safe, until someone shoots Mr. Dimm's son to get to mine! We cannot live like this, Carlinn!" Neither of them noticed her use of his first name, nor that he still held her hands. She felt better for his strength; he felt better for giving what reassurance he could. "Don't ask me to live in fear for the rest of my life, my lord. I cannot do it."

"Of course not. Dimm and I have a plan to capture the extortionists."

Marisol groaned. "Oh no, not another trap. I won't let you use Nolly as bait; I swear I won't."

"You really do get mushbrained under pressure, don't you? You'd never find a place on Old Hooky's staff, that's for sure. If he's hoping for aide-decamp, Foster had better hope he didn't inherit your skitterwits along with your nose."

"What's wrong with my nose?" she asked, diverted as he intended. "And my wits, of course?"

Carlinn patted her hands, got up, and was already pacing. "Your wits have gone begging, my girl, if you think I'd endanger Nolly in the least. No, we'll leave the ransom under the bench, all right, but it will not be real money."

"Yes, it will," she insisted. "Otherwise they

might be angry enough to follow through with the threats!"

He frowned at her. "Blasted pigheaded female." But he kept pacing. "Then we—Dimm and I—stand back and watch who comes to fetch the loot. Then we follow the fake money—"

"No!"

"The real money then, in case the pick-up person is merely a messenger. We see where he delivers the package and, *voilà*, we have the blackmailers."

"What does Mr. Dimm think?" Marisol asked, doubt coloring the question.

"He thinks we might even find Arvid's murderer at the end of the trail. He's off checking now, but he is almost positive that the handwriting on this note matches the message that sent you out to Denning's carriage that day. There's got to be a connection. He also thinks that the demand of two hundred pounds is peculiar."

"It's so low?"

"Right. It eliminates suspects like Boynton. He gambles away more than that before lunch."

"Are you still suspicious of Boynton? I thought he was content now."

"He's still the one with the most to gain if . . ." He let that thought trail away. "But not for two hundred pounds. He'd hit you up in person if that was all he needed. I thought it might be a good idea to send for him anyway, where we could watch him, just to make sure."

"I'll write asking him to come stand watch over Nolly. He never leaves without hinting about some tailor's bill or a new pair of boots, so he'll come."

The earl nodded. "Dimm says the low demand sounds more like some poor sod needs the money to get out of town or something, like Arvid's valet going to the colonies. Dimm doesn't suspect the man—he had nothing to gain except unemployment—but Dimm is looking into ship departures for next week and recent bookings. Maybe he'll turn up something there and we never have to bother with the ransom."

"You keep saying 'we.' You and Dimm have already decided on this plan, then? You weren't even going to consult me?"

"Now don't go getting on your high horse, Duchess. Of course we were. I am. Right now."

"It's too dangerous. And they'll be expecting me."

"No, the note just said leave the money, not that you had to be there. I doubt they'd be wanting to see anyone who might recognize them."

"But that's all the more reason I should go!"

"Definitely not! And don't argue, or I'll have you bound and gagged. Foster gave me permission. He's already aggravated he cannot go help since he cannot hold a pistol or make the carriage ride, so sitting on you is his job. Besides, I need you to stay here to help entertain Miss Sherville."

"I'd rather face the blackmailers."

Kimbrough grinned. "So would I."

Edelia thought Lord Kimbrough's taking himself off to London a capital idea. In fact, she, his sister, and his cousin could all accompany him. She knew he wouldn't wish to leave the women under his protection alone in a neighborhood of such desperate goings-on.

"What, you think you will be safer in London? With all the raff and scaff of the metropolis?"

"But you will be there to protect us, my lord," she flattered, batting her lashes.

"I'm sorry, but I shall be too involved in this effort to trap the hoodlums to be a proper escort."

Edelia wasn't giving up. "Then we'll have time to do the shops and see the sights. You wouldn't wish your sister to appear the gapeseed when she does go up to Town, staring at everything like a cabbagehead. This would be the perfect opportunity for her to gain a bit of Town bronze before the ton returns."

"Miss Sherville, thank you for being concerned for my sister's welfare, but this is not a social call I am paying. It is a very serious matter, possibly even perilous, and will take my full attention. I could not think of having you or Bettina in London at the time."

"And just what am I supposed to do for the remainder of my visit then, with my host nowhere in view?" she demanded.

What she was *supposed* to do was be a gracious guest to her godmother, who had, in fact, issued the invitation. She was supposed, Kimbrough thought, to go for walks and rides and visits to the neighbors, none of which she'd been content with so far. One more week and she'd be back in Bath, thank heaven. Thank heaven twice that he hadn't made any commitment.

To Miss Sherville, the invitation had been as good as an offer. There was no way she was going to wring that proposal out of the slowtop if he wasn't even in the county, though. And for certain she was not going to stay by herself in this benighted place where the nearest neighbors were up to their eyebrows in havey-cavey doings. Not if there was no chance of bringing the Elusive Earl up to scratch. "Perhaps it would be better if I shortened my visit."

"You must please yourself, of course, but I was hoping you would be a companion to the duchess in this trying time. You said you were old friends. I'm sure she'd find comfort in that."

Marisol Laughton? Edelia should sit holding that frumpy blonde's hand? Marisol was the one who married a rich duke and now seemed to have a rich earl sitting in her pocket. "Don't you think you are taking your guardianship of the boy a little too seriously?" she asked spitefully. "I mean, extending your care to the child's mother? That really should be the prerogative of her brother ... or her husband."

The earl loosened his suddenly tight shirt collar. "Her husband is dead, Miss Sherville, and her brother is incapacitated. I am only doing what any gentleman would do in my place."

"How lucky for Her Grace," Edelia sniped, sure now she had lost the battle. "I think I should prefer to go home. Rather than being a comfort, the duchess must find guests an unwanted burden at this difficult time." To say nothing of dangerous. Edelia had no intention of stepping foot in Denning Castle again, not with armed guards and vicious dogs and puking infants who were subject to kidnapping. "Good manners dictate that I cut short my visit under the circumstances."

"But I cannot accompany you home at this time, Miss Sherville. I can put a carriage at your disposal, and outriders, if that is your wish, but I have no male escort to offer. My sister and my cousin feel needed here, helping to look after Foster, so you would only have your maid for chaperone. It is not what I can like, but if you insist . . ."

Edelia was thinking on it. Traveling back to Bath without an engagement ring wasn't what she could like, escorted or no. If she stayed, she might have another go at getting him up to the mark when he returned from London. On the other hand, Kimbrough might be highly titled, as handsome as he could stare, and as rich as Croesus, but there was no denying he was as firmly planted in the Berkshire soil as an old oak tree. With a few squirrels in his upper branches. Oh, he might drag himself to London for his sister's presentation, if the chit didn't run off with that Laughton boy to follow the drum. But after that? He'd stay right here in the country with his outré neighbors, forever and ever. Earl or no earl, Bath was preferable to that.

Miss Sherville was still trying to decide where her best interests lay the day before Kimbrough was to leave for London. Then Lord Boynton came to call. She'd stay. What elegance of fashion, what address, what fulsome compliments he paid!

"What? You've got the Sherville heiress next door, Marisol? 'Pon rep, I knew my luck had changed with old Arvid's passing. She's Golden Ball Sherville's only child, don't you know. And that Grosvenor Square house they own is just sitting there empty. With the father dead and the mother in Bath there wouldn't even be in-law problems. Could even set up my own private gaming hell. Dash it, I always said you were the best of sisters-in-law! Thankee for sending for me, m'dear."

Marisol sipped at her ratafia. "But, Boynton, I didn't send for you about Miss Sherville. It's Nolly's future I'm concerned over, not yours. You've waited this long to marry an heiress. It never occurred to me that you'd be interested."

"Time comes for all men to bite the bullet, m'dear. You've been more than generous, but I can't live off m'sister-in-law forever, don't you know. That's what they make wives for." Boynton patted her shoulder. "And don't worry your pretty head about the little chap, m'dear. Makes frown lines. Tell you what, I'll fork over the two hundred pounds myself. I'm flush this week, what? Better yet, I'll give you a draft on my bank. That way you can set someone to watching the bank when your culprit tries to cash the check. Of course, we'd have cancelled payment by then anyway. I do it all the time." Boynton was grimacing at his waistcoat. "Coral will never do for calling on an auburn-haired beauty. What do you think, m'dear, should I change into the white marcella or the puce brocade?"

Marisol bit her lip. "I'm not sure Miss Sherville shares your enthusiasm for fashion," she hinted. "Edelia is a very proper sort of female."

Boynton adjusted the black arm band he wore. "Right, the gray satin stripe."

"But, Boynton, I believe she's turned down two offers just this year," Marisol tried again. "Edelia is very fussy."

"Of course she is. I daresay heiresses can afford to be as fussy as they want. I suppose I ought to bring the chit flowers. Mind if I gather a posy from the conservatory?"

"I, ah, think that Lord Kimbrough had in mind to make her an offer when he invited her to the Hall." Marisol wasn't sure why the idea bothered her so much, but it did.

"Pooh, he don't need her brass. I do. He's going to London to take care of this little dilemma for you; I'll take care of Miss Sherville for him. Neighborly, don't you know. He'll thank me."

So would Marisol.

Chapter Nineteen

"*Traps* is like women," according to another of Jeremiah Dimm's teachings. "They's some what puts out lures, and they's some what plays hard to get. The ones what turn their backs are the ones what get a man every time. Now, you take lions. You want to trap a lion, you can set out some bait and hope he shows up for you to get a net on. Else you can try to chase him into a corner somewheres, hoping he doesn't turn on you. Or you can do what the natives do, and use your noodle. You find a path your big tabby takes. You dig a deep hole, then you cover it over with leaves and branches, so it looks natural, undisturbed. You put out your bait. Then you go away. You turn your back, he shows up, you got him, and he ain't got you."

Kimbrough wondered how many lions the Bow Street Runner had ever seen, much less captured. Then again, he also wondered how many crooks Mr. Dimm had captured.

The money was the bait. The absence of armed guards and sentinels was the big pit. Natural and undisturbed, that was the key. The plan was fool-proof.

So Carlinn set out for Hyde Park at the fashion-able hour. Of all of London's absurd conventions, he considered, this one was right there with Venetian breakfasts that took place in the afternoon. A man couldn't really ride in the park, the lanes were so congested, and driving a carriage was worse, with all the stopping to raise your hat or bow. Bowing in a curricle was a boneheaded idea in the first place; keeping highbred carriage horses standing around was worse. Most ludicrous of all was walking, for on foot you were then obliged to make chitchat with every passing toady or climber, or pretend to ignore them by striking up conversations with mere ac-quaintances. Either way, you never made progress, so why bother going for a walk in the first place? To be seen, of course, which was the whole point of the Promenade. Which was why Lord Kimbrough never went on the strut, even when he was in Town.

But here he was, bowing and tipping his hat, smiling at dowagers airing their pugs in landaus, and sidestepping young gamecocks atop more horse than they could handle. And it wasn't even the height of the Season. He could see whispering be-hind fans as he passed by, speculation in gamblers' eyes. They all wanted to know what he was doing in Town; luckily his reputation kept them from ask-ing. The earl kept walking, swinging his cane as if he hadn't a care in the world, as if he weren't curs-ing every last popinjay among them. Natural and unperturbed, hah!

He moved through the knots of carriages, horse-men, and strollers, and set out for less congested areas of the park. Following the map, he took a path that paralleled the Serpentine, where nurse-maids and their charges were feeding the ducks and a small boy was sailing a toy ship. Carlinn thought of his ward. This folderol was worth it for Nolly's sake, and Marisol's.

He passed an area less cultivated, where laughter from the bushes told him young couples were enjoying the seclusion. Here he could even notice that the trees were coming into bud and the grass was definitely greener. The whole of winter had gone by without removing his name, or hers, from society's list of suspects in Denning's murder. He quickened his step.

One more turnoff and he was back to a path made too narrow for horses by the benches on either side. Fewer pedestrians walked here, and those who passed were not of the same class as those near the park gates or on the carriage ring. Here was a young woman pushing a pram, a student eating an apple as he pored over a book, and a uniformed park employee scything the grass.

There was the monument, a verdigris knight on a charger so thick with pigeon droppings Carlinn couldn't read the plaque. He walked on, whistling. On the first bench past the monument, a gentleman in an old-fashioned bagwig sat feeding squirrels out of a sack. On the second bench a grandmotherly woman was reading a story to a schoolboy in short pants. The fourth bench held the prone form of a tattered old man whose snores almost toppled the bottle of Blue Ruin by his side. The third bench was blessedly empty. Relieved, Carlinn sat there for a bit, polishing the brim of his beaver hat with a handkerchief until a distant clock struck the hour. Five o'clock. He checked his watch on its fob. Goodness, time to go change for dinner. He replaced the timepiece, replaced the handkerchief, and almost by accident dislodged a small, sealed parcel from his inner pocket. The packet managed to slip under the bench while Carlinn gathered his cane and his hat. He set the hat on his head just so, as if he didn't have to doff it a hundred times before quitting the park. Then, swinging his cane and whistling, he ambled back toward the park gates where everyone and his uncle could see the Elusive Earl heading home. Natural and undisturbed, that was the ticket.

He got into his closed coach and had the driver pull away. Two blocks later he pulled the check-string and ordered the man to turn around, to go back and pull up opposite the gate and wait.

Carlinn had recourse to the flask in the door pocket while he sat there, wishing that he could have been the one to hide in the park waiting for the quarry to tumble into their ditch.

The first one to knock on the coach door and come inside was the young park attendant, scythe and all. "Quitting time," said Jeremiah's youngest son, who was currently employed in his lordship's stables. "Da said it would look peculiar-like was I to stay on. No one's picked up the package yet, though."

The grandmotherly woman, Dimm's sister Cora, stepped up to the coach next, assisted by that young boy some cousin had dropped off in Hill Street, Kensington, and forgotten to fetch. The lad was happy to scramble up beside the coachman, meat pasty in hand, after seeing his aunt seated across from the earl.

"No one would keep a boy out on a park bench past his dinner hour," Dimm's sister declared, "so Jeremiah signalled us to leave. Thank goodness, for I swear we read that story till the sprout knows it by heart. Oh, and the parcel is still there."

They waited some more, until the student, Dimm's nephew studying his anatomy text, reported in. "It's getting too dark to read by, my lord. Uncle waved me off. No one has approached that third bench since you left."

Carlinn put them all in a hackney and sent them home. He drummed his fingers on the door handle. Deuce take it, their pit-trap was growing shallower by the minute. That lion could climb right out again, after taking the bait.

The gentleman feeding the squirrels rapped on

the carriage. "Sorry, can't stay any longer," he said when Carlinn opened the door. "Important meeting at Whitehall. I've been out of nuts for hours anyway, my lord."

"Thank you, your nibs, ah, your honor. I really appreciate your making this effort."

"Like to see this case closed, my lord. Like to see every case closed. Won't happen tonight, by George."

"No, sir, it doesn't appear that way."

The chief magistrate shook his hand and shut the door again.

It was full dark when Dimm climbed into the coach, brushing off his coat and offering the earl a swallow of Blue Ruin. Kimbrough grimaced a refusal. "Did they come?"

"I allus said, no trap is foolproof. They must of recognized one of us, though I don't see how. But they ain't coming today or they'd of been here."

"Hell and confound it. No, they won't come in the dark when we could have constables behind every bush. I suppose I'll just take the money back to the duchess and wait to hear from the extortionists again."

Dimm wiped his mouth on his shirt sleeve. "Well, it's like this, guv. I promised Her Grace I'd leave the brass no matter what, so you'll have a hard time giving it back."

"You mean to say you left two hundred pounds out there for some beggar to find, if the squirrels don't get it first? We'll never know if the blackmailers got the blunt or not, dash it!"

"I promised Her Grace," Dimm repeated.

So Kimbrough took one of the carriage lanterns and picked his path back through the park, avoiding the calling cards left by the carriage horses, staying well away from the banks of the Serpentine, and brandishing his pistol instead of his cane to discourage those who hunted in the park at night. He turned down three propositions

191

from prostitutes, two pleas from paupers, and one approach from a nearsighted pickpocket before reaching the turnoff to the smaller path.

He doused the lantern and stealthily picked his way to the statue, taking up a position near the horse's tail, peering down the path. The packet gleamed white in the darkness, undisturbed by anything but a passing mongrel who sniffed at it, then moved on before Kimbrough had to shout him away. A doxy went by, a sailor on either arm, then a drunk, weaving his way down the path, grabbing onto each bench in passing.

Carlinn held his breath. The blackmailer? No, just a drunk finding his way into the bushes to cast up his accounts. If the fellow didn't land in the Serpentine, 'twould be amazing. If none of the cutpurses and footpads got to him, 'twould be a miracle.

The moon rose, and Carlinn's ire. His fingers on the metal horse's rump were turning blue and, blast, no one was coming to fetch the blood money. He picked it up and went home.

"You did what? Of course they wouldn't come while you were standing there. They must have seen you!"

"Your Grace, no one saw me but some pigeons. I had to throw out a perfectly good hat. They were not coming, period."

"You don't know that! Oh, how could you have taken the money? I mean, so what if you didn't catch them? That wasn't the point!" Marisol jabbed the needle through the gown she was embroidering for Nolly, then back up through the thin fabric. She set those tiny stitches at so furious a pace she never noticed that she was sewing her own gown to the baby's dress.

Carlinn was pacing, as usual. "Oh, sit down, you impossible man. It's enough that you have jeopardized my child's life; you don't have to give me *mal de mer* besides."

"Let me tell you, Duchess, that I did not stand behind the tail end of a metal mount out in the cold for two hours just to put a blight on your life." He sat, but restlessly, drumming his fingers on the chair arm. "It was no pleasure, by Jupiter. And no one was going to come along but some beggar looking for a bench under which to sleep. Your blunt would have made him happy, but that's all. The blackmailers would still be as greedy. Meanwhile, Nolly is safe. Your tormentors will come back, never fear."

"What if they don't? I'll never be able to sleep nights, worrying."

She didn't look well either, he noticed now that he was facing her. Pale and drawn, the duchess seemed to have lost more weight just since he'd been gone. Her dress hung loosely and her hair was more mussed than usual, too. Lord Kimbrough was the last person to quibble over clothes and appearances; he was sitting in Her Grace's parlor in his riding clothes, after all, but he'd been anxious to relate the news. Still, proprieties aside, the duchess's loose and untamed hairstyle, with a ribbon holding back only some of the blonde curls, was disconcerting to him. Not that he would have found fault with the style in a mistress, mind. Instead of reaching out and touching the silky length, he drummed his fingers harder. Dash it, he would not allow her to get to him.

"By the way," he told her, reminded, "Dimm's staying on in London, but he said to tell you he hasn't managed to locate your old maid yet."

Marisol noticed his intense gaze and grimace, and tucked her hair back into its ribbon. She raised her chin. By the stars, Marisol was not going to apologize to him for her appearance, even though she found herself wishing she were in looks for his visit. Besides, if Kimbrough could sit in all his dirt on the dowager's crocodile-legged sofa, then she could leave her hair down when her head ached with fretting. Furthermore, if his clothes could be so unstylish as to give his arms ample room to move, then she needn't be exercised over the fit of hers until she'd regained her figure. It seemed foolish to have her maid alter every gown every week, especially with Sarah so busy. Marisol thought that perhaps next month she'd be ready for a new wardrobe, when Arvid would be dead for six months. Six months was not proper mourning, not by half, but it was all she was willing to give, here in the country. By next month she should have a new maid, too.

"Yes, my Sarah's husband is mending. He wants to go back to Yorkshire where his family has a small textile mill. He'll have a job waiting, unlike so many injured veterans. I am glad for him, of course, but I am sorry to lose Sarah. They won't be ready to travel for a while, but I thought that if Tyson hadn't found a new position, she'd consider returning to my employ, even if I am just a country matron now, quite beneath her dignity."

Marisol Pendenning could never be less than lovely even in her undress, Kimbrough was thinking, putting his first impressions entirely out of his mind. If only he could rid his imagination as easily of thoughts of her undressed altogether. . . . He got up and looked out the window. He was *not* pacing. He was checking the weather. The sky was not quite as blue as her— Thunderation, he was no moonling! He went back to the sofa.

"Dimm says the agency you mentioned hasn't seen the woman, but they gave him her mother's address. He called, but got no information there either. They haven't seen her since Christmas. That valet of Denning's who was supposed to be sweet on her is packing for America, quite openly, nothing furtive. He says he asked Eleanor Tyson to marry him after the murder, but she refused. He hasn't seen her since, he swears, but Dimm isn't sure he's telling the truth on that, for fear of getting her in trouble."

"With Dimm? What kind of trouble could that be? All he wants is to pass on my offer of a job. Certes, it's no big thing. Mr. Dimm says he knows a likely candidate for the position."

"Oh, I'm sure he knows two or three, all relatives of his."

"Blast!" Marisol had just realized she'd sewn the baby's gown to the front of her dress. "Now look what you've made me do, I'm so upset. And using swear words! I never swear, dash it." She started to cut all the stitches she'd just sewn, mortified to look like such a cake in front of him. And the wretch was grinning! "I do wish you'd left the money!"

"Somehow I knew we'd get back to that," he said with resignation. "I did what I thought was best."

"But it wasn't, and you gave your word, to leave real money and all. How could you do such a thing? You listen to me, nod, then go your own way," she complained, as women had for years. "What kind of behavior is that?"

Indefensible, of course, so he didn't try. "I've a bone to pick with you, too. You said this thing between my sister and your brother was only puppy love, childish infatuation."

"Of course it is. Foster is ill and bored and Bettina is sweet and attentive. Helping to care for him gives Bettina a sense of being needed, like a mature woman. Having her admiration restores the pride Foster lost to Arvid and even to you, who stands as his nephew's guardian. Still, he is only twenty and army-mad. He's not ready to take a wife. And Bettina is only seventeen and has seen nothing of the world. Don't worry."

"Strange, you don't listen to me when I tell you not to worry about Nolly. Besides, if there is nothing to worry about, why is Tina suddenly claiming that a London Season is not so important any-more?"

"Perhaps because Edelia is still here, and Boynton now, too. You did tell me to send for my brother-in-law, you know. I'm sorry to have to tell you, and I hope you aren't put out, but those two are as close as inkle-weavers. Edelia even comes to visit Foster now, in the guise of chaperoning your sister in the afternoons when Boynton is between his late breakfast and his early dressing for dinner. London is all the two of them talk about, the latest *on dits*, the newest fashions. Bettina is sensible enough to grasp the shallowness of the tonnish life in Town. It's enough to give anyone a disgust of the place."

"I should take her to Hyde Park at night then to see the pigeons. It would finish the job and I'd never have to go back."

Except to deliver the second ransom demand, of course.

Chapter Twenty

This time the note demanded four hundred pounds brought to the same place, same time, that Friday, without the Runners. It was her last chance to save the little bastard, the message said, sending chills through Marisol's heart. Anyone who could speak so vilely of Nolly could be capable of anything.

She hugged him the harder, and patted the golden curls on his head while he played with the ribbon in her hair. That there were creatures so base they could threaten such a precious little innocent made the world an uglier place. "Don't worry, my angel, the earl won't let anything happen to you." Somehow, to Marisol's surprise, she'd come to believe it was true. Pigheaded and overbearing he might be, but Lord Kimbrough could be trusted. She'd thought never to accept another man's word for anything, never to let another male have authority over her, but the earl was different. He really wasn't like Arvid at all.

This time he swore to leave the money and walk away, after a furious discussion over who should put up the additional pounds. Carlinn felt the blunt should come from him, since his mishandling of the first attempt had raised the ante. Marisol was adamant the duke's estate should defend the duke, that the earl should have no more burden placed on him beyond that of messenger. Resenting the designation of errand boy, Kimbrough had protested. He stormed and he shouted, he paced and he scowled, but he took her money. Arvid would have gone his own way regardless of her objections, and would have flown into an ungovernable rage at her first sign of disagreement. He would never have conceded, or smiled at her afterward. And Arvid's smile never reached his eyes and never warmed her heart, the way Kimbrough's did. "Ah, Nolly," she whispered, tickling the baby's ear, "too bad his lordship is such a stickler for the niceties."

Such a stickler was the earl that he offered to escort Miss Sherville home the very afternoon the note arrived. Her departure date had come and gone, her mother must be missing her, and she should not be subject to more shabby treatment of a missing host. If they hurried, and he rode through the night on the return, he could be in London on time.

Such sacrifice was not needed. Lord Boynton had offered to see Miss Sherville and her maid removed to Bath, at her chosen pace, which involved frequent stops, reservations in advance at the finest inns, and elegant repasts along the way. At the earl's expense, of course.

"Think nothing of it, Boynton," Carlinn told the older man. "You'll be doing me a favor, saving me the trip to Bath. The least I can do is spring for the tab."

Boynton took out an enameled snuffbox and offered it to the earl, who shook his head. When Boynton had succeeded in opening the box with one hand, taking out a judicious pinch, then sneezing into a lace handkerchief—none of which impressed the earl—he said, "Deuced good of you. And can't say I blame you about not wanting to go to Bath. Devilish dull kind of place. Wouldn't be caught dead there, m'self. Actually, suppose I would. Be caught dead, that is. They say it's where old reprobates like m'self go to die. Don't want to end m'days playing silver loo with the biddies, though. Got a better notion, if it don't throw a rub in your plans."

"My plans? What have my plans got to do with anything?"

"Your plans for Miss Sherville. Between gentlemen, don't you know. Wouldn't want to be cutting you out or anything."

Carlinn was able to assure the other man that not only did he have the earl's approval, he had his blessing. "Then Miss Sherville won't feel her trip to Berkshire was a waste. That is, she does reciprocate your regard, doesn't she?"

Boynton puffed out his chest, buckram wadding notwithstanding. "I do believe so, Kimbrough, I do believe. Haven't wanted to put it to the touch yet, of course, not without your leave. You had first choice, what?"

"Sporting of you, I'm sure." Carlinn coughed to cover a laugh.

Boynton didn't seem to notice. "Now that you're giving me a clear field, I'll take the plunge. I mean, Arvid's cocking up his toes like that and all, and my not getting any younger, give a chap pause, by Jupiter. Miss Sherville's a handsome female, what? And knows how to dress. Looks good on m'arm, don't you know. Will look better in that empty house of theirs in Grosvenor Square."

"Ah, part of the dowry, is it? I understood there was enough to purchase any number of London houses."

"Quite, but there's no reason to be wasting all that brass. Need it to keep up appearances, don't you know. Style is everything. Miss Sherville agrees. Well-bred female, thinks just as she ought. Well favored, well dowered; what more could a chap ask?"

Well endowed, Carlinn thought to himself, thinking of another female's soft, womanly shape. Aloud, he just said, "I wish you well."

"And you too, boy-o, happy hunting."

"Hunting? Oh, you mean the ransom note."

Boynton placed his finger alongside his nose. "If that's how you want to put it. Between gentlemen, don't you know. But it happens to the best of us, Kimbrough. Plain as the nose on your face your turn has come, even if you ain't ready to admit it."

Carlinn did have to admit that he knew exactly what Boynton was referring to, but that was as far as he was going. Lud, if this old court card was making book on his fate, Kimbrough's carefully controlled facade must be slipping. It wouldn't do. No, it wouldn't do at all. And it was all that woman's fault. As soon as this ransom mess was taken care of, he'd put her from his mind once and for all. Of course, he'd do his damnedest to see those bastard blackmailers brought to book, and Arvid's murderer, too, so her peace of mind was restored and her name was cleared, so that no one, ever, would think of her as less than a lady. The most infuriatingly exciting, enticing, affectionate, courageous, and beautiful lady of his experience . . . but it wouldn't do.

Dimm was to stay outside the park. He wore his red waistcoat and kept in plain sight, hobbling back and forth near the park entrance. The extra poundage he'd gained recently, from all those fancy teas and lavish dinners, only exacerbated the problem.

"I allus said policing was nine-tenths footwork, but this beats the Dutch. And what am I doing? Nobbut showing the bastards where I ain't." So he limped across the street to the earl's carriage and climbed up next to the driver. He even opened his coat so the redbreast was more visible. "I should be in the park making an arrest," he muttered. To which the driver commented that he'd like to see the day Dimm did anything to earn his keep. Dimm chewed on the stem of his pipe.

Lord Kimbrough was once more making his obeisance at Society's feet. This time the park was even more crowded, the warmer weather drawing the Quality back to London like ants to a picnic. He smiled, he bowed, he refused invitations to innumerable parties and innumerable beds. Behind him he could almost hear the wheels of speculation turning. What in the world was the Elusive Earl doing in London twice in a month? He was only seen in the park, so it couldn't be business; therefore it must be pleasure. A woman, they concluded, quizzing every female to whom he nodded.

Hope even flared that it wasn't a particular woman who drew the earl to Town, but the search for one. A plump matron trailing simpering misses behind her like a row of ducklings even dared suggest he attend her Sylvia's come-out, for they were sure to have much in common. He doubted that. One hard look from the earl had Sylvia—the one in cerise—quaking like a pudding. He moved on, delighted to leave the main thoroughfares behind.

He strode across the grass instead of on the verge by the bridle paths, to avoid the horseback set, nodcocks who called themselves Corinthians because they could sit a fractious beast that didn't belong in the park in the first place, or the peahens trying to show off their seats, their trailing riding habits, and their eligibility all at once.

Bah! Thank goodness not every gentlewoman cared to put herself on display. If he wanted to see fancy equestrian acts, he'd go to Astley's, and if he wanted a bed-warmer, he'd go to Mother Lil's or the opera house greenroom. And if he wanted a wife, well, he wouldn't go back to Bath, that was for sure.

Carlinn checked his watch. Right now what he wanted was to get the parcel to the designated bench. He hurried past the riverbanks where children fed the ducks and the shallows where boys sailed paper boats. At last he was in those deeper reaches of the park that stayed less congested. As he took the final turning, he was pleased to note that the statue was actually being washed down by a park attendant with mop and bucket and damp uniform, not that it would stay clean for long. He was also relieved to see most of the benches were empty. A maid and her young man were enjoying their afternoon off on one of the seats, and a dignified older gentleman read his newspaper on another. A youngish woman in a poke bonnet that hid most of her face sat on the bench opposite the third, rocking a perambulator. She wasn't having much success getting the baby to sleep, Carlinn noted, for he could hear the infant's wails from beyond the monument. He thought for a moment how lucky they were in Nolly. The little duke never carried on that way. Of course, he had any number of adults to cater to his every whimper, but Noel truly was a well-behaved child. Not that Carlinn considered himself any kind of expert, naturally.

He sat on the third bench and checked his watch again and waited for the church bells to mark the hour. The woman across from him was busy with the fussing baby, her head bent over the carriage. Good. At the first stroke of the chime, he removed the packet from his inner pocket. Heavier and bulkier this time, the parcel contained the additional money, plus a plea from Marisol to take the money with her blessings but leave her son alone. Kimbrough slipped the package beneath his seat at the third chime. By the fourth he was on his feet, ready to leave.

Just as the church bells struck the fifth gong,

however, a different noise sounded. "Runaway!" someone shouted back along the bridle paths, and " 'Ware, loose horse." Women were screaming, men were yelling, and hooves were pounding nearer.

The young swain had hustled his sweetheart behind the bench, Carlinn quickly ascertained, and the old gent was on his feet, ready to bolt. The park attendant dropped his mop and came out from behind the statue, peering back toward the intersection. The woman with the baby was shrieking, setting the infant to howling again, on top of the other cries. Carlinn hurriedly grabbed the woman's arm in one hand and the pram's handle in the other and dragged them both over to his side of the path, behind the bench where he could protect them.

"He's coming this way!" the park employee hollered just as a mighty gray stallion, sides flecked with foam and blood, thundered down the path. The uniformed man dove for his bucket of soapy water to toss in the runaway's face, which didn't stop the horse for a second. Then he grabbed for the reins and almost got trampled, without success. The old man waved his newspaper at the brute, and still the animal kept coming without the slightest pause. The bookish-looking beau started out from behind his bench while his companion screamed, but Carlinn ordered, "Get back, you fool!"

Making sure the mother and infant were safely behind him and the concrete bench, the earl stepped onto the tanbark, right in the stallion's way. "No!" He shouted, "Whoa, sir," in tones so loud, so firm, so used to being obeyed, that they finally penetrated the frenzied beast's terrified mind. At least the animal slowed enough to think about running down the large man in his path. The gray's hesitation was long enough for Carlinn to lunge for the trailing reins and wrap them around his fist, digging his heels in the ground as the stallion plunged and tossed his head. By this time the maintenance man was able to grab the cheek strap on the stallion's bridle and add his weight to the earl's to bring the panicked horse to a stop.

"Good boy, good lad," Carlinn crooned, running his hand along the heaving side, where blood flowed from what looked like a bullet crease. "You'll be fine now," he told the animal. "I am sure your rider will be coming along any minute now to take you home."

"I'll walk him a bit, shall I, milord, to cool him off?" offered the park attendant.

"Yes, he's too spent to get up to more trouble. Good job, Isaac."

"And you, milord," said the grinning boy, actually Dimm's son from Kimbrough's own stables.

Carlinn turned around as more people hurried down the path now that the danger was past. The young couple, Dimm's niece Suky from the inn and her brother who was clerking for Stenross, Stenross, and Dinkerly, were helping the older gentleman, Mr. Stenross himself, pick up his newspapers. And the mother and baby carriage were—gone. So was the extortion money.

Diddled, by damn!

"Well, I hope you're satisfied, Your Grace," the earl grumbled. "They've got the money and all we've got for the effort is one scarred stallion." No one had claimed the horse, naturally, especially when he was deposited at the police stable. So Kimbrough took the gray home. He had too hard a time finding a mount up to his weight to leave this one languishing in gaol.

"No," Marisol told him, pouring out the tea. "We've got a little peace of mind and that's worth every bit of the four hundred pounds. Maybe if they read my note, they'll see how much Nolly means to me and leave us alone. If that woman with the baby really was the culprit, she'll understand. I feel much better about the situation now."

She was looking better, too, since he'd sent a note ahead informing her that the money was delivered. Marisol was wearing a blue silk gown that almost matched the color of her eyes, and it clung to her figure enough that he could see she hadn't lost too much weight, only enough to reveal a narrow waist, well-formed legs, and a still-ample bosom.

"In truth, now I can sleep at night without waking up every hour to listen for Nolly's breathing or Sal's growls. I thank you for that, my lord."

He waved aside her gratitude. "You might try calling me Kimbrough then, or Carlinn. I do think we know each other well enough by now, Duchess. You even know how to fix my tea the way I like, without asking."

Marisol found herself blushing like a schoolgirl. She sipped her tea to hide the embarrassment. "And I am sick to death of being *your grace*ed. Please call me Marisol, my—Carlinn." With a faint tinge of color still in her cheeks, Marisol changed the subject away from the personal: "Do you think this will be the last of the threats, then?"

"Only time will tell, but you are an easy mark. The female could not have been acting alone—remember the stallion—hence you cannot bank on her maternal feelings winning the day. I would not want us to relax our vigilance entirely, but yes, I believe you can rest easier."

Kimbrough went home to get his own much-needed rest, but sleep did not come. He kept thinking of lovely Marisol— No, "Duchess" seemed to suit better, especially when she was acting the gracious lady, thanking him for his efforts. He lay in his bed, thinking of her waking up every hour, in his arms, thanking him for his efforts. Every hour ought to do it, for a start. And oh, the efforts he'd go to for her had him breaking out in a sweat. Strange, he'd never once thought of taking Edelia

Sherville to bed, only to wife. Of course, no man wanted a wife who was the subject of lascivious imaginings, did he?

Marisol wasn't getting a good night's sleep either, and not just because she remembered how the earl had kissed her hand and whispered, "Rest easy, my dear." "My dear" was much nicer than Duchess or Marisol. But she still couldn't rest easy, not with the baby crying all night.

It wasn't her baby's crying that kept her up, though, but the crying of the baby left outside the Castle door.

Chapter Twenty-one

"*A* bastard? You mean I went through all that and almost got trampled for Arvid Pendenning's bastard?"

"Yes, and I paid four hundred pounds for him. Isn't he precious?"

Well, no, he wasn't. He was dark and scrawny, with Arvid's narrow eyes and pouty expression. His name was Arlen, the note said, and he was three weeks old. He was also a fussy baby who wouldn't eat well, according to the wet nurse, and hardly slept, according to everyone else in the house. Arlen was quickly settled into the nursery, out of earshot. Poor Sal was in despair, trying to keep her new little herd together and under her watchful eye. Rather than make the crippled dog go up and down the stairs all day, Marisol had brought both children into the morning room, where her maid Sarah was rocking Arlen in a cradle and she was singing to Nolly, to give the exhausted nursemaid Rebecca time for a nap.

When Lord Kimbrough was announced, Marisol dismissed the maid, telling her to go spend time with her recuperating husband. The earl approached the cradle and peered down at the new infant. It was Denning's, unmistakably. One could tell from the petulant curl to the infant's lip. "Fertile bastard, Denning. Sowing his seed in three women at once. His wife, his married mistress, this other woman. Who knows how many other little butter stamps might turn up."

"I wonder who she was, poor thing, that she had to give up her baby." Marisol carried Nolly over to the earl's side and looked down at her husband's illegitimate child. Nolly crammed a fistful of her Norwich silk shawl into his mouth while she was staring into the cradle, wondering if the woman missed Arvid, if he had been kind to her.

"She must be from the lower orders," Carlinn speculated, "that she needed money. A wealthy woman would have gone off somewhere to have the child in secret, then put him out to an orphanage or foster home. If she couldn't, ah, get rid of the problem beforehand."

"I suppose we'll never know. Do you think you could recognize her again?"

Carlinn looked up and started to extricate the shawl's fringe from his ward's mouth. "Silly lad. A gentleman might devour a beautiful lady with his eyes; he doesn't try to swallow her apparel." He turned back to Marisol, who was smiling at his flummery. "No, I cannot say I'd know the woman again. Her bonnet hid most of her face, and then she kept her head down. Not that I would have recognized Denning's lightskirt anyway."

"Mr. Dimm might have. I suppose that's why she wrote that no Runners should come to the park. What does he think? He never mentioned that Arvid had another woman in keeping. I wonder if he knew."

"He didn't say, just that he was going to Bristol on a hunch. Something about wrapping a string around a stone or such."

When the new baby started mewing, Marisol handed Nolly to the earl, as casually as she'd hand him her cape or gloves. She bent to pick up Arlen before he could work himself into a red-faced squall. "Hush, poppet, hush. Everything is going to be all right now. I know you miss your mama, but we are trying our best."

"The doxy didn't seem to have any better luck with the brat than you. Maybe that's why she gave him away." The earl was bouncing Nolly in his arms, getting chuckles and gurgles. "Now, this is what a baby should be!"

"Of course. Too bad they can't all be dukes." Marisol laughed, sitting again and rocking the infant in her arms. Sal dropped down at her feet, tail thumping against the carpet. "I wonder what the mother would have done if we hadn't paid her?"

"Sold him to gypsies, or left him on some parish doorstep, I suppose."

"And we'd never have known. We'd have kept thinking someone meant to hurt Nolly, when the unfortunate girl only wanted Arvid's son to be taken in."

"If that was meant to remind me that I counseled against paying their demands, I stand rebuked." He was dangling his watch in front of Nolly, and told the boy, "Your mother's a hard woman, Your Grace. She never forgets a fellow's lapses, and never misses a chance to gloat. You'd better eat all your porridge or you'll hear about it the rest of your life, how you could have been as big as Uncle Carlinn if you'd only listened to your mama."

He smiled over at Marisol, who really wished he'd stop teasing; it did peculiar things to her insides, like turning them to jelly. "But you were right that Nolly was in no danger," she admitted.

"Ah, a gracious concession. Did you hear that, Duke? In the past six months I have been right one whole time! Amazing, isn't it?"

"Gudgeon, you've been everything wise and kind and brave, and well you know it. I'd tell you how I have come to appreciate you, but shan't, for fear of swelling your head even further."

"A compliment, almost. Nolly, my lad, I think she likes me!" And he tossed the laughing child up into the air.

Blushing furiously, Marisol ordered him not to play so roughly unless he wanted his shirtfront decorated in a fashion Brummell could never approve. Carlinn hastily replaced the child on his lap, where Nolly was content to play with the gold buttons on his waistcoat.

Marisol had rocked Arlen back to sleep in her arms, and now hummed softly to him. Lord Kimbrough watched and listened, until a fierce jealousy swept through him. Denning had two children now, and he was dead! As the earl stared at the duchess, the infant's dark hair a contrast to her golden curls, he got even angrier that it was Denning's child she was cuddling, Denning's bastard besides.

"You cannot keep him, you know."

That brought Marisol's head up with a jerk. The infant thrashed a bit, but stayed quiet. "Excuse me?"

"You cannot keep him, I said. It's too much of a burden. Nolly already takes much of your time and attention. Think of him."

"Are you suggesting I would neglect my son?" she asked, her voice dangerously low.

"No, of course not. I'm only saying that you have enough on your plate without Denning's bastard, too. Why, it will be hard enough to reestablish yourself in Society as is. The ton will forget everything in time if you let them, even Arvid and his lovers, but dragging around the duke's baseborn brat will remind them all over again. You know they won't think kindly of you for making them admit such things happen."

"Why do you persist in this humgudgeon about my vying for Society's approval? I am content here, where I have family and friends and worthwhile endeavors. Let them sneer at me in London. I do not care."

"Very well, I believe you, but think about the boy then. He'll never be accepted. You cannot pass him off as your own; he'll never be anything more than Arvid's bastard, second-rate goods. And his whole life he'll look to Noel, the duke, the heir, the favored son. No boy could help being envious, jealous, no matter what you do for him. That's a hell of a legacy for Arvid to leave the boy, a terrible thing to do to a child. You couldn't be so selfish. You must not keep him."

"Are you quite finished now, my lord?" Her tones could have turned Bath's hot springs to ice. "Are you done with telling me what I may and may not do, even though you have absolutely no authority over me?"

Carlinn kept his eyes on Nolly. "Good intentions. Only thinking of you and the boy," he muttered.

"Are you through? Are you ready to listen to what *I* have decided about Arlen?"

He nodded. But he did whisper in Nolly's ear, "Hard as nails. Remember, I warned you."

Marisol cleared her throat. "Rather than being selfish, my lord, I have been drowning in guilt that I cannot warm to this child the way I ought. I look at him and I see Arvid, his perfidy, his nastiness. I see a mother no better than she ought to be, maybe even a murderess. Little Arlen is not to blame, of course, but he is not an easy child either. Perhaps if he were soft and sweet ... but he is not. Fortunately my maid Sarah is good with him, better than Rebecca, Nolly's nanny. And Sarah has asked if she and her husband can take Arlen with them when they go to Yorkshire. Her husband's injury— Well, the doctors are not certain there will be children for them. Sarah and Ned want to change his name to Leonard and make him their own son, no one's cast-off by-blow. I would be his godmother, and pay for his schooling and such."

"And I'll stand for his first pony! Brilliant, my dear, brilliant! I should have known you'd do what was best for everyone."

"Yes, you should have," she said dryly, then added, "We have sent for Mr. Stenross, to check into the technical aspects of the thing so there is never a question about Arl—Leonard's legal parents, and we'll wait to speak to Mr. Dimm. What if he finds the mother and she wants the infant back?"

"She sold him, for heaven's sake. She won't want him returned. At most she might demand more money, but baby-selling is still a crime, if nothing else. We can threaten her with gaol if she won't sign Stenross's papers. The problem is if he doesn't find her and the woman sells information to the papers, just to hurt you."

"Me? None of this was my misdeed! I didn't bear an illegitimate child, I didn't kill my lover, and I didn't trade my son for a sack of gold!"

"Yes, but people will talk. You can't like being the latest *on dit* forever."

No, *he* couldn't stand being the brunt of tittle-tattle, Marisol knew. Kimbrough was the one who was so concerned with the proprieties that he'd be mortified to find his name in the gossip columns again. He was just like the dowager, who couldn't get Arlen out of the house fast enough, lest she be reminded of her own son's debauchery. And Kimbrough's sister's come-out would be ruined by the hint of scandal, old or new. Carlinn would never do anything to reflect poorly on Bettina's chances of making a brilliant match. He'd never do anything to tarnish his family name or cut up his peaceful existence.

That night it was Marisol's own crying that kept her awake.

Carlinn rode out early the next morning, as was his habit. He took the new gray to evaluate the stallion's recovery, and was pleased to see that the horse was skittish, not mean. A firm hand was enough to keep him under control, even when a rabbit ran across his path. He'd be a safe enough mount as long as the rider didn't lose concentration. The blackmailers could have got him cheap, though, for the otherwise magnificent animal must have been a hazard in the city. With a gun being fired purposely near him, or at him, the wonder was that no one was killed. It was also curious that no one had seen or heard the shooting. Dimm's relatives and associates were still looking into it.

Carlinn rode toward the Castle, expecting to be invited in for a second breakfast. He left the stallion at the Denning stables, after giving instructions for its tending, and carefully brushed off his boots on the way to the front door. Her Grace was sleeping late this morning, however, according to the butler, and asked not to be disturbed. Nolly, Carlinn's second choice, was having a bath, then a nap. So the earl asked after Foster, and was shown up. Foster's smile of welcome only dimmed a bit when he realized the earl was by himself.

"Deuced good to see you, my lord. Dashed flat sitting around, I can tell you. Can't even read the newspapers without someone turning the pages; I tried doing it with my teeth. Only got newsprint on my nose."

"Would you like me to read to you then? I have a bit of time." The longer he stayed, the more likely that Marisol would be up and about. "You must be wanting to hear the latest war news."

Foster rubbed his bandaged hand along the counterpane of his bed. "Well, ah, thing is, your sister kindly offered to stop by this afternoon and do the reading." His face cleared. "But how about a game of chess? I almost had you beat last time. I'm afraid you'll still have to make the moves for me; can't bend the fingers yet with all these wrappings the sawbones insists on. The doctor says soon though. He thinks I can rejoin the regiment before summer. Isn't that capital?"

"Summer in the Peninsula is hot and buggy, full of diseases and mud. Are you sure you want to go? I mean, you've done your bit for king and country already. White or black?"

"But there's bound to be action this summer and I mean to be in the thick of things this time, not on some blasted ship. I had white last time; you can open."

"Your sister will worry." He moved his first man.

Foster was studying the board. "That didn't stop you from going, did it? I mean, all the chaps have mothers and sisters and wives and sweethearts."

"Sometimes all of them. Where do you want to move?"

A few turns later, Carlinn's mind started to wander as he waited for Foster to call his play. Was she stirring yet? Would she come check on her brother before going downstairs? He straightened his cravat. Foster cleared his throat.

"Your turn, Carlinn."

"What? Oh, sorry." He studied the board.

While he pondered his next move, Foster cleared his throat again, which did not aid his lordship's concentration. He looked up.

Foster was rubbing at the bandages again. "I've been meaning to ask permission to write to your sister when I go," he said. "Good a time as any."

"Pardon, you want my permission to write to Bettina?"

"Well, I wouldn't want to do anything harumscarum and give you a disgust of me. It's not the thing, don't you know, for a young miss to be getting correspondence from a man who is not related."

Carlinn allowed as how he might have heard of such a convention. His sarcasm was wasted on Foster, who was intent on making his case.

"Thing is, my intentions are honorable. Not soon, of course. Tina should have her Season. Dance holes in her slippers, don't you know. I've never been a dab hand at cutting a caper, and she's looking forward to it. I'd lay odds she'll be a regular Toast, too."

Carlinn wouldn't take the bet. Bettina was pretty and gay and rich. She'd be a success. Such a success that he had to ask: "Aren't you afraid all those Town beaux might turn her head?"

"It's a chance I'll have to take. That way we'll both know she's sure. Then I'll be asking your permission to pay my addresses. When the war is over, of course."

"And I'd be proud to give it, after you've both seen a bit more of the world, and if you both are of like minds then."

Foster nodded his head and turned back to the board. Then he looked sideways at the earl and queried, "Anything you'd like to ask me before I go?"

Carlinn reached for his knight, then reconsidered. "Like what, chub?"

"Like permission to address *my* sister?"

The knight fell out of his hand onto the floor. "You're beginning to let this courtship nonsense go to your head, bantling. Either that or the hero business."

"Then perhaps I should be asking your intentions, my lord." Foster was only partway teasing. "An eligible bachelor running tame in the household, making morning calls before breakfast—that type of thing can't be good for my sister's reputation."

"You're putting your ugly Laughton nose where it don't belong, Lieutenant," Carlinn barked.

Foster hadn't been in the army long enough to jump when so addressed. Nor had he ever served under Major Lord Kimbrough, for which he thanked his lucky stars. Therefore, he valiantly—or foolhardily—proceeded. "What's the matter with my nose except that new bump in it? I mean, it ain't like Wellesley's honker. Marisol's got the same beak and everyone says she's a beauty. Looks like Noel will have it, too, and I've heard you say he's a handsome lad. Anyway, I thought it was my job to ask about your intentions. Head of the family and all that, don't you know." He grinned. "Luckily I'm not shipping out just yet. You have another month to get your courage to the sticking point."

Kimbrough knocked over the chessboard in his hurry to leave.

Chapter Twenty-two

"Why, Mr. Dimm, how clever of you to find Tyson just when I need a new maid so badly."

Dimm had returned to Berkshire, but not alone. He led the abigail into Marisol's drawing room and kept one hand on her elbow.

"Not 'zactly, Your Grace. That is, I found your maid, Eleanor Tyson, all right and tight, but she's took up a new profession."

Marisol said, "That's too bad," wondering why he'd bothered to bring Tyson then, and why the woman was hanging back after her curtsy, staring at the floor. "What new career have you embarked on, Tyson?"

Dimm answered for the maid: "Extortionist."

Marisol sat back against the cushions. "Those notes? The baby?" No, that couldn't be. Not Tyson and Arlen. Not Tyson and Marisol's husband. Eleanor Tyson had been her dresser for three years; Marisol had trusted her. She shook her head. "No, I cannot believe it."

"It wasn't any choice of mine, Your Grace, I swear," Tyson spoke up. "I wouldn't have hurt Your

Grace for the world, you were always so good to me. But he—"

"Why don't we wait for his lordship to get here?" Dimm suggested. "Magistrate and such. That way we can all hear all of it at once and figger what's to be done."

When Kimbrough arrived, Foster came down, but the dowager took to her bed, preferring not to know any more than she had to. Sarah and her Ned stood quietly in a corner while Aunt Tess was furiously knitting close to the fireplace, where she couldn't hear much, not that her location mattered for that. Marisol would explain things to her later, she said, but little Leonard would need lots of sweaters in Yorkshire now. She refused to consider any other option. The babies were not present. Marisol couldn't bear the thought of Nolly in the room with someone who had sold her own child. Tyson hadn't even asked about Arlen's welfare.

When everyone was assembled, Dimm had his son Gabriel bring in another man, in handcuffs.

"Purvis? Is it really you?" Marisol found that her hands were shaking. She'd written such glowing references for these two, while all the time they'd been plotting her ruin. How could she have been so mistaken, thinking Tyson merely disloyal when the woman was a desperate criminal? To have an affair with her employer, right under his wife's nose, and then perhaps kill him—or have her other lover, the valet, do it—were not the usual functions of milady's abigail. Marisol tried to steady her hands by clasping them together in her lap.

Lord Kimbrough brought her a glass of sherry and stood behind her seat, his strong hand on her shoulder. "Let's hear the whole thing then, Mr. Dimm, before we jump to conclusions."

"Well," the Runner began, "my part of the story starts in Bristol. Purvis here had his name on a ship's waybill, going to the colonies by Robin's barn. The embargo, don't you know. So I weren't half surprised to see him. Then the abigail shows up, the one what's been missing for four, five months. And she's got passage money, too. Wasn't hard to figger."

"But why?" Marisol asked. "I don't understand."

Tyson started to cry. "I swear I never meant to harm anyone." She put her hands over her eyes.

Purvis awkwardly set his manacled wrists at her waist. "Hush, Nell, I'll tell it. It's like this, Your Grace, my lord. I asked Nell, that's short for Eleanor, to be my wife, and she said yes. But His Grace, he said no. He didn't believe servants should marry, he said."

"That's just like the dastard," Foster muttered from the opposite sofa. Lord Kimbrough poured him a sherry, too, which Foster managed to clutch in his bandaged hands.

Purvis went on: "So I waited a bit and then asked him again, seeing as how he was in a rare good humor, what with the baby coming and all. Your baby, Your Grace. The heir, that made him happy to be cutting out Lord Boynton finally. And the duke, he said maybe we could marry, maybe we couldn't. He'd think about it." Purvis stared at his feet. "But he was thinking that if I wanted Nell so bad, he'd maybe better take a second look."

"Oh no."

Purvis nodded. "Yes. I'm sorry, but Your Grace was getting big with the child, and sickly, so his eye was wandering even more than usual. And he did look at Nell. A right pretty lass, my Nell is, too," he said, patting her back with his shackled hands. "And His Grace told Nell she didn't have any choice."

"You should have come to me, Tyson. Eleanor."

The maid looked at the duchess through tear-swollen eyes. "But I saw how he was with you. Everyone knew how he took his temper out on you, poor lady. If you'd crossed him over me, it would only make things worse. I was that worried about you and your baby," she said bitterly.

Now Marisol looked away, embarrassed to have so much dirty linen washed in front of Lord Kimbrough. Understanding, he tightened his grip on her shoulder.

"So I didn't fight him, Your Grace," Eleanor went on. "He said that he'd let us marry when he was done. If I resisted, he said, or cried foul or anything, he swore we'd both be dismissed. So it wasn't rape."

"Of course it was. You had no choice. It was against your will."

"But Purvis didn't see it that way," she said sadly.

"I told you I was sorry, Nell. It was just that at first I couldn't . . ."

"You were not to blame, Eleanor," Marisol insisted with a dirty look to Purvis. "Go on."

"Well, then I found I was increasing, too. When I told His Grace, he laughed and said now I could marry Purvis, and get out. He wouldn't keep either of us on. But Purvis, he didn't want me anymore."

The swine. To Marisol's thinking, there was not much to choose from between Purvis and Arvid. Her glare at the valet spoke volumes.

"But how could I support a wife and child without a position, Your Grace? It wasn't even my child! At least he should have paid. . . ."

"So you made sure he did, eh?" Foster held his glass between two hands and saluted the valet.

It was Marisol who asked, "Which one of you . . . ?"

The maid replied: "First I wrote that note to you, just to get even. Purvis told me where the duke would be and who with. His Grace was bragging something fierce. I wanted you to see what kind of animal he was."

"Oh, I knew, I already knew," Marisol whispered.

"But most I wanted to shame him in front of a real lady, his own wife."

Purvis took up the tale: "When Nell told me

what she'd done, I feared he'd get in a rage, Your Grace. The duke didn't like anyone getting in the way of his pleasures, if you know what I mean. I knew he had taken to carrying that pistol, so I went out to stop you."

"You wanted to protect me?" Marisol asked.

"Yes, and Nell, too, if he figured out she'd written the note. But I was too late. You'd come and gone and so had Lady Armbruster. His Grace was in a rare snit all right. I'd never seen him in such a taking. He was screaming like a banshee, saying I must have been the one to send you after him like that, Your Grace, and I'd pay for it, and you'd pay for it, too. I knew he meant it."

Marisol's shoulder was aching where Carlinn's fingers were digging into the flesh. She patted his hand and he relaxed a bit, but she knew that if Arvid Pendenning were alive and in the room right then, he'd be wishing he were dead again. Hell had to be less painful than what the earl would have done to him.

Purvis shook his head. "I couldn't take his threats no more, Your Grace, my lord. That muckworm, ruining everyone's life that way, and making me turn my back on the finest woman I ever knew. So I told him I was going to marry Nell even if she carried his seed, and if he didn't give us our fair pay, and something to see us by until I could find a place, I'd go to the newspapers and the magistrates and to Lord Armbruster next door. And he laughed. He didn't care, don't you see? He knew he couldn't be arrested for taking liberties with a common maid or withholding pay from unsatisfactory servants. And fornication was as ordinary among the gentry as fleas on a dog. There was nothing I could do."

"So you shot him?"

"No. I didn't have any weapon. I spit on him instead, to show him what I thought of his idea of *noblesse oblige*. I worked for other gentlemen before.

I knew what was right and honorable, and he was none of it. So I spit on him, right in his face."

"Good for you, man," Foster cheered.

Purvis ignored the interruption, still directing his narrative toward Marisol. "You know how he liked everything about him to be perfect?" She nodded. "I thought he'd go off in an apoplexy right there, but instead he took out the pistol and started waving that gun around like a madman. I was afraid it would go off, so I put my hand on his wrist, to keep it pointed away from me. His Grace, he twisted away, screaming at me to take my hands off him like he was god and I was manure. I held on, though, and the gun went off. He was dead, I could see, so there was no point in calling for help. I went back inside but everyone was still at supper, except Nell. No one saw me coming or going, so I kept mum."

"But you could have come forward during the investigation. It was self-defense."

He shook his head at her naiveté. "Who believes a valet? 'Sides, they'd want to know why I didn't speak up first time 'round. I couldn't take the chance, not with Nell depending on me. So I kept my mouth shut. I'm right sorry blame fell on any of you, Your Grace, Lord Kimbrough, Lord Laughton, but what was I to do?"

No one had an answer, so the valet went on: "I had enough put by to emigrate, and a cousin in the colonies who would help us get settled. I thought we could get away if I just kept quiet long enough."

Nell interrupted. "But I couldn't go on a sea journey, not in the middle of winter, not in my condition. Besides, every time he looked at me, I could see Purvis thinking of how I'd lain with His Grace. He didn't mean to, but it made me feel dirty all over again. So I went off on my own with what I had. Said my husband was with the army, and I had no family to care for me. Took rooms in Richmond where no one knew me, and had the baby."

"Who looked like Arvid."

"And who fussed and cried no matter what I did. And I wanted to go off with Purvis, to start a new life without any reminders, and without throwing myself on his charity in case he changed his mind again."

"So you decided to sell us the baby." Marisol couldn't keep the disapproval from her voice.

" 'Twas that or dump him on some church steps and hope for the best. An ocean voyage wouldn't have been healthy for him, and we were going to set up a little haberdashery out west, not near the big cities. Purvis's cousin had written that there was money to be made there, but it was rough and dangerous, with red Indians and all. I couldn't take a baby into that, not after his warning."

"And you needed more money to set up the little business," Kimbrough suggested.

"I figured the duke owed us. Purvis agreed."

"We never meant for you to think we'd harm the little duke," the valet put in. "We neither of us ever meant you ill, Your Grace."

"Yes, I can see. My husband was more evil than even I suspected. All of this can be laid at his door. But what's to be done now, Mr. Dimm? These people were as much victims as criminals."

" 'Spect that's up to a jury, Your Grace."

Lord Kimbrough was thinking ahead to that trial. The press would be lapping up the details like a cat at a milk saucer. Marisol would have to testify, all about finding Denning with Lady Armbruster. She'd have to listen as the sordid details of her miserable marriage were made public. "Must we really have a court case, all the additional notoriety?" he asked. "It was self-defense, we all know it was, and Arvid had it coming. I'd have killed him myself if I knew what he'd done to— Why can't these people just keep going? They're not a danger to anyone else, and they've paid in all the anguish they've suffered at that dastard's hands."

Marisol looked hopeful, but Dimm scratched his head. "I don't know 'bout taking the law into our own hands that way."

"But if I stand by the decision as magistrate? Purvis and Tyson could sign confessions so if they ever came back they could be tried, and legal adoption papers so they'd never have a claim on the boy. It's like deportation to Botany Bay, only in the other direction and with better chance of survival at the end. We can just say Arvid was accidentally killed by a self-inflicted gunshot wound while in a towering rage at his valet. Even the press will accept such a story."

"His nibs might buy it at that, 'specially if it doesn't stir up another hornet's nest at the rumor mill. Just might work."

The manservant pleaded: "There's another boat leaving next week. We can be on it and you'll never hear from either of us again. I swear it, Your Grace."

"And I," Tyson promised.

Everyone's eyes turned to the duchess, as if to leave the decision to her, for revenge or retribution. "Let them go," she said, "after they sign all the papers."

She accepted their undoubtedly heartfelt gratitude, but could do no more than extend her wishes for a safe journey before leaving the room. They'd suffered, but so had she, and at their hands. Besides, neither had inquired about the baby's future. Tyson hadn't even asked to see her son.

Marisol went upstairs to him and to her own child. She dismissed Rebecca and the maid assigned to help in the nursery, leaving her alone with the sleeping babies and the dogs.

It was over, blessedly over. Tyson and Purvis would be on their way by nightfall. Sarah would leave with her Ned and Leonard in a few days, while Dimm's niece Suky from the inn would take Sarah's place as lady's maid. Foster was nearly well enough to rejoin his unit, and Bettina would go off to her Season ... and his lordship would resume his search for a perfect wife.

Marisol and Nolly would finally be alone to start their real life together, just the two of them and Aunt Tess and the dowager.

"And you, Sal." The collie thumped her tail on the floor. The terrier whined. "And you, Max."

Lord, maybe she should emigrate, too, rather than stay in Berkshire waiting for him to bring home an impeccable bride like Edelia Sherville. Marisol sighed, knowing there was no place on earth far enough away to escape her own breaking heart.

Chapter Twenty-three

"*I* have decided to keep Nolly at Kimbrough Hall," the earl declared one afternoon a few days later.

"You what?" Marisol fairly shrieked.

Carlinn studied his fingernails. "My right as guardian, don't you know. I think it will be better for the boy. He needs a man's influence."

The duchess was livid. "He's barely six months old. What are you going to do, take him to a cock fight?"

"And this place," the earl continued, waving one hand around, "is totally unsuitable for a young boy. Dangerous with all those turrets and towers and arrow niches, to say nothing of the broadswords, maces, and battle-axes all over the place. He's sure to get nightmares," he lied through his teeth, thinking the Castle every boy's fantasy playhouse come true. Why, that central bannister was enough to tempt him, even at his age and dignity. He went on: "And then there are all the artifacts that could be damaged."

"Everything dangerous or fragile has already

been put in storage or above the reach of a small child," she said through gritted teeth, wishing she had one of those battle-axes to hand right then.

"No, the little duke is better off with me, at the Hall."

"Better? Why you—you self-righteous toad! You can't even play with Nolly without making him cast up his accounts! And you think you know what is better for my son? You despicable cad, you monster! And you even gave your word not to interfere with his upbringing! I'll fight you in the courts, you bounder! I'll never give him up!"

"I know."

Marisol replaced the china shepherdess she'd been clutching, preparatory to letting it fly. "You know? You did this just to upset me?"

"And you do rise to the bait so charmingly, my pet. I particularly liked that 'self-righteous toad.' But I was not just trying to set the sparks flying. I do know that you'd never part with Nolly, and I would never ask you to."

"What are you saying, Carlinn?"

"What I am saying, no, asking, in my usual bumbling way, is if you would make me the happiest of men, and Nolly's father."

"You are asking me to marry you, just to get Nolly?"

"Now, that is a particularly goosish thing to say, Duchess. Granted the lad is the most adorable, perfect creature ever placed on earth, but even I draw the limits somewhere."

"But—but why, then?" she stuttered, completely baffled.

"Because I think I have loved you forever, and don't want to be apart from you for another day. Because I think of you all the time and wish to spend the rest of my life trying to make you happy."

"But you thought I was shallow and scandalous, a bad influence on your sister. You even thought I was a suspect in Arvid's murder."

"So I was a fool. That cannot come as a surprise; lud knows you've told me often enough. And Tyson forgave Purvis for far greater sins," he added hopefully, staring at her lowered head.

"And far be it from me to be less gracious than my maid?"

"Exactly. Besides, I did buy you this in London, even before we had Purvis's confession." He held out a small box and opened the lid to reveal a gold ring set with small diamonds around a sapphire. "There's the official Kimbrough heirloom engagement ring, but I wanted you to have something all your own. This one matches your eyes." He knelt on the carpet before her so he could see her face. "Blast it, I hate when you cry!" He jumped up and tossed her his handkerchief.

"I know," she blubbered into the square of fabric. "I'm sorry."

"Deuce take it, I'm the one who should be apologizing." He was pacing in his agitation. "I dared to hope . . . that is, I regret if my—my importunities have caused you discomfort. Forget I ever said anything."

"Oh, no, that's not it at all. It's just that you've made me the happiest of women."

"I have? You are? Then I can take it that it's a yes to my question?"

"Oh, yes. I have loved you for ever so long, but never thought—"

Whatever the duchess thought was lost in his embrace. There was no thinking, only feeling, the warmth and magic of his touch, the promised passion, the tender affection and gentle strength and the faintest scent of lemon. If Marisol had to describe heaven, this was it.

"Lud, I've been wanting to do this for ages," he admitted when they paused to catch their breaths. Somehow Marisol was sitting on his lap, on the sofa, their arms entangled. She tucked her head under his chin and gave a sigh of contentment.

"Dash it," he complained, stroking her back, "I'll never understand how you can go from screeching wildcat to purring kitten in the blink of an eye. Do you suppose I might figure it out if I have the next forty or fifty years?"

"You can try, my lord."

"Don't you think you can call me Carlinn, Duchess? But you won't be a duchess much longer, will you? Shall you mind being called Countess instead, my love?"

" 'My love' sounds best of all!" Which required another long interval of less verbal communication.

"What would you have done if I'd said no?" Marisol asked later.

"Oh, I'd camp on your doorstep, frighten away all your other suitors, teach Nolly to say Papa Carl."

She laughed, then turned serious. "And you truly don't care about all the gossip?"

"The gossips can say whatever they want, as long as you say you love me."

"I'll say it over and over, from every rooftop, every day, even if you get more odiously swell-headed."

"And I swear to try not to be too proud that the most wonderful woman in England returns my affection. I'll do anything for you, my love."

"Even move to London?"

Marisol almost found herself dumped on the floor, Carlinn sat up so suddenly. "Good grief, Marisol, you can't want that, do you?"

"Of course not, I just wanted to see you fly into a pelter, my love."

"Touché. But there is Tina's presentation to be considered. We'll have to attend to that."

"Perhaps Nolly and I can stay in the country?"

"What, and make me face the dragons on my own? Not on your life, my girl. Besides, I have no intention of leaving you alone for more than an hour or two, here and there. Anyway, I doubt we'll have much trouble, not with my sister's prattling on about Foster this and Foster that."

"Shall you mind? He hasn't much to offer but his title and his character and what I can provide. Once the war is over, he'll be just another bankrupt aristocrat."

"But Tina comes into a handsome property from our mother when she marries. Foster will have plenty to do handling that. It will give me more time to see to ours."

"Now, that has a nice ring to it. Ours," she repeated dreamily, her head on his shoulder.

He kissed the top of her very disordered curls. "My dear, shall you mind that I'm just a country gentleman, without all those fancy manners? One who looks after his lands instead of his wardrobe? Shall you mind that I didn't woo you with flowers and candy and poems?"

Marisol pretended to think. He didn't give her much time to come to a conclusion. "Too bad. I'll bring you puppies and kittens and new strains of oat and all my love instead."

"Now that you mention it, I do believe that Sal is the only gift you've bestowed on me before today. But what woman could ask for more than what you've offered now? Your name, your ring, your love. I suppose I shall just have to be content, my foolish darling."

After another interval, during which Marisol's hair became thoroughly disheveled, and Carlinn's too, she said wonderingly, "I thought you wanted a proper lady like Edelia Sherville."

"No, I thought I should have a cold, decorous wife like Edelia Sherville. There is a big difference between what I wanted and what I was prepared to accept. I always wanted a lively, loving lady. With a big chest."

Marisol was surprised she could still blush, with said chest being half exposed. "I'm not proper like

Edelia. I'll never make you a perfect wife, you know."

"You're not perfect? Ssh, don't tell anyone. I've been calling it from the church steeple that you are. Except for your nose, of course."

"My nose? What's wrong with my nose?"

"Nothing, my love. It's perfect for kissing." So he did, then asked, "Are you sure you'll be able to put up with me? I know I can be high-handed and dictatorial."

"I'll try, my lord," she answered between kisses of reassurance. "And if not, well, I'll shoot you, of course."

"Sometimes facts is like a boulder," Jeremiah Dimm commented to himself. "They sits right out there, obvious like, and wait for you to stub your toe on 'em."

The Bow Street Runner was in his soft chair, feet up, pipe going, a mug of ale by his side. The little house in Kensington was as quiet and snug as a bear's winter cave. Life was good.

His nibs was happy, for once. He liked the way the Denning murder was tied up so neatly without ruffling any feathers among the peacocks of Mayfair. He was so happy, in fact, that Dimm was promoted to Senior Inspector, and given a healthy bonus. That bonus money was enough to get that last youngster, that cousin's boy, off to school. An architect, he said he wanted to be. Dimm puffed on his pipe and nodded. The boy'd be plying his trade just about the time Lord Kimbrough'd be needing an extension at that manor house of his, what with the way the earl and Her Grace were carrying on.

Now there was a tricky piece of work, Dimm reflected. Arresting Jack Windham, solving the Denning murder—those were child's play compared to getting those two prickly swells together. They were made for each other, any fool could have seen that. But getting them to see eye-to-eye, now that took a real detective. Be damned if that wasn't the high-water mark of his career.

And now his first grandson was the son of a duke, by George. A'course, that was only for private knowing. It was enough that the rest of the world knew little Leonard was having a duchess for a godmother. Countess weren't half bad neither. And the rest of Dimm's brood was fixed for life better than he ever hoped. All those nieces and nephews, sons and daughters, getting established in Berkshire. Even Gabriel was staying on at Lord Kimbrough's invite, as assistant constable with his own little apartment above the one-cell gaolhouse.

That left only Dimm's sister Cora here in Kensington, and Jeremiah had it in mind that Mr. Stenross was a lonely widower. Dimm took another puff on his pipe and raised his mug to his own beloved Cherry, God keep her soul.

He went back to considering the new Lady Kimbrough's offer of the position of caretaker for Denning Castle. He'd have his own cottage by the gatehouse, and a whole staff to look after. And, the countess had added by way of incentive, Mr. Dimm would be right there in Berkshire amid all his sons and daughters, nieces, nephews, and Hambley in-laws.

Dimm blew a smoke ring up to the ceiling and smiled, there in the peace and contentment of his empty house. He'd think some more about her ladyship's offer. Next week.